PRAISE FOR

THE WIDOW'S SEASON

"*The Widow's Season* is far more than what it seems to be at first—a straightforward story of a woman getting used to a crushing loss. It's smarter, slyer, and more unconventional than that. It's haunting—and haunted, too."

—Elizabeth Benedict, author of *Almost* and *The Practice of Deceit*

"Confronts all the twists and turns of grief and loss, love and marriage, and the human heart with honesty, humor, and great intelligence."

—Ann Hood, author of *The Knitting Circle*

PRAISE FOR LAURA BRODIE'S

BREAKING OUT

"Brodie is an excellent guide. Once you open it, her book is hard to put down."

—Jane Tompkins, author of *A Life in School*

"Brodie tells her story with a light touch and an eye for telling detail."

—Jill Ker Conway, author of *The Road from Coorain*

"Brodie is a fine writer, sensitive to nuances."

—Lois Banner, author of *American Beauty*

"A fascinating and highly readable story filled with striking insights into American gender roles and revolutions at the end of the twentieth century. Brodie's book does a wonderful job of demonstrating the pressures for both continuity and change."

—Drew Gilpin Faust, author of *Mothers of Invention*

THE WIDOW'S SEASON

LAURA BRODIE

BERKLEY BOOKS, NEW YORK

THE BERKLEY PUBLISHING GROUP
Published by the Penguin Group
Penguin Group (USA) Inc.
375 Hudson Street, New York, New York 10014, USA
Penguin Group (Canada), 90 Eglinton Avenue East, Suite 700, Toronto, Ontario M4P 2Y3, Canada
(a division of Pearson Penguin Canada Inc.)
Penguin Books Ltd., 80 Strand, London WC2R 0RL, England
Penguin Group Ireland, 25 St. Stephen's Green, Dublin 2, Ireland (a division of Penguin Books Ltd.)
Penguin Group (Australia), 250 Camberwell Road, Camberwell, Victoria 3124, Australia
(a division of Pearson Australia Group Pty. Ltd.)
Penguin Books India Pvt. Ltd., 11 Community Centre, Panchsheel Park, New Delhi—110 017, India
Penguin Group (NZ), 67 Apollo Drive, Rosedale, North Shore, 0632, New Zealand
(a division of Pearson New Zealand Ltd.)
Penguin Books (South Africa) (Pty.) Ltd., 24 Sturdee Avenue, Rosebank, Johannesburg 2196,
South Africa

Penguin Books Ltd., Registered Offices: 80 Strand, London WC2R 0RL, England

An excerpt from this novel was previously published, in slightly different form, in *Shenandoah.*

Cover design by Lesley Worrell
Cover photo by Masaaki Toyoura/Getty Images
Book design by Kristin del Rosario

PRINTING HISTORY
Berkley trade paperback edition / June 2009

Library of Congress Cataloging-in-Publication Data

Brodie, Laura Fairchild.
The widow's season / Laura Brodie.—Berkley trade paperback ed.
p. cm.
ISBN 978-0-425-22765-7
1. Widows—Fiction. 2. Grief—Fiction. 3. Psychological fiction. I. Title.
PS3602.R63486W53 2009
813'.6—dc22

2009002118

PRINTED IN THE UNITED STATES OF AMERICA

10 9 8 7 6 5 4 3 2 1

For Julia, Rachel, Kathryn
and especially John,
may he live to a ripe old age.

Let her take him for her keeper and spy, not only of her deeds, but also of her conscience . . . And let her not behave herself, so that his soul has cause to be angry with her, and take vengeance on her ungraciousness.

—On the proper behavior of a widow
toward her husband.
Juan Luis Vives,
De Institutione Feminae Christianae,
dedicated to Catherine of Aragon in 1523.

PART ONE

Spirit

• 1 •

Sarah McConnell's husband had been dead three months when she saw him in the grocery store. He was standing at the end of the seasonal aisle, contemplating a display of plastic pumpkins, when, for one brief moment, he lifted his head and looked into her eyes. There, in his unaltered face, she glimpsed such an odd mixture of longing and indecision that her first instinct was to rush toward him, to fold her body within that unforgettable green flannel shirt. But she was swept by a wave of tingling nerves and pounding blood so cold, her only response was mute paralysis. In the seconds it took to resume her breathing, he had turned the corner at the aisle's end and was gone.

She heard the broken cry before she recognized it as her own voice, yelling, "David! Wait!" And then she was running after him, her cart abandoned, her pocketbook banging against her thigh.

When she reached the end of the aisle and turned left, she saw nothing but a wall of milk and eggs, mingled with the faces of wary strangers. Immediately she began checking aisle after aisle, finding nothing and nothing and again, nothing. She sprinted to the front of the store and searched in the opposite direction, scanning aisles to her left, checkout lines to her right. Never had the rows of paper towels, canned fruit, and cereal boxes seemed so garish, their cartoon logos blurring with her fractured thoughts.

Rushing out to the parking lot, she yelled David's name again. But among the handful of people unlocking their cars and loading their trunks, there were no dark-haired, middle-aged men in blue jeans and green flannel.

By the time she had reentered the store, the manager was coming down from his elevated cubicle. His bland smile seemed to assure that he had seen all this before. A mother obviously panicked over a missing child. With a small team of searchers he would eventually find the errant preschooler gazing at the lobster tank, or hiding behind a helium canister.

"You've lost someone?"

The words lingered in Sarah's mind. "Yes." She had lost someone.

"What does he look like?"

Her dark eyes kept scanning the store. She had a vague notion that if she stayed near the door she might block David's exit.

"He was wearing his Yankees baseball cap."

"What's his name?"

"David."

"How old is he?"

"Forty-three."

The manager's smile sagged. "Forty-three?"

Sarah stopped to examine the man. She noted his solid black tie, his red-white-and-blue name tag, and his fragile patience.

"He's my husband."

It was almost comical, how quickly the kindness fled from the man's face. In his eyes she was no longer an endearing young mother, in need of a steady arm. She was just another noisy wacko, a middle-aged woman with a wild expression, whose brown hair was falling from its silver clips.

"Do you want me to page him?" The words were more dismissive than curious. Already the manager's thoughts were returning to his computer screen.

Sarah imagined herself waiting at the customer service counter while a stranger paged her dead husband, and gradually the hysteria began to seep away. Why had she come here? What did she want from this place?

"Never mind." Her only thought was to escape to the quiet safety of her home.

Stepping again into the parking lot, she noticed how pale the sky had become. The maple leaves, so bright with fire two weeks before, were crumpled and falling like ash. As she crossed the pavement, the October wind bit through the links of her sweater.

Inside her old Volvo wagon, she shut the door, strapped on her seat belt, and placed the key into the ignition. Then she sat back, closed her eyes, and quietly, very quietly, she wept.

• 2 •

"I saw David today."

Sarah was sitting in her neighbor's kitchen, running her fingertip along the rim of an empty coffee mug. Margaret Blake, a tall Englishwoman with short gray hair, leaned over the stove as she dipped a silver straining ball into a blue teapot. Sarah wondered if her words would provoke a flinch in Margaret's shoulders, or a sudden turn of the head. But she couldn't detect the slightest hesitation in her friend's hands as they reached for the quilted tea cozy.

In the three years since Margaret's younger daughter had left for college, Friday-afternoon tea had become a ritual for the two women. It was a time to talk about gardens and politics, to berate hapless presidents and ineffectual prime ministers.

It was also a time to mourn, because Margaret, too, was a widow. Five years had passed since she had found her husband in the backyard, lying among a pile of pruned crab-apple branches.

Five springs that same tree had blossomed and faded in a floral anniversary, each time prompting Sarah to wonder what had impelled Ethan Blake, a man with a notoriously temperamental heart, to suddenly take up pruning. Had he sensed that something was to be sheared that day? That an old branch needed to be cut away?

Until then his yardwork had consisted of an occasional afternoon with the push mower. She could still see him, wire-rimmed glasses sliding down his sweaty nose as he rocked the mower back and forth around the edges of lilac and forsythia.

From her seat at the kitchen table she had a clear view into the living room, where Margaret had arranged a private memorial on the fireplace mantel. To the right and left stood pictures of her two daughters, ages twenty-one and twenty-four, cheerful testaments to youth and health. Between them, an ebony-framed photograph showed streaks of sunlight pouring through the branches of a crab-apple tree.

Sarah was one of the few people who understood the picture's full significance. She knew how Margaret, arriving home that spring afternoon, had found her husband stretched so neatly on his back, lifeless eyes open to the brilliant sun, that she had decided to lie down beside him—to look up through the crab-apple branches and see what he had contemplated in the last minutes of his life. There, with the twigs in her shoulder blades and Ethan's hand touching her own, Margaret had been so struck with the bright fragments of blue sky, shining like shattered glass through pink petals and black branches, that after going inside and calling 911, she had come back with her camera. And here was the result on the living-room mantel, a triptych monument to life's beginnings and endings.

It must be a British thing, Sarah thought, this pragmatism in the face of death. Margaret Blake was not one to be ruffled by the apparition of a dead man in a grocery store.

"Where did you see him?" Margaret turned and brought the teapot to the table.

"At the Food Lion."

"I thought you shopped at Safeway."

Sarah smiled. How typical of Margaret, to transform the morbid into the mundane.

"I was running some errands on the other side of town."

Thank God it hadn't happened at the Safeway. There were eight thousand people in Jackson, Virginia, and every time she shopped at the local market she ran into English department colleagues, or David's old patients. Even the baggers had familiar faces—the teenage girl with Down's syndrome, the man with the black earring. Sarah would have avoided them for weeks had they witnessed what she was now coming to think of as her "episode."

Margaret sat down and poured two cups of Earl Grey. She placed the teapot on a folded linen napkin and offered Sarah a small blue pitcher of cream, etched with scenes from Canterbury Cathedral. Friends were always bringing Margaret these mementos from their European vacations, as if an atheist from Manchester was going to be nostalgic for Thomas Becket.

"I saw Ethan everywhere after he died." Margaret wrapped both hands around her mug. "In crowds, in traffic. I'd see him in a car that passed and I'd drive like mad to catch up. But it never turned out to be him."

Sarah nodded. The early weeks of her widowhood had been filled with false sightings. Each time she passed a man of David's build and hair color she had felt a brief flash of recognition, invariably broken by the face of another stranger.

"But this was different. This time I recognized his shirt and his Yankees cap. And he stared right at me."

"So what happened?"

"He disappeared."

"Oh."

Margaret put down her mug and focused on the sugar bowl, breaking the hard clumps with the tip of her spoon. With each silver tap, Sarah felt her jaw tighten. What did she need to say to gain a legitimating nod? The only words that came to mind were the same predictable refrain she had repeated for the past three months.

"They still haven't found his body."

And here Margaret did hesitate, just long enough to look into Sarah's eyes. "They will."

In her thirteen years in Jackson, Sarah had witnessed dozens of flash floods like the one that had taken David. Sometimes the water came in the midst of drought, when the land was too parched to absorb a sudden storm. Other days, the downpours capped weeks of steady rain, transforming the area's usually placid creeks and rivers into muddy, frothing torrents. Locals told stories of entire mountain communities drowned in nighttime floods; water climbed the front stairs of double-wide trailers and seeped around bedposts while families slept. But Sarah knew of only a few isolated deaths—a drunk college student innertubing on Possum Creek, a woman in a Honda Civic who tried to cross a flooded bridge and was swept downriver as she climbed from her window.

In "David's flood," as she had come to call it, there were two other victims, a pair of little sisters. They had been huddled under an umbrella at the edge of their backyard creek, watching the water churn and leap, when the muddy bank on which they stood collapsed into the current. Their mother had witnessed it all from the porch of their farmhouse. She had been yelling through the rain for her girls to come inside when the creek opened its gaping mouth.

Sarah shuddered each time she envisioned it. That woman's loss was so much greater than her own. She had no children, and could scarcely imagine the cold horror of watching that umbrella bobbing downstream. One girl's body had been recovered a few days after the flood. The other had been found only recently, tangled among branches and leaves on the banks of the Shannon, into which all streams in the area flowed. The burial had taken place just last week.

And maybe that was the problem. Maybe it was the child's burial that had been troubling her thoughts over the past few days, triggering all of these memories and visions. Sarah had read the newspaper's brief account with a touch of envy, for she, too, had been awaiting a burial. Many nights, alone in bed, she had imagined David's body resting on a bank beneath a grove of trees, water lapping at his ankles. Other times she saw him float from current to current, past fields and cliffs, pastures and houses, *away down the valley, a hundred miles or more*. In her mind, his body never decayed. He was the handsomest drowned man in the world, carried from farm to farm in the Shenandoah Valley, tracked by the eyes of quiet deer.

More and more, her mind was drawn to the river. Each time she drove across the concrete bridge that marked Jackson's town limit, she saw the ripples and eddies below and inwardly gauged the water level. Lately the river's slow current seemed to parallel the hypnotic rhythm of her afternoons—hours of unbroken quiet, stretched on her living-room couch while her mind sank deep into the past. She had always been the sort of person who could get lost in her thoughts, wandering their farthest corners while schoolteachers droned on about trigonometry or trilobites. As a child, she had learned early that imagination was preferable to reality, and that books could be a gateway into labyrinthine daydreams. That was why she had become an English professor, because of her love of fictional worlds.

But these days there was a danger in her daily immersions, for she had less and less reason to resurface, the material world losing its magnetic pull with each new death. Ten years ago she had lost her parents—her mother to cancer, her father to alcoholism—and then there was David, lost to the river while on an overnight kayaking trip. Now there was only Margaret left to reel her in; Margaret, who was rooted in reality like a massive oak. Sarah could hear that Manchester accent at this very moment, calling her back to her muddy tea. Margaret was complaining about the principal at the elementary school where she taught third grade: "The woman goes on about the bloody SOLs as if Moses brought them down from the Mount. And now the state wants us to put 'In God We Trust' on the walls, as if that's going to improve the test scores."

Sarah tried to respond; she enjoyed a good rant in eloquent company. But fast as her blood rose, it receded in a broken wave. She offered murmurs and shrugs to all the usual provocations, until Margaret sighed and put down her mug.

"Have you been sleeping any better?"

"Not really. I still have a lot of dreams about David. Sometimes I'm underwater with him, looking up from the bottom. And lately I've been sleepwalking. Yesterday I woke up and all the items on my dresser were gone. All day long I found hairbrushes and jewelry and bottles of perfume scattered around the house."

Margaret nodded. "Are you taking those pills?"

Ah yes. The sleeping pills. The blue Lunesta with its ghostly butterfly flitting through television advertisements, haunting pillows and windowsills like some glowing angel of Morpheus.

Mr. Foster, from down the street, had given her the pills two days after the flood. He had pressed a vial into her hand at the end of a condolence call, saying "these might help," as if drugged unconsciousness could somehow set the world right, just like in the fairy tales, where women woke from poisoned sleep to find their enemies dead.

"You are the enemy," she had thought to say to the double-chinned Mr. Foster. "You with your presumptuous gifts, your smug sympathy, your revolting flesh." But instead she had smiled and said "thank you" as she closed the door behind him.

David had once tried to give her pills, a year ago when she had slipped into a bad bout of depression. He had come home with a pack of Prozac, "in case you want to give it a try," and although she had liked their shade of green—the name Lilly on each capsule as if they were borrowed from a friend—she had refused to sample the stuff. She was suspicious of men who tried to medicate women, who wanted to shield the world against the specter of female hysteria. It was their own problem if they couldn't bear women's complaints, women's tears, women with lavender moons waxing and waning beneath their eyes. She knew very well how she looked and sounded on her worst days, and to hell with them if they didn't like it. Life was not always pretty and cheerful, with hair curled and teeth whitened and supper waiting on the table. Life was sometimes a bitter Harpy perched on the bedpost.

So now the pills stood side by side in her medicine cabinet, Prozac and Lunesta, like some Wagnerian couple. *One pill makes you larger and one pill makes you small.*

"No, I'm not taking the pills," Sarah replied. And then, with a bitter smile: "I prefer alcohol."

Margaret blew ripples across the surface of her tea. "You should come to my group this week."

"Which one? The Quakers?"

"No." Margaret laughed. "I'm only a fair-weather Friend. I haven't gone in months. But I'm hosting my bereavement group this Sunday. I think you'd like some of the women."

"I thought you gave up on them years ago."

"Not entirely. I still see them a couple of times a year, just for the companionship. Some of the older women are very funny."

Brilliant. A gaggle of humorous widows.

But Margaret promised to bake scones and lemon bars and chocolate cake, and when Sarah thought of the cans of creamed corn waiting in her half-empty cupboards, she acquiesced just long enough to say that yes, come Sunday, she would think about it.

• 3 •

Walking home in the first shadows of twilight, Sarah saw two skeletons hanging in the Fosters' poplar trees. Silly String cobwebs cluttered their rib cages, and their skulls drooped in shame. On the porch, two sheeted ghosts, apparently fled from the desecrated bones, sat in wicker rocking chairs.

It looked like the aftermath of a lynching. But so it must always be in a house with three young boys. Each year the Foster brothers celebrated Halloween with a grisly exuberance. Purple blood dripped from their pumpkins' howling mouths.

The other two houses that separated Sarah from Margaret had porches neatly trimmed with baby pumpkins and dried corn husks. And that would have been the extent of her own decorations this year, had things been different. She would have managed a few straw flowers and a bowl of polished gourds—something tasteful and completely devoid of imagination.

In the early years of their marriage, she and David had driven out to a local farm to choose their pumpkins. She preferred long, thin ones with melancholy expressions; David liked round jack-o'-lanterns with cackling smiles. The challenge lay in contriving annual variations on these themes—serrated teeth and crossed eyes and teardrops shaped like moons. David always did the carving, as seemed to befit a doctor, although he hadn't touched a scalpel since medical school. When the operation was complete, they inserted candles, turned out the lights, and sipped hot cider while the pumpkins glowed on the kitchen table.

She couldn't remember when that tradition had ended. Each fall seemed busier than the last, until it was an achievement just to buy a pumpkin, let alone carve it. Halloween was for children, and children were the elusive ghosts that had haunted their marriage.

One year they had forgotten Halloween entirely until the Fosters' youngest boy arrived at their door with an ax in his skull. A cerebral jelly made from peeled purple grapes oozed through his hair. Sarah apologized profusely as she dropped a Ziploc bag of Oreos into the boy's pillowcase of candy. She knew that the local children rated the neighbors according to the quality of their Halloween treats—from full-size Snickers bars down to anonymous orange-wrapped toffees. The boy's derisive gratitude indicated that the McConnells had sunk to the bottom of the neighborhood ladder. Had she thought of it, she would have given him money, a few quarters to buy his silence, but seeing more children approach at the curb, she and David had locked the door and retreated to the basement.

That had been a good Halloween. They had stayed up past

midnight, sitting in the dark, drinking beer and watching *Tales from the Crypt*. She could still see David's blue eyes lit by the television screen, and with that memory came the image of his face in the grocery store today, bent slightly toward her, as if he had something to say, something she needed to know.

She hadn't told Margaret about David's expression. She hadn't explained how his eyes looked torn, how his mouth seemed on the verge of speaking. Perhaps that detail would have made his appearance more credible. But why did she need Margaret's approval? And if she craved legitimation, why hadn't she told Margaret the whole story?

In truth, this wasn't the first time it had happened. David's ghost had first appeared back in August, on the day of his memorial service. It had been a strange affair, a ceremony without a body or clear date of death. Three weeks had passed since the flood, and although the rescue teams had found David's kayak, paddle, and cell phone, his corpse remained the sunken gold no diver could recover. Still, Sarah clung to a small hope of his return, and when his relatives and friends suggested a memorial service, she had inwardly deplored their need for tidy endings.

That afternoon Sarah's sister had brought a poem, her niece had brought a flute, and David's friends and colleagues had brought memories that they shared in an open-mike ceremony interspersed with nondenominational hymns. The event was held at the college chapel and led by the campus minister, a young man who had no qualms about ushering David's Unitarian soul into his own vision of a Presbyterian heaven. In the minister's eyes, David's career as a college physician, battling daily cases of bulimia, chlamydia, and alcohol poisoning, merited a divine reward.

Listening to the man's impression of her husband's work, Sarah was reminded of how far David's life had wandered from his Peace Corps days. When they had first met in New York, he had been eager to take arms in the endless battle against infant mortality. The rural clinic outside of Jackson had provided him with a front line, and for five years he had come home with tales of tooth decay that rivaled the parasitic horrors of his time in Mali.

The misery of Appalachia had both depressed and exhilarated him. Breast-feeding was his mission, home repairs his necessary pastime. And so it must have seemed like a silent rebuke, each night that she lay in bed reading real estate guides, admiring crown molding, ceramic tiles, and finished basements. She was not the fisherman's wife, insistent on steady progress from cottage to mansion to palace, but she did ask for that initial leap beyond the thin carpet of their two-bedroom starter home, and David shared her dreams enough to take note of the college physician's impending retirement. When old Dr. Malone finally moved to Florida, the decision to apply for the job had been David's own. Once the contract was signed, the two of them had been rewarded with invitations to faculty cocktail parties, a 401(k), and a mortgage supplementation plan, but unspoken between them lay the knowledge that David's youth was gone. He had traded the children of the poor for the children of the wealthy, and the hours he spent volunteering on the hospital board were slim penitence.

The pearls around Sarah's neck felt especially tight that August afternoon as she stood in the broiling heat outside the chapel doors, receiving a line of kisses as if she were the hostess of a grim party.

Each cheek that pressed her own seemed to siphon a little more air out of her lungs, and when the crowd began to dwindle she retreated to a wooden bench on the opposite side of the building. There, in the shade of an ash tree, a breeze offered its own whispering condolence, carrying with it an odd sensation.

She felt an unexplainable conviction that David was nearby. The impression was so strong that she began to look around, beyond the chapel's hedges, down the wooded walkway toward the white-columned library. She didn't know what to expect—a smiling ghost underneath a tree, or a sad, translucent face framed in a classroom window? For a moment she even stared into the sky, where each strangely shaped cloud seemed to harbor a secret. When nothing revealed itself, she walked to the corner of the chapel and pressed her hand against its cool limestone. She began to trace its perimeter, imagining David fifty feet ahead, turning each corner just as she approached, until, at the front entrance, she did encounter a handsome dark-haired man—David's brother, Nate, who placed her hand in the crook of his elbow and said that it was time to go.

Later that night, after her friends had exited the house, leaving the refrigerator filled with salads and casseroles, Sarah gathered a stack of towels and washcloths and took them upstairs to the guest room. There, her younger sister, Anne, had settled under the covers.

Anne was a blessing—a public librarian with a summer schedule flexible enough to allow her to stay for a few days. Her husband had driven their two girls back to Maryland after the service, leaving the sisters to ply their work of memory and consolation. They had survived funerals before; a cemetery in South Carolina provided the backdrop for their lives. In response, they had learned to be mutually protective. Sarah had been present for the birth of Anne's daughters. Now Anne was present for the death of her husband.

That evening Sarah had kissed Anne good night as if she were her own child. She had pulled the white comforter, sprinkled with violets, around her sister's shoulders and brushed her fingers through Anne's hair. What was it that created the aura of progress in her sister's life? Was it only the children with their annual rituals—birthdays, school pictures, and dental appointments? More than anything else from her youth, Sarah missed that sense of growth, the idea of life moving forward in a steady procession—first grade, second grade, third grade, fourth. Why else had she gotten a doctorate, except to perpetuate the illusion of advancement?

As a child, she had measured life according to her latest report card, viewing those slim pieces of paper as a social contract, each A a promissory note for a season of happiness. She had been such a diligent student, ever willing to follow the path laid out by the public schools, grateful to be given a path at all, naively assuming that the world was obliged to reward so many years of obedient effort. It was only in high school that she had begun to grasp the truth, that there was no guarantee of happiness at the end of her slow march, and that graduation was a precipice from which most of her classmates would drop like lemmings into the labor market. But she was off to college and eventually graduate school, deferring reality with degree after degree, each one a higher precipice from which to fall.

Sarah patted her sister's comforter, then walked downstairs to her bedroom, leaving the door open while she sat down at her vanity. The face that stared back from the mirror was tired, but still pretty. At a distance, she flattered herself, she might pass for a woman in her twenties, except that in her twenties she had not twined gray strands of hair around her index finger. She yanked one out and stretched it before her eyes, silver and glinting.

In college her hair had hung halfway down her back, a dark barometer that curled into turbulent waves on humid summer afternoons. Her hair had been a source of power, the altar at which half a dozen boys worshipped with penitent fingers. But now, as she released her tortoiseshell barrette, her sensible cut barely brushed her shoulders. *I am like Samson,* she told herself—shorn and blind and angry enough on some days to pull the temple walls down on her own head. Except that there was nothing especially heroic about her life. What could be extraordinary in the life of a woman like her?

She pulled her bangs up to survey the thin lines that spread from the corners of her eyes up toward her brow, like the rays emanating from a child's sun. Lifting a jar of eye cream, she dipped her pinkie inside and began dabbing greasy white polka dots around her eyes, rubbing them into invisible swirls. What did it mean, she wondered, to be thirty-nine, childless, and widowed? What did it mean to be alone for the first time in her life?

It was then, caught in a moment of self-pity, that she saw him. In the back of the mirror's reflection David passed through the house behind her, quiet as a shadow.

The vanity stood opposite the bedroom door, so that it reflected down the hallway, toward the living room. There, David had come and gone in an instant, headed across the hall toward the kitchen.

For a moment Sarah remained frozen in her chair. She had an instinctive sense that she should not move or look behind her. She knew the fate of Orpheus, who turned too soon. Instead, she began to examine the mirror, touching the spot where David's image had appeared, as if his spirit were somehow trapped inside the glass. When at last she did turn and look down the hallway, no one was there. Tying her bathrobe around her waist, she rose and walked slowly down the Oriental runner, into the kitchen.

The light above the stove emitted a small glow, revealing familiar objects in familiar places: the refrigerator, the clock, the glass table, the ceramic tiles painted with wildflowers, arranged in intermittent diagonals above the granite countertop. Her eyes settled on the French doors that led to the patio. They were closed, but not locked. She never locked them. Never before had she worried about what might be outside.

But on that night, walking across the linoleum and reaching for the knob, she had stopped short. Did she really want to see what was outside? To look upon her husband, back from three weeks in the cold river? She thought of "The Monkey's Paw," a story she sometimes taught her freshmen. She remembered the mutilated son knocking at the door, and slowly, slowly, she drew her fingers back.

The kitchen's light blinded her to what was outside; across the door, her face was multiplied in a dozen dark rectangles. She cupped her hands around her eyes and leaned forward, her nose almost touching the glass before the shadows outside began to assume recognizable shapes. A dogwood tree, a juniper bush, a wrought-iron table, a bird feeder. She jerked away, suddenly chilled. The problem wasn't what she had just seen, but all that she had seen before. Her mind was littered with television scenes of bloody hands slapped against windows, or frantic eyeballs meeting a looker's gaze. *Ridiculous,* she told herself, but she couldn't shake the fear.

Another minute passed as she debated her options. Her glimpse of David probably wasn't real; it was probably a mirage concocted by a sleepless brain. But why was her mind chanting: *Let him in, let him in*? When she looked down she saw her hand move like a foreign object, reaching for the knob. Her fingers touched the brass, felt its cold metal, and with a swift twitch, they turned the lock.

And then she ran—down the hallway, up the stairs, and into the guest room. She climbed into bed next to Anne, pulled the covers to her chin, and tucked her knees to her chest.

Sarah never told Anne what had happened that night. Four days later, when it was time for her sister to take a train back to Maryland, Sarah stood resolute. Everything was all right. Not to worry. She would take some time to organize things, then drive to Maryland for a long visit. Give her love to the girls.

After waving the train off, Sarah drove back to her house, intent upon one thought. Heading straight for the linen closet, she gathered the bedsheets and began to move from room to room, covering every mirror. She had read somewhere that in previous centuries mirrors were turned toward the wall after a death, for fear that they would reflect evil spirits. In Victorian England, mourners wore their jet jewelry with a matte finish, to avoid the unfortunate faux pas of discovering a dead man's face in a woman's brooch.

Now she understood the superstitions of ancient cultures, the impetus for séances and Ouija boards, and the necessity of burial, so that the dead might sleep in peace. She couldn't say which was more troubling—the state of her husband's soul or the state of her own mind, for she suspected that all those mourners with their mirrors reversed did not dread spirits so much as the look of their own haunted faces.

Anyway, the sheets were a bad idea; the covered mirrors resembled ghosts tacked on the walls. After two days she took all of the mirrors down, dismantling her vanity with a Phillips-head screwdriver. She lay them on the guest-room bed, where they stared vacantly at the ceiling. That left only the mirror in her bathroom, which was screwed into the wall. She decided to leave it up, but to look into its reflection only in the brightest light of day, with the television set blaring in the background. If David wished to appear beside the toilet or in the bathtub while Regis Philbin commented on the morning news, so be it. She would reduce his ghost to something domestic. She would not be afraid.

She thought of the mirrors now as she stood in front of her house, the last structure before the street dead-ended in a wooded cul-de-sac. Two months had passed since the night of the memorial service, and although in that time she had often felt the sense of being watched, she had never again seen a full-bodied apparition inside her home. Her precautions had either been highly effective or completely unnecessary.

Sarah leaned her head back as she assessed her house: a

two-story beige Victorian with white trim, pine-green shutters, and wraparound porches. She could describe it with a Realtor's precision, having spent two years researching the local housing market. Once David had signed his contract with the college, she had begun to examine properties in town and in the country—ranch houses, farmhouses, Cape Cod cottages. Colonial, Victorian, Georgian, contemporary. She had studied the merits of heat pumps and copper pipes, wells vs. springs, thermal windows and shingled roofs.

This house had not been her first choice. She had fallen in love with a three-bedroom contemporary in the style of Frank Lloyd Wright—a stone-and-cedar jewel on a private hill a few miles from town, with a backyard terraced south in raised flower beds. She'd felt almost giddy, showing David the solar heating, the picture windows, the granite countertops. But when they stepped onto the back patio, he had laughed. "A swimming pool? Who's going to take care of a swimming pool? Oh, Sarah." He rolled his eyes. "You can't be serious?"

"It's only a lap pool." Her volume had dropped to a murmur.

"And what about all those flower beds?" His arm swept south. "Who's going to take care of them?"

"I will," Sarah replied, but already the coneflowers seemed to wilt beneath David's critical eyes.

"Sure, you'll take care of them for a few months, until the novelty wears off. After that, the beds will be full of weeds, and we'll be stuck paying a pool guy."

She remembered his indulgent smile as he put his hands on her shoulders and looked into her face. "It *is* beautiful. I *know*. And if we were retired, with all the time in the world, this house would be perfect. But how many hours are you going to have for weeding once we start a family?"

Walking to the pool's edge, David had knelt to stroke his hand through the heated water. "You know that a pool is the worst thing to have with a toddler around."

He was right, of course. David was always right. Or at least, David had an air of certainty that made him sound correct, and that always made her feel mildly ridiculous.

Was it possible to love a man who made you feel ridiculous? Of course, Sarah assured herself as she looked up at her huge Victorian house—the house David had chosen. Love was complicated, that was all. Or was love simple, and marriage was complicated? In seventeen years of marriage David had often left her feeling frustrated, and furious, and disgusted, yes—but he had also made her feel beautiful, and protected, and loved. And oh, what she would give to feel loved right now.

She hoped Mrs. Foster wasn't looking out her window—staring down the street and seeing Sarah at her driveway, wiping her eyes with the sleeve of her sweater. She remembered when David had first shown her this neighborhood. He had declared it perfect—the mature trees, the well-groomed yards, the elementary school within walking distance. This hundred-year-old house, he had explained, was the ideal family home, with four bedrooms, a large backyard, and a finished basement where children could shout at one another in privacy. "Isn't it big?" Sarah had asked, thinking, Isn't it boring? But David had explained how the rooms would shrink with each child that occupied them, until at last she agreed. This was the perfect place for children. She imagined them filling the space like a current of warm air.

On their closing date, signing page after page in the lawyer's office, she had been ten weeks pregnant, and had already bought a nursery border of ducks and teddy bears. She could still remember that sense of ease, the threads of her life coming together in one complete tapestry: the house, the child, the successful husband, the part-time teaching job that would keep her intellectually alive while she raised her children past their preschool years. It was the last time in her life that she had felt content.

Eight days later when she woke in a small puddle of blood, she had consoled herself with statistics. One in three pregnancies ended in the first trimester; the trick was to last well into the fourth month. But four was a magic number, the unattainable goal her body could never achieve. She thought she had managed the feat when her third baby reached fourteen weeks. Pulling a kitchen chair into the nursery, she had spread the wallpaper border like a celebratory banner. One week more and she was standing on that same chair, scraping at the teddy bears. *Curettage, curettage,* it sounded like ballet.

How ironic it all seemed, to have spent so many years tending to her brain, memorizing the required facts, polishing her sentence structure, believing that if she were smart enough her life would culminate in some glorious fulfillment. And then to be betrayed by the lesser parts of her body, to fail in a task mastered by the most brainless of women, by drug addicts and child abusers and the dithering cheerleaders from high school. In the end, they had all outdone her.

Now, as she looked at her enormous house, with its latticework and porch swing and white-pine rockers, she knew what any stranger would assume—that nothing could be wrong in a place like this, a structure so symmetrical, so clean and creamy. No one would guess that behind those walls each empty room represented an unrealized life, each window a gaping frame for an absent child who should have been waving to her at this moment. She could sometimes hear their voices in the upstairs bedrooms—the crying of an infant, the babbling of toddlers. "The pipes are noisy," David would say. "The wind whistles on the tin roof." But Sarah had assigned faces to every sound.

With David gone, she had sealed off the upstairs, shutting the heat vents, closing the doors, and huddling in her bedroom with real estate guides, wondering if she should find a house with less space to heat, less grass to mow. All around her, life was shrinking into something small and hard, a shell into which she was retracting, newly invertebrate.

Sarah gathered her letters from the mailbox and inspected the return addresses as she walked along the driveway. Bills, credit-card applications, and three more notes of sympathy; they kept trickling in from distant acquaintances around the country. She walked up the porch steps and over to the door, reaching into her purse for her key, but the knob turned in her hand. She would have to be more careful about using the lock.

Leaving the mail on the hall table, she walked into the kitchen and put her pocketbook on a chair. Grace, her Persian, soft and gray as a pile of ashes, curled around Sarah's legs as she opened the refrigerator. "Hungry, my love?" She pulled Grace into her arms and rubbed her nose behind the cat's ear. The refrigerator's depleted shelves reminded her of her abandoned shopping cart at the Food Lion. By now some resentful bagger would have reshelved her linguine and oranges, her Cabernet and Zinfandel and Australian

Shiraz. She took out a leftover bowl of tuna salad and placed it on the floor for Grace, then removed a half-empty bottle of Chardonnay. Taking a glass from the cupboard, she stepped out onto the patio and sat at the wrought-iron table.

The yard was in its last gasp of autumn glory. A row of thick, burning bushes that separated her property from the neighbor's privacy fence had turned a deep ruby red. This was the only time of the year when those bushes distinguished themselves. Her other shrubs were spring and summer bloomers—rose of Sharon, crepe myrtle, pink and white azaleas, all framed with ten inches of grass.

She would have to learn how to use the Weedwacker. And the staple gun, the chain saw, the blowtorch. Despite all her talk of feminism, she had never changed a tire, never checked her antifreeze, or even lit a pilot light. There had never been a need; David had handled all the "men's work." The one time she had tried to use the Weedwacker, yanking at its starter cord a dozen times and yielding nothing more than a guttural cough, David had come outside and lifted the handle from her fingers. "It's all right. I can do it." With one turn of a knob, one jerk of the cord, he was off trimming around the porches. That was his nature, always in control.

As the alcohol lingered on the back of Sarah's tongue, goose bumps rose along her forearms. It was happening again—that unmistakable sense that David was there, watching her. Where was he this time? The bedroom window? The neighbor's roof? The feeling was becoming so common it bordered on the ludicrous. For once, however, she felt a rare bravado. Perhaps it was the wine, or perhaps her growing resignation, but Sarah rose from the table, lifted her glass into the air, and spoke aloud: "Come out, come out, wherever you are."

For a few seconds the yard remained absolutely quiet, even the mockingbirds pausing to listen. And then, from behind the burning bushes came the crunch of leaves. Someone was standing there, shifting his weight.

Run, she told herself. Run into the house and lock the door. Run straight through the hall and out the front, down the street to Margaret. But the longer she waited, the more resolute she became. After all, what did she have to fear? David, the good doctor? Or did she fear her own death? No. The miscarriages had changed her attitude toward death. She didn't fear it; she despised it. She hated how it had planted itself in her body, making her its walking vessel. Sometimes in her angriest moments she even hated God—what had she ever done to Him, to have cast so many shadows upon her life? With that thought she put down her wine, walked to the garden shed, and retrieved a hoe.

She carried it to the face of the middle burning bush, six feet tall with leaves so thick she could not see beyond them. Carefully she inserted the handle of the hoe into the shrub like a giant thermometer until it hit the fence on the other side with a dull thud. She repeated the gesture four times, imagining a man on the other side, contorting his body to avoid the thrusts of her horticultural sword. At last she dropped the hoe, raised her hands, and inserted them into the bush, watching her fingers disappear into the red leaves.

She had a vague idea of what she might touch. Something cold, something sharp, a set of teeth. She both dreaded and desired another pair of hands, to grab her own and pull her in. But all she felt was a mesh of branches. With a sudden jerk, she divided the bush to the left and right, and looked straight through to the fence beyond.

There was another crunch of leaves, a blinding rush of wings, and when she opened her eyes she saw a pair of blue jays ascend into the darkening sky.

• 4 •

Early the next morning, while the eastern horizon lingered in a predawn blue, Sarah woke to a slow tapping. In her dream David's blue-white knuckles were rapping at the window, but when she sat up, the sound became liquid. Barefoot and dizzy, she slumped into the bathroom and discovered a wet towel dripping from the shower rod. Where had it come from, this foreign object? It hadn't been there last night, of that she was certain, but when she pulled it from the rod and wrung it out into the tub, the action felt familiar.

Back in her bedroom, she noticed that her windows were shut tight—she usually kept them open to the night air—and when she pressed her toes on the carpet beneath the windowsill, it was damp. A storm must have passed after midnight. She must have risen to shut windows and sop up puddles throughout the house. It was strange that she couldn't remember, but the line between sleeping and waking had grown tenuous in recent weeks.

Outside, the lawn glittered with frosted rain, carrying her mind back to the morning of David's death. Then, too, a thunderstorm had emerged in the early hours, and she had trudged around the house with a towel, closing windows that faced north and west. David had been gone on an overnight kayaking trip. He had wanted to spend two days paddling the Shannon south through the Blue Ridge.

She had driven him to his put-in point the previous morning, helping to carry the kayak down to the water's edge. One last kiss, given carelessly as she tucked his wallet into the Velcro pocket of his life vest, and she had stepped back to watch him perform the brief ritual of preparation. She could still see him, tightening the chin strap on his helmet; stowing his camera, sandwiches, and cell phone in a waterproof pack at the back of the kayak; pulling his spray skirt around his torso, and finally wading into the water and settling into the boat. Usually the midsummer water was too low for paddling; kayaks scraped rocks at every rapid. July, however, had been unusually rainy, and even the Shannon's long stretches of flat water flowed at a steady pace. With a shove of his paddle, David was away from the bank, waving to her as the current caught him. He planned to paddle for five hours that day, and to stop midway through the next county, where they owned a cabin by the river.

Normally Sarah would have gone with him; they knew the importance of the buddy system. But she had agreed to help with registration for the college's summer scholars program, and David was determined to take advantage of this one free weekend. She had asked him not to go, told him to wait for an afternoon when a friend could come along; even now she was annoyed at his over-confidence, his refusal to be delayed. But what was the use in chiding the dead?

That night David had called from his cell phone. The river had been gorgeous. He reported seeing two deer, several trout, and a few children plunging from a rope swing. In the early evening he had set up an easel on their cabin deck, painting the trees along the river's edge. Art was a lifetime passion that David could only indulge on occasional weekends. The cabin was his main studio, and the basement, with its high windows, his second choice. If David was painting, all was well.

And so, when the thunder woke her that July evening, she had not worried. She hadn't thought of the river, slowly swelling, changing color and pace. Only now, with the trees still dripping, her mind was full of rivers. As she settled back into bed, she imagined swirling currents, clogged with leaves and fallen branches that metamorphosed into mossy arms, pulling her down.

• 5 •

At eleven o'clock Sarah was still lounging in her robe, crawling in and out of her covers while cups of tea replaced the empty wineglasses on her bedside table. Each morning she seemed to stay in bed a little longer, poised somewhere between depression and luxury. Ever since childhood she had loved to read and nap in her sheets, slowing time to a groggy limp. Her happiest summers had been spent as a freelance writer during graduate school, when she had taken her laptop to bed. Afloat in a sea of pillows, she had clicked the mornings away, sometimes falling asleep with the screen open on her belly. David had suggested that she draft a special clause in her health insurance for bedsores.

Now, with *The Washington Post* spread across his side of the bed, she could have easily drowsed until noon. But when the digital clock read eleven-thirty, she remembered that Nate was coming down from Charlottesville for lunch. She had invited him to look through David's things, to see what clothes might fit, what childhood mementos might hold special meaning. Her bathroom was filled with masculine odds and ends that she wanted to pass along: shaving cream and black shoe polish and Old Spice.

With the thought of Nate's arrival, she was instantly out of bed and flipping through her closet. A visit from Nate required more than her usual jeans and sweater. It called for something casual but pretty, sufficient to show that she was not falling apart. She looked through skirts, blouses, and pants, before settling on a loosely cut light blue dress. Was it too summery for October? Her entire wardrobe was probably too summery for a widow. Stepping into a pair of sandals, she weighed and rejected the idea of makeup; it would be an achievement just to brush her hair and find the barrette that had fallen under the bed.

Five minutes later she was lying with her cheek pressed against the carpet, intent on a shimmer of mother-of-pearl beneath her dusty headboard. She took a pencil from the bedside table and stretched her body flat, inching the barrette around the abandoned books, socks, and cough-drop wrappers, all the while thinking: Was this necessary? Why did she need to dress for Nate? But the answer was obvious. Every woman dressed for Nate. To stand beside Nate wearing shabby clothes was to look like a chain-link fence propping an arbor of roses.

Nate was a beautiful man, a man whose face had determined his fate. As a child, his dark hair and blue eyes, combined with an eloquent tongue, had left a wake of charmed teachers, moonstruck girls, and one mildly disgusted elder brother. According to David, Nate was a sweet-tempered boy ruined by the flattery of schoolmates.

Sarah couldn't say whether David's assessment was fair; she

had always felt an unspoken sympathy for her brother-in-law. Now, as she clipped the barrette in her hair and walked into the kitchen, she paused at the photo of Nate and David that hung on her refrigerator. In any other family Nate would have been the ideal son—handsome, popular, and bright. But the McConnell brothers had been raised by a pair of philosophy professors who valued the life of the mind more than the wonders of the flesh, and who maintained, from their own awkward youths, a lingering prejudice against prom kings.

David was the son with whom they sympathized, a young man intelligent but not cocky, attractive but not beautiful. David's face was somehow more authentic than Nate's. When the two stood side by side, Nate looked like an artist's flattering vision of David's flawed features.

While Nate had ruled his high school social scene, at home he was always second best. His B's were shadowed by David's A's; his election as president of his college fraternity was a bleak lampoon of David's induction into Phi Beta Kappa. Although Nate had earned a fortune as a Merrill Lynch broker, his wealth seemed obscene beside David's idealism.

Sarah heard Nate's car arrive as she stirred a pitcher of lemonade. She smoothed her dress, pinched her cheeks, and regretted, for the first time, the absence of mirrors in her house. Tucking loose strands of hair behind her ears, she opened the front door and was struck by the color blue. Blue jeans, a blue pin-striped oxford shirt, and blue eyes that looked, today, surprisingly kind. Nate seemed to have descended from the clear autumn sky.

"How are you, Sarah?" He brushed her cheek with a light kiss.

"Royal Copenhagen," she murmured. It was David's favorite cologne as well.

As she closed the door behind him she saw a silver Mercedes parked at the curb. He had switched cars again in the two months since the memorial service.

She took one of the three white deli bags from his arms. "Let's eat on the patio."

Nate had brought a small feast—roast beef on rye, turkey on wheat, bagels and lox, pints of chicken salad, potato salad, herb cream cheese, and tabouli. A few baguettes. Enough food for a week. Was it obvious to everyone that she had been surviving on peanut butter?

She poured two glasses of lemonade, and placed Nate's on a napkin. "How are things at your job?"

He shrugged. "The market's a nightmare. I've got folks in my office crying, like *I'm* the one who told them to put their entire life's savings into stocks."

Sarah nodded as she lifted a bagel. Compassion was the chief quality that had always distinguished David from Nate. David had an intrinsic desire to alleviate suffering; she had sometimes been impatient with his need to make things right for other people, people who had no care for themselves, or for him. But for Nate, business was business, and if a couple lost half of their nest egg, what could he do about it?

"And how's Jenny?"

Nate had been dating a blond travel agent for the past few years. He liked to tag along on her trips to the Caribbean, sipping complimentary piña coladas while she assessed meals and maître d's.

The two had seemed otherworldy at David's memorial service, so tan and healthy, death was as remote as the Arctic Circle.

"We're seeing other people. She's in Egypt this week."

"Oh, I'm sorry." Sarah had thought the two of them might get married, Jenny being the only woman who had ever held Nate's attention for more than a year. But Sarah could not imagine Nate in Egypt, with throngs of beggars jostling at his sleeves. Impoverished crowds were David's fascination.

"What have you been up to?" Nate handed her the cream cheese.

For one brief moment she thought to tell him the truth. To say "I've been chasing your brother around grocery stores, and searching for him in bushes." But Nate wasn't the sort of man who inspired confidences.

"I'm getting back to some of my nonprofits. I told the college that I'd organize their Thanksgiving food drive, and I'm on the board for Habitat. We're raising money for two new houses that are going up this spring."

"So . . ." Nate smiled. "What are you raffling?"

Ah, thought Sarah, how well he knew the do-gooder's annual routine. "You wouldn't want any of the prizes. There's a big Victorian dollhouse, a wedding-ring quilt, things like that."

"The prizes don't matter." He pulled a fifty-dollar bill out of his wallet and tucked it under the tub of chicken salad. "Habitat's a good cause, and I never expect to win."

She gazed into the face of Ulysses S. Grant, thinking how the cash machines never gave out fifties. Nate must be going inside to flirt with the pretty tellers.

"Have you thought about going back to work?" he asked.

she found a scrap of red silk, and unfolded a small treasure. Turning toward the closet again, she held out a gold ring and was about to speak when her breath caught in her throat.

David was standing there, smiling at her. He looked as he had ten years ago, gray hairs returned to black, dressed in the dark sport jacket and light blue shirt that he always chose for special dinners. As he stepped toward her, reaching for the ring, their eyes met, and suddenly his face was swimming, changing into Nate's, standing there in her husband's clothes. Nate's fingers touched hers as he took the gold band.

"Dad's wedding ring," he said. "I'm glad David took care of it."

He slipped the ring onto his empty wedding finger, then held up his hand for Sarah to see. "The shape of things to come?"

Her heart was still pounding. "The clothes fit you well."

"I think I can wear some of the shirts and coats. I don't like sweaters much, but maybe this one." Nate pulled out a dark blue woolen sweater, handmade in Scotland. Excellent choice. She could see his expert eyes assessing David's wardrobe, settling on all that was best, and determining that most of it was not worth keeping.

"There are some ties you should look at." Sarah rose from the bed and walked into the closet, her left shoulder brushing against Nate's chest. "A few of these also belonged to your father." She pulled down a brass tie rack.

"Yes." He laughed. "The fat ones." But again he was fingering fabrics, reading tags, assessing value.

She had to escape this air of acquisition. "I'm going to get a box."

Downstairs in the basement Sarah settled onto the sofa and closed her eyes, struck by how Nate had looked like a beautiful young David. Again he leaned toward her, reaching for the ring with those immaculate fingernails. When she opened her eyes, she was confronted with all the leftover furniture that could accumulate in seventeen years of marriage. A pullout couch, a minifridge, old lamps and end tables, a TV with a twelve-inch screen. In the corner by the window, a large white bookshelf was stocked with paints, pencils, chalk, a portfolio of drawings and watercolors, and strips of wood that David used to hammer into frames. An easel leaned against the wall, and to its left, a long bin overflowed with oil paintings.

Sarah walked over and began fingering through the portfolio. In college David had experimented with charcoal drawings of nude women—sleeping, bathing, stretching. She had never known the models, never asked for their names; they were probably the fleshy product of a young imagination. By the time he reached medical school, David had been embarrassed by his pages full of breasts and buttocks. He had switched to watercolors of elderly men, the paint running down their cheeks in folds of flesh pulling earthward. Sarah held one at arm's length—a black man at a bus stop with drips of paint carving veins into his neck, his coat a bundle of wrinkles.

She had fallen in love with David during his watercolor phase. There were both living in New York. He had been finishing his first year of residency at Columbia just as she was wrapping up her senior year at Barnard, and they had met at a reception following a poetry reading. She couldn't recall the poet's name—they passed through Barnard in an endless processional—but she did remember her first glimpse of David, alone at the far end of the hors d'oeuvre table.

She could always tell when a man was watching her, ever since her fourteenth birthday when she had "blossomed" (her mother's word) from a knobbly stalk into something rounded and soft. Overnight she had become an object of male assessment, a fact more annoying than empowering, because too often the eyes that followed her belonged to old men, or ugly men, or men with anxious faces whose only pleasure seemed to rest in the ability to stare. And so she was relieved, on that evening in May, to glance down the table and find that this particular gaze came from a young man in his twenties, neatly dressed, even handsome, who grinned when their eyes met.

She remembered David's opening line as he walked over. "Toddler food," he had said, nodding toward her paper plate filled with red, seedless grapes and Cheddar-cheese squares. With hand outstretched he had introduced himself, saying how much he enjoyed Ted Hughes (*that* was the poet, how could she have forgotten), and would she like to go with him to the café across the street where the food was much better?

Sarah had never before encountered such unabashed confidence. All of her college dates had been sweet, bumbling boys with apologetic gestures. But David was a twenty-six-year-old vessel of optimism, arriving on the scene at the perfect moment, because she had been slouching toward graduation with her habitual dread of endings, on the lookout for another well-worn path to tread. She hadn't expected that path to include a man—at least, not so soon; it violated the Barnard creed. And yet here was this handsome doctor in training, emerging like her private Polaris, and yes, she would follow him to the café, and back to his apartment, and on to whatever promised land his gods had foretold. Four months more and they were living together; another year and they were married.

She supposed it was foolish, to have gotten married so young. If she had lived on her own for a few years, she would have been more prepared for her present solitude. But two things in life could never be scheduled—love and death. And anyway, the foolishness of her youth was happier than all the calculations of her middle age.

Sarah put the portfolio down and moved on to David's recent work in the bin, oil landscapes with fuzzy boundaries between trees, river, and sky. Here were the Blue Ridge Mountains that stretched east of Jackson, fold after fold of purple and gray. And here was Stuart's Pass, cutting through the Alleghenies that slanted in the west. None of David's work was abstract; one could always say with certainty, "Here is a cliff, here is a chimney," but everything was subject to motion and change.

She stopped at a painting of a dark-haired man in his forties—David's only self-portrait, and not his best work. The features were correct, but the mouth lay flat and empty. Only the eyes were alive, challenging her with a slight sense of humor. Staring into them was like opening a porthole on a sinking ship.

She turned at a creak of the stairs, and found Nate watching her.

"David did beautiful work." He crossed the room and looked over her shoulder. "When we were kids he was always drawing—everything he saw—people, plants, things in the house. He said he'd be an artist when he grew up."

Sarah nodded. "He was still considering it in college. But he didn't think he could support himself as a painter. Or he couldn't support a family."

But there had been no family. No soft-skinned infants. No baby hands with dimples where the knuckles should have been. No orthodontist bills or college savings plans, soccer camp or music lessons. Only an increasingly dissatisfied wife, turning inward.

"I think it was a cop-out," Nate went on. "People who sell themselves short always use the family as an excuse. He should have stuck with his dreams."

Of course, thought Sarah. How easy it is to romanticize the life of the artist when you're driving your Mercedes back to your luxury condo.

"He was a very good doctor." She flipped past David's portrait, into more landscapes.

"Yes, but there are lots of very good doctors around." Nate wouldn't let it go. "Painting was his gift. He should have kept at it."

Should have, should have—her life's mantra. She pulled out a landscape, the view from the back of their cabin. To the right, a fishing pole leaned against the railing of a short dock. To the left, the river disappeared behind a row of sycamores.

"Have you been back to the cabin?" Nate asked.

"Margaret and I went out there the week after the flood. I had a notion that I wanted to lie down on the last bed that David slept in. You could see where he had been the night before, the covers were just yanked up, and the sheets were poking out."

Nate smiled. "David never liked to make his bed."

"Yes, so I tucked the sheets under the mattress and straightened out the bedspread. I folded the covers down and fluffed the pillows. I guess it was sort of silly, but Margaret was great. She helped unplug all the appliances and empty the trash. David left a lot of stuff like apples and bread and milk, so we had to clean out the refrigerator. And on the easel there was an unfinished painting of geese on the river. One brush was still soaking in a jar of water, like he thought he'd come back in a few days."

Why was she telling him all of this? Her shoulders trembled and Nate stretched out his arms, but she held up her palm. "It's all right, I'm okay." She wiped at her eyes with the back of her hand.

"Do you think you'll go back there again?"

She nodded. There was something appealing about the cabin's solitary quiet, the retreat from Jackson's manicured fishbowl. "I'll have to go back, because I left David's paintings on the walls, and I'll need them for the exhibit."

"I got your note about that. When is the opening?"

"In about three weeks, on the Friday before Thanksgiving. You should be getting a postcard in the mail any day now. Have you ever seen the local gallery?"

"No."

"It's not much compared to what you'd find in Washington or New York, but it's nice enough. The owner, Judith Keen, used to be a curator at the National Gallery before she moved out here. She's a friend of ours."

"Acquaintance" was more accurate. Judith hadn't even known that David painted until she came to the house in August on a condolence call. Normally Judith shied away from locals who pursued art as a casual hobby. They came a dime a dozen in Jackson—retired women who roamed cow pastures with brushes and palettes and folding chairs.

Sarah had been surprised when Judith pitched the idea of a one-man show. The gesture seemed too sentimental for the high-brow curator, with her tight skirts and high heels and blouses all black and white like some sandy-haired version of Cruella de Vil. Her gallery was supposed to be a beacon in the wilderness, and the most David had ever done with his art was to donate a few paintings to local charity auctions. But Judith had oohed and ahhed so much when she saw the paintings in their house, praising David's use of light, and insisting "I had no *idea*," that Sarah had agreed, an exhibit would be a nice tribute.

She put the landscape back into the bin and stepped aside. "Find a few you'd like for yourself. And you should look through these photographs. They're all from your family." She lifted some albums from the bookshelves and placed them on the table beside the couch. "Would you like a drink? I'm going upstairs." Nate shook his head and she retreated in search of Chardonnay.

An hour later Nate had chosen a dozen pictures and two paintings. One was an oil landscape with a barn and fence, beautifully done, though Sarah never would have guessed that the subject would appeal to him. The other was a watercolor of Helen, David and Nate's mother, bent over a garden of daylilies.

"Yes, that one is nice." She should have known that he would choose it. Helen was the great love of Nate's life; beside her, all girlfriends shriveled to insignificance. She used to come to Virginia to flee the winters of her native Vermont, made so much colder after her husband's heart attack. Many evenings while David was off at medical emergencies, Sarah and Helen had spent hours by the fire, comparing book-club lists, lamenting the state of undergraduate grammar, and sharing stories about the McConnell brothers.

Nate never knew how much his mother admired him, how she had marveled at his beauty as he grew from toddler to teenager, wondering how her body could have produced such symmetry. Sometimes when he exited a room Helen would raise her eyebrows at Sarah and say: "A thing of beauty is a joy forever." Keats's line had a wonderfully ironic ring on those days when Nate was feeling sullen; his mother's presence had a way of reducing him to sulky petulance.

If Helen had lived, Sarah now thought, Nate could have been the only son. He could have monopolized his mother's attention, become her raison d'être. Or perhaps a dead brother would have been harder to compete with than a living one? Regardless, Helen had succumbed to breast cancer three years ago, leaving her sons without that point in the family triangle to hold them together. In the last year, the two brothers had scarcely spoken.

Sarah knew that it was a betrayal, to let Nate acquire this symbol of love between David and his mother. David had completed Helen's portrait as a Mother's Day gift, trumping Nate's fresh flowers with these painted lilies. But Nate would treasure it; all images of Helen were sacred.

"Keep them for the exhibit." Nate put both of the paintings back into the bin. "Just mark them for me."

By late afternoon Sarah was helping Nate pack boxes of clothes, books, and videotapes into his trunk. His visit had been more pleasant than she expected. He had taught her how to start the Weedwacker, and had trimmed the entire yard. He had checked the fluids in her car, and had shown her where to pour the oil.

"Are you going to be all right?" he asked as he stood beside his car.

"Of course." She gave him an awkward hug.

And then he did a strange thing. He lifted his right hand and combed it through her hair, pulling her bangs back from her eyes and stopping behind her ear, where he cupped his palm and held her skull as if it were a brandy snifter. He tilted her head toward him ever so slightly and leaned forward, kissing her gently on her left cheek.

Before she had time to think, he was in his car and down the street, leaving her blushing on the curb. She hadn't been kissed so tenderly in years, and the effect was wrenching. Her mind was caught between annoyance and puzzlement, wondering what sort of game he was playing. But her skin, still tingling with the soft pressure of his lips, whispered "More, more, more."

• 6 •

What woke her at 3:13 that night? There was no thunder, no rain on the roof. All was quiet as she sat up in bed, her knees pulled to her chest. She knew she had been roused by a loud noise, some sort of crash. It sounded as if it had come from the basement.

David is in the house, she thought. He's looking for something. Soon he'll be coming up the stairs. He'll turn the knob on the basement door and step into the kitchen with cold, damp feet. Wet indentations will sink into the rug as he walks down the hall.

He wants to come back to bed. He's so, so tired. He wants to get under the covers and warm his hands.

"Enough." She switched on her bedside light. She had to stop scaring herself with these morbid visions. David was not some clammy ghoul. He was a good man, and if his ghost was in the house, she should go to meet him.

She rose from her covers and reached for the terry-cloth robe that hung on her bedpost. As she tied the belt around her waist, she turned to face the open hallway.

There was nothing to be seen, of course. There never was. She walked down the hallway and into the kitchen, turning on every light. The furniture, the wallpaper, the carpets, all emerged from the shadows in their usual shapes. The patio door was locked; she always locked it now. That left only the basement door, waiting beside the pantry. It occurred to her that on the night of the memorial service, when she had seen David's ghost enter the kitchen, she hadn't thought to check the basement. She had been so drawn to the patio doors, so certain that he was standing on the other side, she had not considered that he might have gone downstairs. Now, with her hand on the basement doorknob, she wondered if she should hurry back to bed. Perhaps she should get under her covers and wait until morning; whatever was downstairs could be confronted in the daylight.

"Nonsense." If something or someone was in her basement, she should know about it. She took a deep breath, yanked open the door, and stared into the darkness.

Something was rushing up the stairs, something that howled. She managed two steps backward before the object wrapped itself around her legs. "Grace." She knelt and lifted the cat to her chest. "Did I leave you down there?"

The cat jumped from her arms and trotted down the hall while Sarah switched on the light and walked downstairs. As the furniture came into view, she spotted the problem on the opposite side of the room. A glass jar, filled with paintbrushes, had fallen off the shelves and shattered on the tile floor. She walked over and picked up the largest pieces, holding them gingerly in her hand. When she turned back to the stairs, she gasped.

David was watching her from the couch. His eyes were staring, his lips slightly open. His face looked unusually pale. It took two seconds for her to register that this was only his self-portrait, propped up against some pillows. Nate must have left it out, although it was strange—she thought they had been careful to put everything away. Looking down, Sarah noticed that her hand was bleeding. In her surprise, she had clutched at the broken glass.

"Shit." She went to the couch and with her free hand she picked up the self-portrait and returned it to the bin, next to the painting of Helen and her daylilies. Then she walked back upstairs, turned off the light, and dropped the pieces of glass into the trash can. Bent over the kitchen sink, Sarah watched her blood mix with the water as it flowed down the drain.

• 7 •

At seven o'clock the next evening Sarah sat on her porch steps, trying to muster the enthusiasm to visit Margaret's widows. She had dressed for the occasion, ironing a white blouse and crisp tan slacks, and what a shame it would be to have ironed for nothing. Ironing was such a rare event, done only because she envisioned the other widows in impeccable clothes—sixties-ish dowagers with light makeup and heavy jewelry, all trying to fill the empty spaces in their lives with conversation. God, how she dreaded the banalities to come, the insipid tenor of rich women's angst. But if she didn't make an appearance, Margaret would worry. She would think that Sarah was depressed or antisocial. And it wasn't true—not this time. It wasn't depression that held her back as she stared at the stiff leaves of her magnolia. It was a distinct fear that Margaret's friends would look into her heart, measure the depth of her sorrow, and find it lacking.

Over the past few months she had come to suspect that she wasn't truly mourning the loss of her husband. She was mourning the loss of an idea, a vision of how her life should have been. And that vision had not been swept down the river three months ago; it had been dying slowly over the past several years, with each small dream that she had abandoned.

Her dreams had never been overly ambitious. No—Sarah shook her head as she wiped a dead moth off the step beside her. She could not be accused of overreaching. During her first few years with David, living in New York, she had worked as an administrative assistant at a shelter for battered women. By day she had typed grant proposals and answered the telephone; by night she had stuffed fund-raising letters while watching TV. How righteous she had felt, and how incredibly bored. In her mind, the physical battery of wives began to blur with the economic exploitation of women such as herself, young idealistic females who did society's dirty work of caring for the needy, earning minuscule salaries or nothing at all.

When David was offered the position in Jackson, he had said that it would give her a chance to start again, but still she hadn't wanted to move. She already knew about small-town Southern life, the awkward blend of transplanted Yankees and Confederate flag-wavers. After her childhood in South Carolina, New York had seemed like progress. She felt that she was climbing a geographical ladder, if not a professional one. But who was she to block her husband's path? David had a career; more than that, he had a calling. And what did she have in New York, except a job that was going nowhere?

Jackson had proven to be more cultured than she expected. She had signed on as marketing director for a community theater that specialized in Appalachian folktales. But the group's financial health was never better than precarious, and after four years of treading water, Sarah had traded the world of nonprofits for its academic equivalent, a PhD in English.

What a luxury that had been, a six-year immersion in poetry from Beowulf to Bishop. Granted, the commute was tiring—three days a week across the mountains to Charlottesville—but she had compensated with weekends stretched in bed beside a pile of novels. Words had always been her most faithful companions, and her curriculum vitae boasted all the prerequisites for a brilliant future: published articles, conference papers, a dissertation fellowship. When her first foray into the job market yielded nothing, she hadn't worried. It often took several tries to land a tenure-track position, and at thirty-four she wanted, above all, to start a family. Part-time teaching at the local college would be ideal while she raised her children past their early years. She could still remember David's comment when he read her framed diploma: "I guess we're smart enough now to make a baby." At the time, it had seemed funny.

Once, in a footnote to a pregnancy guide, she had found a term for herself: the *habitual aborter.* She liked its criminal ring; it matched the darkness of her mind over the past few years, teaching expository writing to college freshmen who had never mastered subject-verb agreement. She had thought that adjunct teaching would be freeing, even fun, but instead it was a purgatory that paralleled her body's limbo—pregnant, not-pregnant, pregnant again. Her career and her family seemed equally stunted, which might not have mattered had she been younger, with plenty of time for life to unfold. But her thirty-ninth birthday had arrived like a plague, a hideous reminder that by forty a woman should have something to show for herself: a book, a child, an assistant deanship. Something more than a remodeled kitchen.

She had never been able to explain her misery to David. He was the sort of person who had witnessed other people's shortcomings, but had never tasted the bitterness of failure for himself. She felt that her miscarriages were tainting his perfect world, a barren wife being the most ancient blight of all, and she sometimes suspected that the acidity of her mind might be poisoning her womb; no life could grow within a body so bitter. Some nights David would stay at work just to avoid her tone at the dinner table. She recognized the fear in his meager excuses, the dread of a middle-aged woman turned prematurely sour, and for days at a time she was able to check her anger, talking airily about Asian babies, Russian babies, Romanian orphanages. But inevitably the knife edge of her temper would return.

So what should she tell Margaret's widows? That she was mourning her youth, her muted intellect, her unborn children? That she missed her husband less than she missed the early years of their life together, when each day had promised something new? In recent years their marriage had hardened into a daily routine, without accusation but also without passion. She supposed that was inevitable in most marriages.

Perhaps she should go back inside her house. Stay at home and pass the evening without speaking. She had done it before, gone for days seeing no one, living in silence, wondering if her vocal cords would atrophy. Before her the future yawned, a pale tundra in which her only conversations would be with telemarketers. That thought was sufficient to lift Sarah to her feet. Enough of this brooding. She would arise and go now, go to meet the widows, if only to hear her voice speaking aloud.

By seven-thirty a handful of strange women had assembled in Margaret's living room. Four were well over fifty, their husbands lost to a mixture of recent illnesses and old wars. Two younger women had been widowed in sudden accidents, a car crash and a waterskiing incident. "One if by land and two if by sea," as Sarah's morbid brain put it. Inside the kitchen she leaned against the round oak table, filling a platter with cheesecake squares and blueberry scones while Margaret recounted her guests' tragic histories.

"Patty is interesting, though a bit pompous. You might know her, she's the thin one with the red curly hair? She teaches in the sociology department."

Sarah shook her head.

"Anyway, she saw her husband through two years of lung cancer, and now she's made widowhood into a research topic. I think she's working on a book."

"So anything we say can be used against us?"

"Exactly." Margaret arranged some cheese and crackers on a lazy Susan. "Try to sit near Adele. She's the one with white hair and a peach jacket. Always dresses as if she's going to a garden party. She's eighty-two and her mind is sharp as a pin. Her husband died in Korea and she ran his hardware store for thirty-two years."

"Fascinating." Sarah rolled her eyes as she bit into a scone.

"Any woman who's lived through World War Two, Korea, and

Vietnam is going to be a lot more fascinating than you or me." Margaret put the lazy Susan into Sarah's hands and steered her shoulders toward the door.

Inside the living room, the conversation was centered on one of the older women, Ruby, whose husband, Bob, had died without leaving a will. The omission was especially troublesome, since Bob had a son by his first marriage who didn't approve of Ruby, and who was fighting her in court.

Sarah liked this Ruby woman—a petite, graying bulldog who used words like *greedy bastard*. Profanity was always entertaining when it fell from the mouth of a septuagenarian. Sarah lay the cheese and crackers on Margaret's coffee table, scanned the room for Adele, and settled into an armchair beside the only woman in peach.

It seemed that Bob's son wanted to liquidate everything. He thought they should hold a massive estate sale, transforming his father's life into a pile of money that could be divvied up. But Ruby refused to abandon the house, and insisted that she would spend the last years of her life within the space she had called home for the past decade. Stubborn Bob Junior, who had grown up within those same walls, resented his stepmother's intrusion, and now lawyers were scripting the family drama while their fees whittled away at Bob's estate.

Ruby's tale sparked a flurry of lamentations about wills, annuities, and government entitlements, all of which made Sarah newly grateful for Nate. He had handled everything after David's disappearance—insurance, taxes, Social Security. Nate had filled out all the paperwork, consulting with David's accountant and the college's personnel office, and scouring desk drawers for every policy, every receipt. Sarah had only to locate the "sign here" stickers at the bottom of each form.

David had left her with an insurance policy for four hundred thousand dollars, a sum he had chosen back when they were planning a family. Add that to the college's death benefit and her monthly Social Security checks, and widowhood had proven to be an enormous windfall. She planned to give half of the insurance money to the college, to establish a memorial scholarship for each year's top premed student, but thinking about the money only made her restless. Margaret's widows sounded more like an investment club than a bereavement group.

Sarah wondered what these women were really thinking. Did they feel lonely or liberated? Bottled up with rage, or drowning in apathy? She, who loathed group therapy, found herself wanting less talk about money and more about misery. She wanted someone to break down.

Perhaps that was why, when Ruby tipped her head and asked, "How are *you* doing?" she let the truth drop so abruptly.

"Not so great. I think I'm being haunted by my husband's ghost."

She expected silence. She thought her words would stain the atmosphere like a glass of red wine spilled on the carpet. But the reaction was just the opposite. The group seemed to bubble into life.

"Have you seen him?"

"Do you talk to him?"

"How does he look?"

She told them about the two occasions when she had seen David's ghost, and explained how she had often sensed his invisible presence, and all the while the women nodded, as if she were giving a recipe for chocolate chip cookies. When she finished, the red-haired professor spoke for the first time.

"It's not that unusual. Statistics show that widows are the most likely demographic group to report contact with the dead, everything from sightings of apparitions to vague feelings that ghosts are present."

"Of course," Ruby interrupted, clearly impatient at words like *demographic,* "women are much more psychic than men."

"I don't know about being psychic," the professor pressed on, "but women are more pious, and that makes them more likely to believe in ghosts, whether or not they're real."

"They're real all right." An older widow spoke up. "I saw one in my grandmother's backyard in Missouri, when I was eight years old. It was Thanksgiving morning and I was inside, reading in a window seat, and when I looked out there was a man standing under the big elm. It was my grandfather, clear as day. I recognized him from the pictures in Gran's bedroom. He died of a heart attack before I was born, right in the middle of a church service, and Gran always said that meant he'd gone straight to heaven. He was still wearing his Sunday best when I saw him, and it was windy, and his hair was blowing, and he looked cold. But he was gone in an instant, like it was just a thought that had flashed across my mind."

"I've never seen my husband," the woman added after a while. "I've waited for twenty years, but never a glimpse."

The water-skier's widow sighed, and spoke in a quiet voice. "The only time I see Greg is in my dreams. Sometimes I'll be talking to him, and it seems so real. Then I remember that he's dead, and I tell him so. That always wakes me up."

Around her the group murmured its assent. Dreams were the

widows' common denominator, the alternate world where life and death mingled. The redheaded professor launched into Freudian implications, while Sarah recalled visions of David, floating down the river.

She felt a hand touch her own, and turning to her left, Sarah found Adele leaning toward her, her dogwood brooch almost nicking Sarah's shoulder.

"I've spoken to my Edward many times in the past forty years. Sometimes I'll wake up and he'll be standing beside my bed, still wearing his uniform. And I'll say, 'Eddie, you go on now and rest easy. I'll be with you soon enough.' "

The old woman leaned back in her chair and chuckled, as if she had just told a marvelous joke.

Sarah didn't know whether to be pleased or appalled. She had almost come to accept David's appearances as a sign of mental breakdown, a delusion sparked by her isolation. But here were these women insisting that she wasn't crazy, she was normal. Somehow the idea didn't soothe her; a touch of insanity was preferable to the status quo.

She glanced over at Margaret, who was leaning against the kitchen doorway. "What do you think?"

Margaret hesitated, apparently choosing her words more carefully than usual.

"I think it's going to be hard for you to have any closure until David's body is found."

"Which means you think this is all in my head?"

"I didn't say that."

"But you don't believe in ghosts?"

Again Margaret hesitated.

"I believe there is a lot more going on in this world than we can comprehend. Whether or not that includes ghosts, I don't know. But I'll say this much—if you are really seeing David, there must be a reason. Either he is somehow trying to reach you, or you are trying to reach him. Most likely the latter. There's probably something unresolved in your mind."

It was ten o'clock when the group disbanded, waving and hugging and exchanging book titles on yellow Post-it notes. After everyone had left, Margaret retrieved a flashlight from her pantry and walked Sarah back to her house. There was only one streetlight at the start of the road, and its lavender glow faded as they walked to the end of the cul-de-sac, the beam from Margaret's flashlight bobbing like a buoy.

When they reached Sarah's porch, Margaret stayed on the lawn and shined the light up the stairs as Sarah unlocked her door.

"Thanks for inviting me," Sarah called back. "It wasn't so bad."

"Your enthusiasm is breathtaking."

"Tea at my house this Friday?" Sarah switched on the hall light.

"All right; and, Sarah?"

Sarah turned back and saw Margaret looking up at her with a slight smile.

"If David shows up again, tell him I said hi."

• 8 •

Two days later Sarah was walking through the Safeway, filling her cart with bags of Skittles and SweeTarts. It was Halloween, and her shopping was motivated by guilt. Upon entering the store, she had seen Mrs. Foster hoarding enormous amounts of fruit: "The kids are having a party . . . I'm making caramel apples." At Sarah's vague nod Mrs. Foster had added: "Do you want the boys to stop by this year?"

The question was meant kindly, but Sarah couldn't help imagining Mrs. Foster three years ago, inspecting her children's candy for razor blades and opened wrappers, and discovering a Ziploc bag of Oreos.

"Of course, have them come. I'd love to see their costumes." The neighborhood mothers were probably doubtful about her house this year, advising their children to leave poor Mrs. McConnell alone. Soon she would become the Boo Radley of the town, her life the subject of whispers, her address branded unlucky. Its location at the end of a street already made her house an inefficient stop on the Halloween route, unless the children were guaranteed a good payoff. And so she piled on the candy, imagining herself as the witch in "Hansel and Gretel."

Widows were often accused of witchcraft, so Sarah mused as she inched past the Laffy Taffy. There was something frightening about a solitary woman, something that made her fit for burning. Many cultures blamed widows for their husbands' deaths. Maybe this year she should retrieve her pointy black hat from the attic; some of the parents might appreciate the irony. She doubted it. Better not to put ideas into anyone's head. Better instead to stock up on these bags of miniature Snickers bars. She would greet Halloween with a bright porch light, a bottomless bowl of candy, and a smile calculated to assure the neighbors that she was utterly harmless.

The children began to emerge from their houses shortly after six. First came the Foster brothers, all three, even the fourteen-year-old, whose only costume was a rubber George Bush mask. "Terrifying," Sarah said as she extended a wooden salad bowl full of candy. She guessed that their mother had sent them together to pay their respects before they disbanded to their separate activities. All were unfailingly polite, taking only one piece of candy from her bowl.

"No, no, take more. I've got plenty inside." Their fingers spread into claws and depleted her bowl to half its depth. She would have to limit the next children to two pieces each.

Sarah had never before seen so many trick-or-treaters. She counted seventy-six in the first two hours, an insignificant number compared to the main residential drag, where the totals regularly topped three hundred. In recent years the town had been overrun by county dwellers, children from small farms or new rural subdivisions where each house was separated by at least six acres. Too hefty a trek for a single piece of candy. In the wealthy neighborhoods of Jackson children ran from door to door accumulating hoards of sweets, while their parents waited down the street in dusty pickups. Jackson's older residents complained that they were frightened by the unknown urchins and their lurking vehicles. Most of the old folks turned off their lights on Halloween and hunkered down, as if the children were a passing storm.

At Sarah's house, half of the faces were familiar. Mrs. Foster seemed to have spread the word that she was accepting trick-or-treaters, because all the local children made a point of coming down the street, saying "Thank you, Mrs. McConnell" and "Happy Halloween, Mrs. McConnell" with rehearsed precision. Sarah welcomed princesses and fairies, vampires and superheroes; Harry Potter reigned supreme.

By nine o'clock the stream of children had slowed to a drip. Her doorbell rang at intervals of five, eight, and ten minutes, rousing her each time from a tepid Poirot mystery movie. At nine-thirty, as the last child was leaving, she stepped out on the porch and scanned the street. Three houses down, heavy-metal music thumped through the Fosters' windows. Teenagers roamed the back lawn, drifting in and out of the bushes. Many pumpkins will be smashed tonight, she thought vaguely as she turned off the porch light and took the bowl of candy into her bedroom.

After changing into her nightgown, she settled under the sheets with a Mr. Goodbar. The body count for Poirot had reached three, but the inspector was unruffled. He conducted his search for clues as if it were a treasure hunt, confident that the prize was waiting at the end. She hated this cinematic version of predestination, where some characters were always fated to triumph, while others remained trapped in a cycle of despair. Clicking through the channels, she passed World Federation wrestling, CNN, the ubiquitous *Law & Order* rerun, and finally stopped at her nightly destination: the Weather Channel.

It had become a fascination in the past three months, to mute the sound and stare in silence at the ever-changing maps. She believed in weather as a measure of fate, the meteorologists a priestly caste with their hieroglyphic rain clouds, lightning bolts, and snowflakes. Her life had been irrevocably changed by a storm, and she suspected that she was one among many—not so much the farmers and fishermen, who lived by the skies, or the owners of coastline property who dwelled in the shadow of each hurricane season. Her sect was more select. She counted herself among the landlocked city dwellers and smug suburbanites, with their lightning rods and Tyvek walls and monstrous SUVs, who, in the midst of their well-insulated complacency, had found their lives altered by heatstroke or hailstorm or an ill-timed lightning bolt. They were the recent converts to the cult of weather, for whom each symbol on these maps represented another tragedy.

Sarah had just switched off the TV when a knock came at the door. The clock read ten-fifteen, too late to indulge any greedy newcomers. She rolled over in bed and closed her eyes, willing the child to vanish. But there it was again, three knocks, slow and heavy. Sighing, she pulled on her robe. She would have to tape up a sign—OUT OF CANDY—to keep the stragglers from knocking until eleven.

When she opened the door the darkness was startling. She had forgotten that she had turned off the light, and now she wondered what sort of child would stand at a pitch-black porch. Remembering the teenagers down the road, she braced herself for a Halloween prank. Something disgusting would be left on her mat, something squishy or smelly or dead; the children would be watching from the bushes, waiting for her scream. It was best not to disappoint them. With a sigh of resignation, she switched on the porch light and looked down. Nothing was there. Glancing to the right and left, she saw that all of the rocking chairs and potted plants were in their proper places; nothing had been altered, nothing left behind. The floodlight pouring from the eaves revealed no one on the porch, the walkway, or driveway. It seemed to be a case of knock and run, and she was turning to close the door when she saw something move in the shadows.

It wasn't a child. That much she could tell as her eyes settled on the black outline. It was a man, hidden underneath her vast magnolia. She was about to run and call the police, when the figure seemed to sense her impulse. He crossed from shadow into light and stood at the foot of her porch stairs.

She felt as if the air had been sucked out of her body. Her left hand reached out and she grabbed the side of the door, hugging it to her chest as she stared at her husband, standing there with his face glowing like the moon.

Sarah closed her eyes, guessing that this apparition would disappear as swiftly as all the others. But when she opened them again David was still there. Something about his steadiness helped to overcome her initial wave of shock. He didn't speak or move, but his body looked so tangible, it seemed to give substance to her own legs. She thought of what Margaret had said, how there must be something unresolved between them, and the thought gave her courage.

She pulled the door back, shielding herself with it as she opened a path into the house. Then she met David's eyes, and with a voice barely audible she whispered, "Come in."

PART TWO

Flesh

• 9 •

He hadn't meant for any of this to happen. So David claimed as he sat across from Sarah at their kitchen table, unfolding the long story of the past three months.

"I planned to see you the next day," he began. And Sarah listened, all the while asking herself: Could a ghost have such solid flesh? Could his weight creak in a chair? There was nothing amorphous about David. She's couldn't see through his skin. He smelled like a man who hadn't bathed in a week. Still, she couldn't shake the sense that he wasn't quite real. She'd read enough old legends to be suspicious of anything that came knocking on Halloween.

Back in July, David explained, when he left on his kayaking trip, he had expected to be gone only one night. Sarah was scheduled to meet him at five P.M. just north of the Buck Island Dam, where the Shannon widened into a small lake before dropping down a forty-foot concrete wall. There, a line of red buoys steered paddlers away from the precipice, toward a muddy portage point on the western shore. On Sunday Sarah would be waiting under the poplar trees, reading a paperback novel, sipping at something, probably bottled water. She would stand and wave as he approached, and together they would carry the kayak up from the river, across the road to the gravel parking lot. They would tie the boat to their station wagon, stow his paddle and gear in the back, and he would change into a clean T-shirt and tennis shoes. Halfway through their sixty-minute ride back to Jackson, they would stop to eat dinner at the Mexican café in Walker's Draft. Everything was arranged; life was predictable.

On the first day, all had gone according to plan. The Shannon, which alternated between class-two rapids, rippling rock gardens, and long stretches of flat water, was flowing at a perfect level. Water splashed his face and arms at every rapid, but nothing about the river was intimidating. In the calm sections he leaned back and let the current carry him beneath canopies of maple and oak. As he floated into the hills and meadows beyond the outskirts of Jackson, the subdivisions gave way to occasional farmhouses perched above the floodplain. He paddled underneath one highway overpass whose metal beams hummed a steady alto, and at the next bend a cluster of children hailed him from a rope swing, briefly coming to swim at his side like a pod of dolphins. No other paddlers appeared that day. His only companion was a great blue heron, flying from tree to tree fifty yards ahead.

The river was a temple of meditation. Lulled by its steady current, he formed resolutions as if it were New Year's Day. He vowed to exercise more, clean the attic, pressure-wash the porches. Above all, he needed to step back from his job. For the past two years he had spent hundreds of hours chairing committees and heading a push to build a new student health center, and although the causes were worthy, there was only so much joy to be gained from architects' drawings. He often thought that a private practice would be more fulfilling; then he could follow his patients' lives from diaper rash through acne, all the way to heart disease. But every time he imagined it, the insurance industry waited like a troll under the bridge. Besides, the answer to his restlessness did not lie in another variation on medicine. It waited in sunny afternoons, fishing, painting, and planting trees on their acres by the river. He wanted to visit friends out west—to hike through canyons he had seen only in *National Geographic*. And perhaps, if he worked fewer hours, he could salvage his marriage.

He and Sarah had been happy in their first decade together, satisfied with the present and hopeful about the future. It was only in recent years that they had lost their joint sense of purpose. Now they were held together by a web of social obligations, in which they fluttered like a pair of desperate moths. Sarah's trap was especially cruel, victimized by her own biology. Last year, as he watched her settling into a permanent funk, he had brought home a pack of Prozac, but her response was so biting, so completely ungrateful, he had never uttered those two syllables again. Now *divorce* was the unspoken word that hovered above them, the angel's sword waiting to fall.

The river slowed at a deep swimming hole, and David steered to the sandy bank, threw his paddle on shore, and stepped into the cool water. Pulling his kayak up the narrow beach, he sat and stared at the river. Six years ago he and Sarah had stopped at this same bank. They had shed their swimsuits and life jackets and folded their bodies together in the water, ripples multiplying around them like sound waves.

"We're scaring the fish." Sarah had laughed as she unwrapped her legs from his waist. Her voice in those days had a softer tone; the thought of its low music made him dig his toes into the sand. He needed to bring Sarah back to the river. She hadn't been paddling all summer, and only once the previous year. He needed to bring her out to the cabin, to get her into the water.

Water was an instrument of renewal, a medium for rebirth. And God knows Sarah needed a change. She was becoming unbearable, the way she lashed out at him like a cornered animal. After the first miscarriage he had been full of sympathy, bringing flowers, cooking dinner, rolling his own mourning into a tightly squeezed ball. All his energy had been devoted to keeping Sarah on an even keel. But after the second loss her grief was sharp as razor wire, a twisted perimeter holding him at bay.

Let her come to the river, David thought as he waded back into the water. He could play John the Baptist and give her a good dunking . . . No—he had to stop that bitterness. It was sad, how love was always tinged with aggression.

At two-thirty he reached their cabin, its backyard marked by a small dock extending from a muddy ledge. To the right and left the woods encroached, but here the sun fell on a wide clearing dotted with black-eyed Susans. He dragged his kayak up the bank and flipped it in the tall grass, laying his life jacket and spray skirt on top to dry. Fifty yards up the sloping yard, a bluish gray cedar cabin stood shaded by pine and oak, its back deck the only sunny spot fading in the heat. David walked around to the front and removed the spare key from its hiding place under a cracked brick beneath the shrubs.

Inside, the cabin air was thick with humidity, each piece of wooden furniture sweaty to the touch. He moved from room to room, opening windows and turning on ceiling fans. In the living room he paused at the sight of his brushes and paint, stacked near the window. For the rest of the day he would sit on the deck, sketch the trees, and try to see the world anew.

Only one thought troubled him as he settled outside with a beer in his right hand and a sketchbook in his left. Whatever peace he achieved this day could not be sustained once he returned to work. On Monday the summer school students would be lined up outside his door, sick from their weekend bacchanalias, while he and the nurses commiserated over cups of bitter Folgers.

A flock of Canada geese arrived at the dock, honking and flapping. David went inside, found his binoculars, then came back and focussed on a black head with shimmery eyes. How to begin to draw this creature? He studied the proportion between its large body and small head, measuring the width of its white chin strap with the lines on his knuckles, before counting the rows of feathers across the bird's back. The goose obliged by extending its neck, displaying a five-foot wingspan, so that David was struck by a vision of Raphael's angels, layer upon layer of feathers bridging the human and divine.

That evening as he drifted into sleep, he thought of the birds sleeping in the trees around him—finches and titmice, robins and wrens, cardinals male and female. Deep in dreams of feathers and flight, he barely registered the storm that passed in the early morning. When he woke he heard only the slow, repetitive call of mourning doves. Which was why, when he walked onto the deck with his first cup of coffee, he was startled by the river's change. The water was high with muddy bubbles foaming at the shore; clusters of pine straw and leafy branches flowed by at a fast clip. Now the rapids and rock gardens would be submerged; the swimming holes would look like frothy cappuccino. So be it, David sighed. He had paddled muddy water before, and the river's pace promised a quick trip. The usual five-hour journey to Buck Island would take half the time. If he left by two o'clock he could still meet Sarah on schedule, and perhaps the river would recede a little by lunchtime.

He went inside to set up his easel, planning to work by memory. Yesterday's blue-green water and gregarious birds were gone, but in his mind the river remained transparent down to its flickering trout. He opened his sketchbook and examined the pencil drawings of splayed tail feathers, puffy breasts, and one long beak extending from a small forehead. Then he dipped his brush into a circle of gray oil and marked the canvas.

It was noon by the time he stepped outside, his back and hands aching for release. Leaning against the deck rail, he rubbed his neck, lifted his eyes, and was surprised to see dark clouds forming in the west. The possibility of another storm hadn't crossed his mind. Hurrying into the cabin, he changed into his swimming trunks and stuffed his clothes and gear into his waterproof pack. He pulled the covers across his bed and shrugged at the unwashed dishes in the sink as he filled his water bottle. If he was going to stay ahead of the weather he would have to get on the river now.

Down at the water's edge, he turned his kayak right side up and stuffed his gear behind his seat. As he waded into the river, the current yanked at his boat; he climbed inside and was off, the sun in his face and the clouds lengthening at his back.

The river wrestled against his paddle, alive as any body he had ever tended. He imagined himself as a drop of blood flowing through an artery, but it was a cold-blooded creature that he inhabited; yesterday's sun-warmed current had been replaced with chilly rain. His boat was rushing down the veins of a snake, twisting its way through the mountains, and at each turn he steered clear of the meshes of fallen limbs that extended from the banks in impromptu dams, waiting to overturn him.

He was fifteen minutes downstream when he heard the first roll of thunder. The storm was still distant, but the wind was blowing in his direction. Paddling faster, he mulled over the best plan if lightning were to surround him. He had heard of a family of canoeists, electrocuted as they stood on a damp island in the middle of a lake, trying to wait out a storm. The best course was probably to take shelter under the shortest trees, crouching on the balls of his feet, to minimize contact with the ground.

When the first raindrops tapped his shoulders, he paddled harder, not looking back. But when the rain began to pelt down on his helmet, he turned his head and saw the dark clouds extending for miles. A lightning strike in the mountains convinced him that it was time to get off the river, but he hadn't counted on the strength of the current. As he tried to paddle toward the bank, he felt the inexorable force of the water, pulling him downstream. He would have to wait until the next sharp bend in the river. When the channel veered left or right, he would paddle straight ahead toward shore. Squinting forward through the rain, he tried to spot the best place to carry out his plan.

It was then that he heard it—a roaring like a jet engine, two hundred yards downstream. He was approaching a rock garden where the river dropped fifteen feet, while to the left, two crumbling stone walls jutted skyward. He recognized the tall stone ruins of the canal locks which had once enabled large boats to navigate the Shannon's shallow rapids. As the water hit the locks it was turning in upon itself, spitting back upward in a ten-foot geyser.

David began paddling with all his strength toward the left bank. There was no beach to aim for; the river was now swirling at the base of sycamore and maple trees as the bank sloped sharply upward. But the trees seemed to be reaching out, urging him into their arms, and in his rush to avoid the churning rapid, he did something stupid.

Seeing a large maple lean its branches down to the river's lip, he steered toward it, and as he passed under one of the limbs, he clutched it with his right hand. The idea was to stop his forward motion, to grab onto something solid and hold tight. But although he succeeded in abruptly halting the forward momentum of his upper body, his legs and hips, strapped into the kayak, raced on in front. With his chest leaning back and his waist yanked forward, he found himself instantly flipped over in the river, racing toward the rapid upside down.

As his head rushed forward in the darkness, he thought to attempt a roll, something he could manage in flat water and swimming pools. But with the river screaming around his ears and his mind disoriented, he reached instead for his pull cord, yanking his spray skirt away from the kayak. Emerging from the muddy water with a gasp, he reached for his boat but felt it being swept away. He was thirty yards from the geyser, with no chance of reaching shore; he would have to swim the rapid and hope that it spat him out safely at the other end.

His only thought was to get his legs downstream and lift his toes into the air. He had heard of paddlers fallen into rapids, who tried to stand up and had their feet trapped in rocks. Either their knees were broken backward or they were held underwater and drowned. Now, as he was swept toward the edge of the rapid, he took a huge breath of air and released his paddle, watching it disappear over the ledge. Then he was falling into the vortex, sucked vertically downward, legs first.

Underwater, his body tossed like a puppet. He tried to scramble upward, scratching toward sunlight, but the water's force pummeled him back down. He was caught in a hole, and in the midst of his panic he remembered what he had been taught in his earliest kayaking lessons—don't try to swim directly upward. Swim down toward the bottom, then make your way to the side, away from the hole, before attempting to ascend. With his breath almost gone he tried to swim downward, though the rush of water was so confusing he could scarcely get his bearings. Touching rocks at the bottom and the canal wall to his left, he began to pull himself to the right, away from the hole, but it was pointless. The water was pouring down in every direction, his lungs were bursting, his arms weakening. Even as he dragged himself along, rock by rock, he could feel his mouth opening, his lungs ready to breathe water. He imagined the mud settling into his windpipe, his blood fading to brown, and he lurched about with a last flutter of panic as he felt the water enter his throat. Then his mind grew dizzy, his muscles relaxed, and he saw Sarah waiting under a poplar tree, reading her paperback. The water rolled him over onto his back like an old log, and now Sarah was standing, waving at him. She was coming down to the river's edge, urging him ashore. *Hurry up please, it's time.*

And suddenly his body and soul were reunited on the water's surface, thrown clear of the hole. He was floating with the current past the locks and away from the heaving rapid. Am I dead? he wondered. Is this my corpse? But the sound of his gagging interrupted his dream.

With aching legs he kicked toward shore, thankful for the life vest that kept him bobbing. As he neared the bank, he reached again for a sycamore branch hanging over the water, and this time he was able to hold fast. He pulled his body forward leaf by leaf until his feet touched river bottom. Then he staggered out of the water, onto the wet leaves, and allowed his legs to buckle as he coughed up phlegmy streams of muddy water. On his knees for the first time in a decade, he rocked back and forth, hovering between moans and prayer: "Oh God, oh God, oh God."

· 10 ·

David rested on the bank for almost ten minutes, the rain forming puddles around his knees. Finally he stood and tried to get his bearings. He had lost his kayak, his paddle, his food and water and cell phone, but he still had his wallet, Velcroed into the breast pocket of his life vest. The thought of the salvaged credit cards and wet green dollars gave him an ironic sense of substance. He had his Visa; he would live to see another day.

But which way should he go? His rendezvous point with Sarah was several miles downstream, past an unpopulated stretch of river. He didn't think he could walk that far with his legs still trembling. He remembered passing a cabin on this side of the river, shortly after the rain began. That was his best bet for a telephone.

Ten minutes into his slow walk home, the bank ascended into a steep, rocky cliff, and David had to climb with it, pulling himself from ledge to ledge, gripping the trunks of saplings. From the ridge above the river he saw no houses, only trees and hills, rolling into the distance. The lightning had passed; that was a blessing. He had only to endure the cold misery of trudging through woods in soaked clothing. Another half mile and the ridge descended through a steep gully, where a stream flowed into the river. What was usually a clear trickle from an underground spring was now a seven-foot-long jump. He paced up and down the edge of the stream, looking for the narrowest crossing, then took a running leap and almost made it, one foot landing on the leaves, the other sinking into the water, wrenching his ankle.

"Son of a bitch!" He fell forward and clutched at the pain. "Motherfucking son of a bitch!" He raised his face to the clouds and released a long, wordless howl that dwindled to nothing beside the roar of the muddy river. And then he began to laugh—how pitiful, the fury of one man against the rage of nature. Rising to his feet, he spotted an adequate walking stick not far from his hand, and accepted it as a sign of providence.

When he reached the strange cabin he saw no lights or cars. The door was locked, a few windows were shuttered, and he briefly thought of breaking in. But these hunting cabins rarely had telephones; if the owner was not around with a cell phone, it was pointless. The best he could hope for now was to return to their own cabin and ride his trail bike up to the general store, four miles away.

As he continued through the woods he noticed muskrats and mice, scurrying along the river's overflowing bank. He felt aligned with them, one more refugee from the flood. When a snake startled by his foot, he recognized the danger of stepping on a copperhead so far from help, and he trod more carefully on his throbbing ankle.

He hadn't realized how far he had traveled from the cabin. Although he had been on the river for only thirty minutes, the speed of the current had carried him several miles downstream, and when he finally saw his backyard clearing, visible in green flashes between the pines, it seemed like an oasis—a fluorescent hallucination.

Inside the cabin he peeled off his wet clothes, threw them on the bathroom floor, and turned on the shower. His skin was too numb to tell whether the stinging stream was hot or icy, but when the steam began to rise, he sat on the tub floor, letting the water pour down his face and chest and knees, thawing him cell by cell. After twenty drowsy minutes he realized that he was in danger of falling asleep, spared by the river only to drown in his tub. He turned off the water, dried himself with a towel, and lay down in his bedroom, wrapped tight in a warm comforter. The digital lights on the radio clock read four-thirty; the general store closed at five on Sundays. It was too late to ride there and use the phone. Anyway, he was too exhausted to move. Sarah would be frantic, but for now, his only desire was to feel the miracle of his lungs, breathing in and out.

The clock read five-thirty when David woke, and as he waited for his mind to clear, he thought that he had slept for less than an hour.

But gradually he noted the voices of birds, and the glow of dawn falling through the window. Pulling on a T-shirt, he walked into the living room and opened the door onto the deck.

The river was still high and muddy but the sky was clear, all traces of storm swept away. Around him the world was dripping—from the trees, the eaves, the corners of the bird feeder, and the sound triggered again the deep sense of calm he had experienced on Saturday. Pleased by the rain-soaked boards beneath his feet, David spread his arms, lifted his eyes to the sky, and thought, I am Adam, newly created, Lord of my garden.

With three hours before the general store opened, he carried his easel and palette outside, wiped off the deck furniture, and brought out a cup of coffee. Never had the trees glistened so brightly, their branches a slick ebony. His eyes followed the spread of one sycamore's limbs, from arteries, to capillaries, to each leafy cell nodding at the water's edge. He watched the lowest leaves bob in the current, thinking how his body was equally fragile, little more than a floating stick.

All morning David painted his ideal river, green water sprinkled with white flecks of sunlight, tree shadows skimming the surface. When it was time to leave for the store, he felt disappointed. His painting wasn't finished, and neither was his soul's rejuvenation. But Sarah would be sick with worry and his patients would be waiting, so he stuffed his wallet into his front pocket, walked outside to the storage shed, and lifted his mountain bike from the stacks of flowerpots and lawn chairs.

It had been years since he and Sarah had ridden together on these mountain roads. Shortly after buying the cabin they had gotten matching bikes, hoping to explore the area without the accompaniment of a car engine. In the first few years they had spent long afternoons pedaling logging trails, startling chipmunks and deer. Once, an adolescent black bear had paused in their path, assessing them with slow curiosity. David could still remember his reaction—a mixture of awe and vulnerability. Far from the hard shell of his car, how would he protect his exposed arms, and his wife's bare throat?

But on this morning there were no bears, no deer. His eyes were trained on the gouges in the muddy road, where the flash flood had swept gravel into the woods. Rocks and puddles jolted his kidneys, so that by the time he reached the first cluster of houses outside the village of Eileen, his calves were spattered like a Pollock canvas.

Inside the general store, he waved at the woman using the pay phone in the back, but she gave no sign of acknowledgment. He bought a donut, a bottle of orange juice, and a local paper, then walked outside to the picnic table and spread the news before him.

The lead story described the new dean of students at the college, a former Yale professor who had arrived in town with a clear mission to curb the excesses of the Greek system. Good luck, David thought, opening his bottle of juice. Scanning down the page, he stopped at the headline FLASH FLOOD CLAIMS THREE. Two small girls had been swept down their backyard creek. Sad, very sad. Then he read the name of the third victim: *David Robert McConnell.*

Goose bumps prickled along his arms as he stared at the words *missing and feared lost.* He recalled that odd sensation in the river, when the sun appeared like a divine revelation and he felt his spirit rising to the surface. Here, in the infallible medium of print, was the confirmation of his death.

Reading on, he learned how Sarah had called the police after waiting an hour in the rain, trying to reach him on his cell phone. Poor Sarah. He walked inside the store again and glared at the woman on the telephone. She turned away.

Back at the table David read the final paragraphs. The police had found his kayak and personal belongings along the banks near Buck Island. Today rescue teams would drag the deep water above the dam, using dogs in the boats to try to sniff out the corpse. They'll never find me here, David thought, and as he imagined their futile searching an unexpected smile tugged at his lips. It occurred to him that he didn't need to contact the office right away. No one was going to be expecting him at work that morning. Death had granted him a holiday, and he felt like a child, waking to an unforecasted snow.

Of course he would have to call Sarah. By now she would be stricken. But even as he rose once more to check the telephone, a strange sensation held him back. From some remote corner of his mind, one emotion surfaced—morbid curiosity. How *would* Sarah react to his death? Would she be overcome with grief? Miss him terribly? Would she care as much as she had cared for all those babies? Or would she, deep in her quiet soul, feel relieved? They had been struggling on the edge of separation for so long, perhaps this was an opportunity—perhaps, an act of God.

And then the impulse came, so concrete it almost hurt—an unmistakable desire to run away. Of course it was ridiculous. He had a wife, a job, a mortgage. He was a responsible person, known for doing the right thing. But what *was* the right thing for a man in his midforties, when his marriage and work had stagnated? Wasn't there something else that he had envisioned for his life, some dream that might still be possible? All around him the trees were whispering invitations, encouraging him to fade into their shadows, and as he watched their branches nod, David sat back down.

• 11 •

Ten minutes later he was pedaling to the cabin, the telephone growing distant behind him. He assured himself that this retreat was only temporary. He would finish his painting, rest a little, and return to his life the next day. The painting could be a gift for Sarah, an atonement for his selfish absence. She was his Penelope, waiting for her shipwrecked husband.

But that night, as the sunset spread across the treetops, he assumed Penelope's role himself. Leaning over his easel with a moist rag, he daubed out the geese he had painted that afternoon. His work was not complete; he would need another day.

The next morning he woke early, painted for an hour, then rescued his fly rod and tackle from the cobwebs in the storage shed. Dead beetles fell from his hip boots when he shook them out. He reached a gloved hand down into the toes to feel for mouse nests, before donning the boots like plaster casts and lumbering off through the woods. A few times the tip of his rod caught in honeysuckle vines, but eventually he emerged at his favorite fishing hole, where the river descended in wide, stairstep ledges. There he tied his lucky fly, waded in above his knees, and began whipping the water's surface, his line whistling a tuneless song. Initially he thought of Sarah, and all the excuses for his disappearance, but after the first bite, nothing else mattered for the rest of the morning.

Walking back two hours later with a pair of trout in his bucket, David glimpsed the green patch of his backyard and froze. A policeman was standing on the dock, pistol holstered at his side.

Of course, David thought as he crouched behind a tree. He should have expected this. Someone would have to be dispatched to search the cabin. They had probably combed the woods from Buck Island to this spot, maybe with dogs—dogs that had caught his trail on the bank near the canal locks, and had led them all the way to the cabin's back door. Maybe the dogs would catch his scent now and howl him out, sheepish and apologetic, the ludicrous truant.

The policeman on the dock removed his hat, and David relaxed. He knew this guy. It was Carver, Carver Petty, a black man in his late thirties, the favorite local cop among the college crowd. Carver was the kind of man who never arrested students for public drunkenness, unlike his overly zealous colleagues. When he found college kids vomiting in park bushes, he drove them to the campus hospital, where they could sleep it off under a nurse's observation.

"You're a good man," David had often said, taking some staggering freshman off Carver's hands. To show his thanks, David had offered free medical care for Carver's nine-year-old daughter, saving them the copayment at her pediatrician's office. She had been raised by Carver ever since his wife walked out eight years earlier. Luckily the child was blooming with health, her problems limited to mild bronchitis in the winter, poison ivy in the summer. David sent them home with free samples of hydrocortizone.

So now Carver had come to investigate the cabin, the last place where Dr. McConnell was known to be alive. David tried to remember whether he had left any signs of current habitation. He hadn't eaten breakfast, so there was no food on the table, no radio playing, no door propped open. There was only his painting, still wet on the easel. He wondered if Carver had noticed; perhaps he was waiting for the doctor to show himself.

As David wondered what to do, he watched Carver place his hat over his heart, look out across the river, then wipe his eyes with his left hand. And with that small gesture of grief David knew that he was safe.

An hour later he was alone and back at his painting, scraping away a layer of feathers with his palette knife. Tomorrow he would return home, so he told himself. It would be the third day, the proper time for the dead to rise. He could appear to Sarah first, and perhaps she would forgive him. Or perhaps not. The time for forgiveness might be long gone.

The next morning, threading through the woods on a slow walk, David tried to concoct a plausible story. Amnesia was comical, a broken limb too easily disproved. Hypothermia, however, gave him pause. Now there was a logical diagnosis. He could claim that after his near drowning, the rainy hike had left him bedridden with severe chills, compounded by a twisted ankle. He had attempted a trek to the general store on the second day (which would explain why he had missed Carver's visit), but the swelling had been so bad he'd had to turn back after a mile.

David was reviewing his symptoms with professional detail, nearing the western side of the cabin, when suddenly he stopped. Margaret's blue Accord was parked in the drive, which could mean only one thing. Sarah had come looking for him. She would see his dishes in the sink, the painting on his easel, and the game would be over. Sarah would recognize the signs of life.

He wondered if he should walk into the cabin and confess everything, trusting that the women's wrath would fade over time. And perhaps that would have been the right thing to do, but instead he found himself sneaking up to the kitchen window, peering through the glass from behind a rhododendron. He saw Margaret throwing away his food—the ham, the mayonnaise, the apples and tomatoes. She must hate me, he thought as he watched his supplies disappear into her plastic trash bag. But then he considered Sarah, standing beside his easel, examining the brushes soaking in turpentine. And oddly enough, her eyes were not angry, her mouth was not prepared to scold. She appeared sad and contemplative, an expression he had witnessed in hospitals and at gravesites. David realized that he was looking at two widows, come to clean the mess left by a dead man, and for the first time since his absence, the shame swept over him.

He crouched with his back to the cedar boards and pressed his fingers against his temples. What an idiot he was. What a son of a bitch. He, the doctor, was causing pain.

Had Sarah been alone he would have revealed himself at that moment, but he dreaded Margaret's disdain. In the face of her pragmatic nature his retreat into the woods seemed pathetic. He would have to wait for some future occasion when he could speak to Sarah alone.

Glancing into the window, he saw her approach his bedroom, and he circled quietly to the northern side of the cabin. Through unwashed glass blurred with a spiderweb, he watched her smooth the mattress, pull the sheet tight, and fold it down six inches, perfectly horizontal. She tucked the edges under the mattress, fluffed two pillows and placed them over the fold. Then she sat on the bed and stared at the closet.

If she cries, I will go to her. He never could bear to see Sarah cry. Whenever she was troubled he had always hurried to correct the problem with a joke, a bouquet, or a prescription. That was why he had felt so helpless during the miscarriages, why he had stayed in the basement at night while she cried in bed. Because all he could do was offer cups of chamomile tea, kiss her forehead, rub her shoulders, clean the bathroom and the bloody sheets.

It all came back as he searched Sarah's face for hints of anguish. There were no tears, no sobbing. Her expression was stoic, which made him stare all the more. Did this woman really miss him? Sarah was so difficult to read. Not like his young female patients, who seemed to welcome college as the age of display, saying "Look at *this*, doctor. Look at *me*." His wife never invited observation, which was one of the things that appealed to him. Sarah had layers of reserve that shielded a heart which was genuinely, intensely warm—whenever he could reach it. In these past few years it had gotten harder for him to touch that heated core, she guarded it so closely. Still, he felt an odd thrill in looking at her, trying to interpret her subtlest gestures. Of course he recognized this spying as a shallow temptation. Doctors knew the horror and the fascination of other people's tragedies; the spectacle of human suffering was a sadistic pleasure.

David pulled himself away and walked back into the woods. Fifty yards past the cabin he sat at the base of a small hill and waited for the sound of a door closing, the start of a car's ignition. When he heard the clatter of Margaret's tires spinning on gravel, he looked back and watched a flash of blue metal, carrying Sarah far away.

• 12 •

That night in the cabin David felt, for the first time, unmistakably dead. For the past few days he had reveled in the possibilities of a new life, but now he mourned the old one. He tried to reassure himself that there was still time. Time to confess, to return to his previous routine. But how could his former life be anything other than diminished?

Tomorrow he would have to go to the general store, to replace the food that Margaret had thrown out, and there he would face the telephone, waiting like the wife he was neglecting. That would be the moment of reckoning, the point of no return.

All night he slept fitfully, thinking of Sarah sitting at the foot of this bed, surveying the room with those sad, dark eyes. It was cruel to let a woman mourn for a living man, cruel to leave her alone in their empty house. But their marriage had already been a form of grief, and any momentary joy she felt in his reappearance would not last long. He told himself that their best hope for happiness was to change their lives, and this was a change beyond imagining.

By sunrise his mind was already set. He would stay at the cabin and try to create a new life, something Sarah might want to share. When the time was right, he would return to her, and ask if she wanted to start again.

On the ride to the store, he considered everything that he was leaving behind. The college would be fine without him; several physicians in town would be happy to take his place, and his student patients came and went so frequently, he had made few strong connections. For serious ailments, undergraduates usually went home to their family doctors, and as for the faculty, most of them avoided the college waiting room, dreading sick students who might plead for extensions.

All in all, he felt surprisingly few obligations toward other human beings. His friends were so busy with their jobs and children, they wouldn't have much time to mourn, and Nate had so many consolations between his women and his wealth, he would never suffer for long. Only Sarah had the capacity for extended grief. Sarah, with her memories, her poetry, her inconsistent philosophies. He could not leave her in limbo. Eventually he would have to go to her, to explain everything and give her the power to decide what should happen next in their lives.

At the store he withdrew two hundred dollars from the ATM. He guessed that Sarah wouldn't notice; she never balanced her checkbook and maintained only an approximate notion of what the totals should be. Their funds were always sufficient, and when the bank sent its monthly statements she simply glanced at the balance and threw the sheets onto his pile of papers to be filed. Widowhood would probably change her habits, but that would take months, and by then they would have spoken. In the meantime, the money machine would serve as his accomplice.

He was going to need more supplies. Two pairs of underwear were insufficient to start a new life, and the general store offered meager groceries—canned fruit, Wonder Bread, milk cartons with overdue expiration dates. He needed warm clothes, medicines, and hardware. He needed, alas, a Wal-Mart. Sarah almost never visited the one on the outskirts of town. If he went there in the early morning, he could probably avoid anyone he knew.

David planned his shopping for the following Tuesday, and prepared by growing a seven-day beard. When the time came, he wore a baseball cap, his knapsack, and black sunglasses that darkened the sunrise to a midnight glow. He pedaled along side roads as much as possible, averting his face whenever a vehicle passed. The mountains were grueling and his legs were weak; he had to push his bike up some of the hills, so that the forty-minute car ride to Jackson took nearly three hours. It was almost nine o'clock when he arrived at the supercenter, an hour behind schedule, but when he scanned the parking lot for familiar cars, he recognized none.

Inside the door, he angled his face away from the security cameras. Removing his sunglasses, he hurried through the aisles, indiscriminately grabbing fishing line and hooks, underwear and socks, a sweatshirt, blue jeans, a spatula, tape. Each minute was an excruciating exercise in paranoia. He cringed at every possible encounter, maintaining an aisle between himself and all other shoppers, but it was a needless precaution. The strangers remained isolated in their own concerns, more attentive to prices than to people.

The only person who looked him in the eye was the checkout

girl, who smiled and asked, "Credit or debit?" He had automatically run his card through the machine—the Exxon Visa that Sarah rarely used. Now he would have to sign his name on a piece of dated paper, the first tangible proof of his life after death.

"I'm sorry. Can I pay with cash instead?"

"Sure. Just press cancel."

Outside, next to the riding mowers, he emptied his plastic bags into his knapsack, and was surprised at how few of his provisions fit inside. Glancing around, he kicked off his shoes, pulled his new blue jeans over his shorts, and tied the sweatshirt around his waist. He stuffed fishing line into his pockets and tied tube socks around his handlebars, looking like some kind of bike-riding homeless man. But no one stopped, no one stared. Silly, to have imagined himself as a magnet of attention. He could probably ride through town as unnoticed as every other ghost.

Only at the parking lot exit, when a blue Accord pulled up on his left, did he feel his stomach clench. There was Margaret, the ubiquitous woman, concentrating on the red light. Slowly, very slowly, avoiding sudden movements, he turned his handles to the right and coasted into the gas station on the corner. He stood behind a pump and watched until the last trace of blue had disappeared down the road, then he pedaled ferociously away from town.

A mile later, where the fast-food restaurants gave way to farmers' fields, he stopped by a meadow of Queen Anne's lace and dropped his bike in the grass. His heart was pounding, his hands sweaty. At the edge of a barbed wire fence, he stared out across the pasture, and wondered if Margaret had noticed him. Surely she would have stopped and stared. He could still see her silhouette, an arm's length away, and how strange it felt, to be fleeing from neighbors, cringing at all human contact. His exchange with the checkout girl had been his first scrap of conversation in seven days. With no telephone at the cabin, no television or computer, the bedside clock radio was his sole companion, its reception so weak all he could pick up was the local country music station. He preferred the sound of whippoorwills and even the cawing of these crows that now gathered before him, hopping among the goldenrod.

• 13 •

Two weeks later as he sat on the deck, thumbing through a newspaper from the general store, David came across the announcement of his memorial service. Saturday, four P.M., Jefferson Chapel. In lieu of flowers, donations were being accepted at the Rural Development Medical Clinic.

He read the item three times, wondering if he could get away with another trip to town. The service didn't appeal to him so much as the idea of seeing Sarah, and trying to gauge her feelings. But going to town was risky. His Wal-Mart escapade had left him stupidly fearful, dreading a knock at the door—Margaret or Sarah or Carver. But as each day had passed in solitude, he had become more convinced of his invisibility. The human brain manipulated visual data into objects that were comprehensible and expected. No one had expected to see him at Wal-Mart, just as no one would be looking for him at his own memorial service.

The next day he packed his knapsack with bottled water, a bag of trail mix, and a paperback novel. He had shaved his beard several days earlier, but his sunglasses and baseball cap made him confident. Most of the people who knew him would be inside the chapel. If he came late and kept his distance, the chances of detection were slim.

At five minutes to four he arrived in the woods at the edge of the college campus. Leaning his bike against a pine tree, he followed a circuitous route, shying away from the busy quad with its imposing perimeter of brick buildings from which a colleague might suddenly emerge. When the stone chapel appeared, he veered to the opposite side of a hedge twenty yards to the left. There he stretched on his side in the grass, pulled the book from his knapsack, and tipped his head toward the pages so that the ball cap shadowed his face. Behind his sunglasses he closed his eyes and listened to the sounds floating through the chapel windows. "Amazing Grace," "Be Still My Soul," a collective recitation of the Twenty-first Psalm, then a long stream of speakers, distinguishable only as alto, tenor, and bass. A half hour passed before he heard the young reverend, his volume higher than the others, using words like *Christ, redemption,* and *heaven.* A breathy flute whispered Gounod's "Ave Maria" and the air was hushed in benediction, broken by the organ's cry of "Onward Christian Soldiers."

He turned and looked through the leaves as the human record of his life emerged from the chapel doors. First Sarah and her sister, Anne, arm in arm; then Anne's husband and two daughters, followed by Nate with his latest blonde. The reverend gathered them into a receiving line as the congregation passed—administrators, faculty members, several student patients. His squash partner, his dentist, the owners of his favorite restaurant. Three cousins, two college roommates, most of Jackson's medical community. He felt a grim satisfaction at the size of the crowd.

Sarah seemed to be enduring the condolences with admirable patience, accepting a handclasp from the dean she despised, a kiss from Mrs. Foster while her boys kicked at the shrubs. When most of the mourners were gone, she walked alone to a wrought-iron bench, and David followed on the opposite side of the hedge. In her face he saw none of the collapsing misery that had come with her miscarriages, only a drawn, tired expression.

Suddenly he crouched, for she had done something strange. She had stood up and turned in his direction, as if called by a familiar voice. Her eyes scanned the hedge, then stared into the sky, and finally she walked back to the chapel, placed her hand against its exterior, and began tracing around its edge, disappearing from view. He returned to his original vantage of the chapel entrance and watched Sarah appear around the corner. Nate offered her his elbow and escorted her to the car, while his girlfriend followed five paces behind. The three of them climbed into a blue Accord, and for the second time that summer he watched Margaret whisk Sarah away.

Show's over, he thought. There would be no funeral procession, no headlit drive to the cemetery. There was nothing to bury or burn, no corpse to slather with grisly makeup. He supposed they would all congregate at his house, and he wondered if he should follow.

Behind him, the five-thirty sun leaned toward the Alleghenies. If he didn't leave soon he would be pedaling through the mountains in complete darkness. Still he hesitated, because in watching Sarah, the dark, addictive pleasure had returned. Shameful as it might be, he wanted to know what was going on inside her head, what secrets she might reveal in her unsuspecting quiet.

Ten minutes later he was headed home, not on the usual roads, but through fields and alleys that led to the woods beside his backyard. On a slope overlooking the eastern side of the house, David rested his bike on the leaves and knelt behind a screen of blackberry bushes. To his left, a row of parked cars revealed the identities of Sarah's visitors. His accountant drove the silver Audi; the BMW must be Nate's. The maroon station wagon belonged to his favorite nurse, Anna Marie.

On the patio, mourners circled Sarah while Margaret poured iced tea into crystal-blue glasses. Nate stood farther down the yard, beside the butterfly bushes, running his fingers along his girlfriend's naked arm. Strange, thought David, how the trees' shadows formed a boundary between himself and the sunlit world. Although his name kept rising from the crowd, a curtain had fallen between his life and the drama below. When he sat against a white pine and closed his eyes, he felt that his exile was complete.

After two hours all of the cars were gone except for Nate's. David walked down from the slope, leaned up against the house's back wall, and glanced into the kitchen. Anne was fixing a pot of tea—good, reliable Anne. She was arranging cups on a tray, filling a purple sugar bowl. He moved to the living room window and watched her carry the tray to the coffee table. She poured a cup for Sarah, who was sitting on the sofa, and two more for Nate and his girlfriend in the wing chairs across the room. David smiled as his brother sipped politely; Nate was no tea drinker.

Around him, the twilight air felt chilly; it would be a cold night sleeping in the woods. To his right, concrete steps led to the basement door, and quietly, very quietly, he walked down the stairs and tried the knob. The door was unlocked; that much hadn't changed in the past three weeks. He walked across the dark space and stretched out on the couch. A half wall separated the top of the stairs from the main room; if someone came down from the kitchen, he would have a few seconds to hide behind the sofa.

Evening faded into night until the room was completely black, but he did not turn on a light. Instead he lay there listening to the voices above. Occasionally a word emerged—"yesterday," "ceremony," "river," "David." The rest were a haze of syllables, mixed with footsteps in the kitchen. This, he thought, is what it must be like to be buried—to lie underground, paralyzed in the darkness while the living murmur overhead.

He heard a change in tone, bits and pieces of good-bye. Footsteps crossed the hallway and the front door closed, followed by a car's gradual departure. The two sisters were left in the kitchen, the lilting alto of their voices punctuated by the clatter of dishes in the sink. Water gurgled through the basement pipes as a toilet flushed, then footsteps moved across the floor and up the stairs.

Another fifteen minutes and the house was silent. Sitting up, David switched on the lamp and waited for his eyes to adjust. They settled on the bookshelves on the opposite wall, filled with old paperbacks. At the cabin, the only decent book was an anthology of short stories that he had read twice over the past few weeks. The others were house rejects, third-rate novels and college textbooks. David walked to the shelves and touched the books' spines. Here were the sort he wanted, time-consuming classics: *War and Peace*, *Huckleberry Finn*, *David Copperfield*. Sarah would not need them for her women's studies classes. He stacked them by the couch, along with a pile of *National Geographics*, a Penguin edition of Shakespeare's tragedies, and Fielding's guide to North American birds.

When he stepped back to assess the books, something was missing. Perhaps it was his brush with death, or the silence of the woods, but for the first time in his adult life he wanted to read the Bible. Upstairs they had a beautiful copy, a gift from his mother on his twelfth birthday. "Required reading," she had called it, "if only to understand Shakespeare." After listening for the slightest sound in the house above, David took off his shoes and approached the stairs.

He ascended one step at a time, testing each stair for creaking joints before planting his weight. At the top, he turned the knob and silently pushed the door, just a crack, to check that all was clear before he entered the kitchen. He left the door slightly open, so that he wouldn't have to turn the knob again on his way down, then he glided into the living room, took the Bible off the shelf, and rearranged the other books to hide the gap. He paused to thumb through the New Testament, where the words of Jesus appeared in flaming red, as if to keep Christ's blood forever on one's conscience. *Our friend Lazarus has fallen asleep, but I go to awake him.*

David's eyes leaped at the sound of feet. Sarah was coming down the stairs, her legs now in view. How stupid of him, not to have realized that she might still be up there. A few steps more and she would have a clear vantage into the living room. He thought to hide, but any movement might attract her attention, and so he stood still as a lamp, watching her fingers trace the banister, down, down, curling to the right, away from him, into the hallway. She never looked up. He listened to her bare feet walk down the hall and into their bedroom, then he waited for the door to close, but the sound didn't come. Sarah was opening her closet door, walking in and out of their master bathroom. With a click, the hallway dimmed, and he knew that she had turned off her overhead light, leaving only one lamp, probably the one on her bedside table. He waited again for silence, then swiftly, with Bible in hand, he crossed from the living room into the kitchen and tiptoed downstairs, closing the basement door gently. From the corner of his eye he had seen Sarah at her vanity, her back turned, apparently oblivious to his presence. He sat motionless on the couch, hoping for silence.

After a little while he heard her feet coming down the hall. She was entering the kitchen, standing near the basement door. Obviously she had seen him. At any moment the door would swing open, the overhead light switch on, and Sarah would descend. So be it. It was time. They were alone, the house was quiet. Three weeks of separation had tested their marriage. Explanations, wholly inadequate, raced through his mind. But just as he was settling on his opening words, he heard the rapid patter of feet, running back along the hall. Strange. He waited another ten minutes, but the danger seemed to have passed.

David set the clock radio beside the couch for five A.M. Tomorrow, in the half-light, he would wake and leave Jackson before anyone might recognize him. In the meantime, he pulled a crocheted afghan up to his shoulders, lay back against the pillows, and opened the Bible. *In the beginning God created the heavens and the earth. The earth was without form and void, and darkness was upon the face of the deep; and the Spirit of God was moving over the face of the waters.*

* * *

Ever since that night, he had known that he must return and speak to Sarah, but only in the past week had he finally come back, sleeping in the basement at night and watching from the woods by day, trying to study her face, to sense if she would want him. He had watched her eat on the patio, walk down the street, read in bed with glasses of red wine. And yes, he had watched her undress at night, hair falling into her eyes, hands rubbing lotion up her calves, knees, thighs.

The encounter at the grocery store had been wholly accidental; he didn't think she ever shopped in that part of town. For one brief moment he had considered revealing himself then and there, but instead he had panicked and run through the swinging doors in the dairy section, into the storage area, where he had weaved through cardboard boxes and out the delivery entrance. That evening he had lain awake in the basement, certain that it was time to go upstairs. Still, he fretted over her response, the anger and the shock.

Only tonight, on Halloween, as he sat in the woods and watched the children come and go, had he felt the time was right. Seeing her open the door to all visitors, he had hoped for the same warm reception. His was the spirit returning on All Souls' Eve, come to tell a tale of death and resurrection. All that was left now was to ask her forgiveness.

· 14 ·

At last he was silent, studying her from across the table. And she, too, had nothing to say for a long while, struck by the strangeness of this body sitting in her kitchen.

It looked like her husband. He had the same eyes and hands. And his story, though infuriating, was consistent with her knowledge. It explained his appearance in the house and at the grocery store. It confirmed her sense of being watched. And explanations were crucial, weren't they? Every problem needed to be solved, every oddity framed in a logical context. God forbid that her life be filled with mystery.

But still, there was something surreal about this midnight visitor, with his unnaturally pale face and too-convenient story. Why did his words sound so much like the narratives in her mind—the meticulous fictions she had constructed over the past three months to explain his long absence? She had concocted so many intricate tales, so many logical reasons for why he was gone and how he would return, that now David's story seemed like the merest echo of her own thoughts.

She could tell that her silence was starting to unnerve him. Underneath the glass table his hands were folding and unfolding. *Good, let the bastard squirm. Let him rot in hell. Better to have been a corpse than a spy.*

"What are you thinking?" he asked.

Sarah took a long breath. "Why are you here?"

He seemed surprised. "I wanted to see you . . . to know if you were okay."

"You've seen me several times, and you say that I looked okay."

"I wanted to talk to you and explain what happened."

"To make yourself feel better."

"That's fair enough. But I thought it might make you feel better, too."

It didn't, and Sarah wondered why. Any normal woman would have been desperate to see her husband again, overjoyed at this miraculous reprieve from widowhood. She had longed for a miracle as deeply as any mourner, and a part of her wanted nothing more than to walk over to David and embrace him with a hard, ferocious love. But all she could think of was the old admonition: *Be careful of what you wish for*. Because there was nothing normal about a husband who hid in the woods, who spied on his own memorial service and watched at windows. None of it seemed like the man she had married. And besides, she didn't buy this sudden urge for confession.

"Why are you here *now*?" She looked into David's eyes and for once he answered without forethought.

"You turned off the power."

Sarah leaned her head back and laughed. Of course. Every October they closed the cabin and turned off the electricity. This year she had forgotten until she got a phone call from her neighbor Rich, who worked for the power company. When asked if she'd like the cabin's power shut down for the winter, she had said yes, thank you. That had been twelve days ago, time enough for the cabin to thoroughly chill. She pictured David's breath crystallizing on his lips as he shivered in bed, and the image blended with all her previous visions of his corpse.

"So you want the power back on?" Her tone was sarcastic.

"Yes. But it's not just that. Really, Sarah." He raised his hands above the table and reached toward hers, but instinctively she pulled her fingers back.

"I want you to come to the river. I want us to be alone together, away from everything. Come with me to the cabin."

How eerily his words seemed tuned to her desires. She had wanted to leave this big house for so long, to flee the tepid sympathy of minor acquaintances, but she felt a great resistance to David's will. Thus far he had controlled the entire sequence of events. He had abandoned her, spied on her, transformed her into an object of neighborhood pity. She owed him nothing, the son of a bitch. But anger required energy, and along with her disgust came an overwhelming sense of exhaustion.

"I don't know." She looked around the room in search of things concrete—her refrigerator, her trash compactor, her gleaming marble countertop. It occurred to her that in the past few years of her life, cleanliness had replaced ambition. She had tended her kitchen like a substitute child, washing its surfaces and dressing its windows, seeking a sense of progress in updated cabinetry.

This was not what she had wanted for her life.

"I am tired," she murmured.

"Of course." David raised his palms in a gesture of conciliation. "Think it over. I'll sleep in the basement tonight if that's all right, and I'll head back to the cabin tomorrow morning. You can decide whether or not you want to join me. But, Sarah"—and now he was leaning toward her—"I want you to know that I didn't plan this. I wasn't trying to leave you. This path just opened before me and I had to follow it. I know that's not an excuse. There are no excuses. But please, come to the river."

With that, he rose from the table and walked to the basement stairs. She listened to his feet descend, then folded her arms on the table and laid her face upon them.

• 15 •

The next morning Sarah woke in bed with Grace at her feet. Rectangular blocks of window light slanted down her bedspread, returning the house to its mundane pastels. The clock read seven A.M., and she was about to roll over and close her eyes when she remembered the man in her basement. His eyes came floating back, along with the rhythm of his voice, and she imagined David as her Ancient Mariner, the restless spirit reciting his long mea culpa. Water, water everywhere.

She stood up, waited for the dizziness to pass, then walked to the kitchen. The room bore no mark of the figure who had occupied it the night before. A pair of blue ceramic turtledoves, branded *S* and *P,* once again dominated the glass table. Their mundanity challenged any thought that this might have been the site of a miracle—a dead man come home. Opening the basement door, she listened for sounds of life below. There was no noise of a man dressing or snoring, no sound of a television tuned to the morning news. As she walked down the basement stairs, the room emerged item by item—the unruffled couch, the dusty books, the pillows and afghan arranged in their usual manner. She found no note, no scent, no mess, nothing to cling to as evidence of David's visit.

It was to be expected. All ghosts must flee at sunrise. But had she even risen from her covers last night, or was it all a product of her elaborate imagination? And what was the difference between reality and dreams, in a life spent mostly in bed?

She sat on the couch and rested her face in her hands, her skull fragile as a glass jar, blown thin at the rising flame. I need an aspirin, she thought—no, she needed something stronger. A few Bloody Marys might banish a persistent ghost. Still, one idea rocked back and forth with her swaying body: *He's alive, alive, alive.*

She thought to jump into her car and follow David out to the cabin right away, but that impulse died as quickly as it came. She would not chase after the man who had widowed her. David had kept her waiting for three months; he could wait for at least twenty-four hours. Time enough to think things through. For now, only one action was needed—she reached for the basement telephone and dialed the power company.

All day long Sarah did not dress or shower. She paced the house in a long white robe, thinking, I have become the anxious spirit, and David is the living man. But what sort of man would hide at a cabin for months, never calling his wife or friends?

In high school she had dreamed of living as a modern-day Thoreau. Alone in the woods in a rustic cabin, her only companion a body of water—that was the setting for genius. Never mind the cold, the hunger, the loneliness. The pains of self-reliance could be forgotten when daydreaming in a heated bedroom.

But David was forty-three, with a wife, a job, a mortgage. Too old to be indulging in a Boy Scout fantasy.

She took their wedding album down from the living-room shelf and marveled at the dark-eyed bride whose hair was wreathed with baby's breath. Pearl buttons ran from her breasts to her navel, and at her feet, a two-foot train of Victorian lace spread in an ivory puddle. Beside her, Anne wore salmon silk, while above their heads the Spanish moss served as mistletoe. The pictures were filled with kisses from uncles and cousins and friends, a clownish kiss from David with wedding cake smeared on his lips. But it wasn't the kisses, the crumbs, or pearls that struck Sarah most. It was the smiles, the unrestrained enthusiasm of it all.

In recent albums her expression was more subdued. She was standing at a table covered with salads and cold pasta—a departmental potluck. Their host was roaming with a camera, and she had paused to indulge him while David turned his back. It seemed that their joys had been tempered, their pleasures qualified. Age, she told herself, does not appear first in wrinkles or gray hair, but in the dulling of one's smile.

She returned the albums to the shelf and paused to examine the paintings that decorated their living-room walls. David had always wanted the opportunity to become a full-time artist, to immerse himself in the road not taken. Few people ever got the chance to thoroughly transform their lives; it was so much easier to maintain one course, stifling regrets along the way. She couldn't fault him for trying something different, and yet, a man of courage should have acted publicly. He should have announced to the college, and to the whole world, that he was giving up medicine in order to paint. That would have taken guts—to endure the incredulous stares and indulgent smiles, and to let the entire town witness his success or failure. But how could he have done it with a wife at home, sitting in their enormous house, expecting the bills to be paid?

Sarah liked to imagine that she would have been supportive, willing to move back into a two-bedroom cottage and muddle through on her adjunct pay. And maybe in her twenties it would have been possible, when life was still a grand adventure, not rooted in material goods. But truthfully, if David had come to her in the past year and said that he wanted to give up his job to become an artist, she wouldn't have tolerated it. Sure, she might have acquiesced in a muttering way, but all the while she would have held him back—a nagging, resentful anchor.

Sarah shook her head as she stepped away from the paintings. Why did she always blame herself? David was the one at fault here—the sneaking voyeur—no matter how reasonable he might sound, how full of self-justifying logic. Her husband was a self-righteous man; even death had not humbled him.

At eight o'clock Sarah settled into bed with her remote control, lying in darkness while the local forecast crawled across the bottom of her screen. Somewhere between the wind speed and the barometric pressure she heard a voice close to her ear calling, "Sarahhh . . . Sarahhh," and she swam up from the half-world between waking and sleep, sensing that the sound was in her room, coming from the shadows beside her bed. David was back.

"Leave me alone." She wrapped a pillow around her ears, but a crackle in his voice made her sit upright, and she saw red lights blinking on the answering machine. "I know you're there, Sarah. Please pick up . . . I need you to come to the river. The trees are still turning, you would like the colors." A long pause followed, both of them listening for the other. "Come to the river, Sarah," and the machine cut off. She remained silent while the memory of his voice evaporated, then she leaned back into her pillows and imagined mountains green and gold, with drops of bloodred maple.

The next morning she reached across her bed and pressed play, thinking to conjure David's voice by daylight, but there were no new messages. Strange, she did not remember erasing his plea, but she did recall something else: he had no telephone. It was a dream. All of it, dreams.

Time to call a therapist, she thought as she walked into the kitchen and put on the kettle. Time to call Margaret and confess the whole story of her resurrected husband. The two of them could drive out to the cabin and search for David's ghost in the closets and underneath the beds. And when they didn't find him they could make a plan for Sarah's future, a strategy for tethering her mind to this world.

No, she couldn't call Margaret. If David was real, then she shouldn't expose him, and if he wasn't, why shame herself? One quick trip to the cabin could confirm or dispel all her delusions. Then why did she hesitate?

Sarah sat at the table for half an hour, trying to read the tea leaves at the bottom of her cup. She knew the reason for her fear, although she wouldn't say it aloud. It was not that David might be a hallucination; that idea was almost comforting in the power it granted her imagination. No—she dreaded something more obscure, something between life and illusion. What bothered her was the possibility that what had returned to her on Halloween night was a wandering spirit, a half-life caught in a purgatorial state.

Sarah had always believed in spirits. She had believed in them as a child, apologizing to the ghosts of birds and moles killed by her tabby cat, burying their frail corpses in blankets of pine straw. She had believed even more in adolescence, standing beside her grandmother's grave on Kiawah Island, in a cemetery where spirits seemed to hiss in the Atlantic breezes. But her first true sighting had come in this very house, four days after her mother's death. She had woken past midnight to find a hazy figure sitting at the foot of her bed, pale and translucent, neither female nor male, hardly a face at all, but somehow parental. She hadn't woken David, sensing that the visitor was there for her sake alone, and the vision had faded as her eyes became accustomed to the darkness. But she had told him the next morning, eliciting a single, indulgent nod. In all his medical school dissections, his years of flashlit searches into throats and ears and eyes, he had never encountered anything so amorphous as a soul.

How strange it would be if David, the unbeliever, had now become a ghost. How strange and how terrible. Because Sarah not only believed in ghosts, she feared them. She dreaded their loneliness, their longing and disappointments. In her experience, ghosts always seemed to want something—something that could never quite be given.

Another twenty minutes and she bowed to her inertia. A body at rest remains at rest, she thought as she carried a bagel to her bedside table and crawled beneath the covers, the weather maps flashing green and blue across her face. Drifting in and out of sleep, she heard the telephone again, one . . . two . . . three rings. The machine clicked on and Sarah waited for David's coaxing syllables.

"Sarah? Are you there?"

Judith Keen's crisp Boston accent had the snap of a hypnotist's fingers.

"Hello, Judith? I'm here, let me turn off the machine."

"I'm glad I reached you." Judith didn't pause. "I've been meaning to set up an appointment to go through David's work. We've got less than three weeks before the show, but Tom Bradley says he can frame most of the paintings if I get them to him at the beginning of next week. I was wondering how Monday looks on your calendar."

"My *calendar*," Sarah answered, "is nonexistent."

"Well then. All right. How about if I come by your place at ten o'clock to start picking things up?"

"Fine."

"Wonderful. I'll see you then."

That decided it. Sarah rose from bed and opened her closet. She had a task and a deadline that required her to go to the cabin. Half of David's paintings were stored there; a few of his best pieces hung on the walls. Armed with a practical reason for her visit, she could face him with dignity, not like some fish he had lured with a pretty fly. There, in his presence, she would know whether he was real, or whether her hand could pass through his chest and wave him off in a pillar of smoke.

• 16 •

Driving into the Appalachian foothills, Sarah felt the wind pushing at her doors. Damp red leaves blew onto her windshield, then somersaulted away over the sunroof. The trees were whittled down to lace, revealing glimmers of the Shannon to her right, backed by rocky cliffs that spanned the opposite shore. When the road leaned to the left, the river disappeared behind her, but always she came back to it, following its path through layer upon layer of the Blue Ridge.

After thirty minutes she reached the eastern side of Hogback Mountain, where a cluster of white wooden houses, a Baptist church, and a tiny brick post office constituted the village of Eileen. Turning right onto Possum Run, she passed the general store that had provided David with his necessities; its picnic table and drink machine stood silent and conspiratorial. The road was draped with arching trees that threw shadows across her hood. Pavement gave way to gravel, with driveways every three hundred yards or so. They had bought the cabin for its invisibility. Even in winter, with the trees bare, there was no glimpse of other houses, no hum of distant highways. No postmen, no garbagemen, no salesmen or evangelicals. Only a cluster of mountain laurel and rhododendron to mark the beginning of their property.

As she turned into the driveway, she noted how the summer rains had carved into the road, leaving long trenches that scraped the bottom of her car as she wound back toward the river. When she pulled up at the cabin's side she was a little disappointed to find no one there to greet her. She had imagined that David might be waiting at the window, but perhaps that was a woman's fate. Even so, the sound of the first car to arrive in months should have brought him out from any corner of the house or yard.

She stepped from the car, noticing the leaves that clogged the gutters, the pine straw on the walkway. She tried the doorknob and found it locked. Lifting a brick from underneath a holly bush, she took out the spare key and let herself inside.

The cabin appeared just as she and Margaret had left it. To her right was the open kitchen, its pine-green Formica uncluttered and clean, a washrag hanging over the silver faucet. To her left stood the back of the sofa, checked green and white and peppermint, draped with the navy-blue afghan she had crocheted in college. A braided rope rug lay in front of the sofa, and a cane-backed rocking chair sat beside a stone hearth that reached up to the ceiling's exposed cedar beams. To the right of the hearth, David's easel still held its unfinished painting, brushes soaking in acrid jars.

She entered the room and rested her purse on the kitchen island, where three wooden stools were tucked neatly in place. Five more paces and she stood at the polished pine dining table with its four polished chairs, shining with sunlight that poured from glass double doors leading onto the deck. Opening those doors, she stepped outside, surveyed the mildewed deck cushions, the locked shed to her left, and the empty dock at the foot of the yard. The river beckoned, and she walked down the deck stairs and waded into the grass.

Ahead of her, the dock needed repair. Splintery boards formed curling grins, and the railing listed to port. Stepping carefully across the planks, she walked the fifteen feet out to the dock's limit. When she glanced back, the cabin looked small and sad, its closed windows a pair of sleeping eyes. He is not here, she thought. He was never here.

Deep in the river the limbs of a tree reached up from the bottom, making her wonder what it would feel like to drown. Not in the metaphorical sense—she knew a little of that already—the sensation of darkness closing in, the muffled hearing, the constriction in her lungs. Half of the people around her seemed to be drowning daily, in their worries, their jobs, their uncontrollable excesses. But all of life was not metaphorical. There were real rivers, real lakes, real lungs breathing real water. It could not be peaceful, to drown for real.

She closed her eyes, lifted her face, and let her cheeks absorb the rare November warmth. Soon enough the weather would be chilly as her mood, but a scrap of summer was left in this day. In front of her, the river swelled into a swimming hole, deep enough in high water for headlong dives. To her left it narrowed into a mild rapid, where the water greeted the rocks in an ancient tongue. Its clicks and rolling consonants formed incantations, and Sarah's mind joined the spell, repeating three words, over and over: *David Robert McConnell.*

A few minutes more and the snap of a branch switched open her eyes. Someone was walking along the riverbank, crushing the fallen leaves. She peered into the trees upstream and saw a moving shadow, scarcely human, a patch of shifting darkness. As she looked more carefully the figure assumed legs, arms, and fingers, each new appendage touching her with dread.

What had she conjured from the forest? She rose and hurried off the dock, gauging the distance she would have to cover to reach her car. This was stupid, so stupid, to have driven alone to the middle of the woods at a dead man's invitation. Nothing good could come of this.

To her left, the figure was gaining height, hair, and clothes, and when she turned to look at the forest's edge, where the trees gave way to clearing, a fully formed man emerged in the sunlight, with a fishing rod in one hand and a bucket in the other. It was David, still wearing his green flannel shirt.

When he saw her, his face broke into a reassuring grin. He approached within a few feet, laid his bucket and rod in the grass, and wiped his hands on the bottom of his shirt. "Thanks for coming."

What was this brave new world, where dead men returned with smiles and open arms? He took two steps forward, ready to embrace her, but she moved back.

"I didn't come for you. I came for your paintings." David lowered his arms. "Judith wants to have an exhibit of your work."

"A posthumous show?" He smiled, and reflexively she smiled back, but stopped short.

"Well . . ." David sighed. "Follow me." When he knelt to lift his bucket, Sarah glimpsed two glassy-eyed trout floating in bloody water.

Inside, he laid the fish on a cutting board and walked into the bedroom: "I want to show you something." Sarah followed, noting how the bed was neatly made, just as she had left it three months before, but within the shuttered closet David revealed a cache of charcoal sketches and chalk drawings she had never seen. He stepped back into the hall and opened the door to the second bedroom, where half a dozen oil paintings leaned against the wall—detailed depictions of the surrounding landscape.

"You've been busy," she said.

"I've run through most of my supplies. I was hoping you could get some more."

Ah yes, his girl Friday. Running errands, buying supplies, helping to make things easy. That would make him happy, the selfish idiot. And yet, as she knelt to study the landscapes, some of the bitterness started to fade. These were better than anything he'd done in the past ten years. Three months of solitude had allowed him time to pore minutely over his canvases, experimenting with color and light and texture.

"They're lovely," she said, impressed by how each goose feather was carefully delineated. Inside the second bedroom she thumbed through the charcoal sketches, stopping at the final work. Her own eyes stared back, dark and brooding. She was lying in bed among disheveled covers, turned slightly toward the viewer, drowsy and dream-filled. Light filtered through her bedside curtains, illuminating strands of hair that circled her breasts. The effect was tender, wistful, and utterly foreign.

David watched from the door. "Choose what you like. Or better yet, take them all. But stay for lunch."

Inside the main room she sat at the table, watching David clean his fish. He sliced the tail, fins, and head with surgical precision, and scooted them to the side of the board. Then he split open the white belly and scooped out its organs, shaking them into the trash. "I've become quite a fisherman," he said as he pulled out the skeleton. "It's the only fresh food I can get right now. During the summer the general store sells local vegetables and eggs. But now it's filled with chips and hot dogs."

She watched in silence as he washed the blood from his hands.

"I saw the paper's announcement," he continued. "About the exhibit. How did that happen?"

Sarah shrugged. "Judith came out to the house on a condolence call. She saw some of your paintings and seemed genuinely impressed. So I took her into the basement and let her look through everything. She said she had no idea you were so talented."

He laughed. "I suppose it's flattering."

Sarah turned her face away, toward the river. He had no right to be pleased with himself, this man who ran away from his commitments, who snuck into houses and listened to other people's conversations.

"What is your plan?" she asked. "Are you going to come back?"

He turned off the water, took two beers from the refrigerator, and placed one in front of her. "I don't know if I could come back at this point. I know I couldn't get my job back. They wouldn't want a doctor who takes a three-month sabbatical without asking anyone. And I don't know about the neighbors. I guess we could tell them that I had some sort of nervous breakdown." He twisted the cap and took a long swallow. "But you've already got the insurance money, right? And the college's death benefit? We'd have to return all that. I suppose we might be accused of insurance fraud."

Sarah winced. It had never occurred to her that she might be blamed for this, that she could be viewed as anything other than a passive victim.

"I'm giving half the insurance money to the college. To set up a scholarship fund in your name."

David laughed again. "I don't think that will satisfy the Allstate men."

Her nails dug thin crescents into her palms. "So what is it that you want?"

David peeled a thin strip of label from his bottle. "I thought we might go kayaking, the way we used to. Or go biking up into the hills." He paused to look into her eyes. "I'd like to go back to the way things were ten years ago. Or not back really, but forward to someplace different."

Sarah merely stared. "You've set us up for insurance fraud because you're feeling nostalgic?"

"No one will ever know," he said, "unless you tell them."

When Sarah didn't answer, he rose from his chair. "I don't have any plans beyond this week, or even this afternoon. I just wanted to see you."

He walked out to the deck to turn on the grill, and all the while her eyes followed, impressed with his aura of health. David no longer seemed to have the pallor she had noticed when he sat in her kitchen. Here, his cheeks were bright, his face rough-shaven, his arms muscular. To the left of the hearth a two-foot log pile testified to his major pastime; he must have started chopping when the power went out.

It would serve him right, thought Sarah, to go home and turn off the electricity, change her bank account, cancel his ATM card. Let him see how long he could survive on his fishing rod. But much as she wanted to hurt David, to crush his arrogant soul, a part of her still loved him—loved him now even more than in the past twelve months, because now there was nothing predictable about her husband. Nothing was left of the old routine. He had endowed their marriage with a sense of mystery.

David served the grilled trout with a slice of wheat bread and a thick chunk of Cheddar cheese, and Sarah ate in silence, appreciative of the meal's simplicity. A few times she thought to say something conciliatory, but no words came. When he was done, he pushed his plate aside and looked out toward the river.

"I can't describe how it felt to rise up out of that water and be able to breathe. It was like I was a new person. I'd been given a new life, and I couldn't go back to the old one. Staying here seemed like the best option. Maybe it was a mistake, but it's done, and now I'm trying to deal with it."

Sarah carried both of their plates to the sink. "I understand your motives. I just don't know if I want to be a part of this."

An hour later, as he helped her pack the paintings and sketches into her station wagon, she tried to speak lightly: "You know, there are better ways to get a marriage back on track."

And then she was in the car, starting down the driveway. It occurred to her that she had never touched David, never tested whether her fingers would meet solid flesh. When she looked into the rearview mirror, he was gone.

· 17 ·

Ten days later Sarah stood in the Walker Street Gallery, watching Judith's bracelets slide down her forearms as she perched on a stepladder, adjusting the track lighting that fell on one of David's river scenes. Judith was inching the light toward the precise angle where it could shine on the water, making dabs of gold and silver paint glitter like sinking coins. Three centimeters to the right, one to the left, and Judith stepped down. She glanced at Sarah, who smiled and nodded.

This space of white walls, blue carpet, and movable room dividers had come alive over the past three days. Charcoal sketches filled the garden alcove; the opposite wall blazed with oils. Each corner had a distinct mood which Judith planned to complement, on opening night, with matching hors d'oeuvres—caviar to echo the charcoal, lemon tarts beside the watercolors.

Margaret, who had volunteered to do much of the cooking, scoffed at Judith's culinary schemes—"How about smoked weenies next to the nudes?" But Sarah trusted in Judith's vision. Enveloped in these walls of shifting color and form, she felt newly appreciative of David's talent. Here she could walk from piece to piece and trace the evolution of her husband's obsessions.

"What do you think?" Judith walked to Sarah's side and examined the space, wall by wall.

"You've done a wonderful job."

"I've done nothing. Here I've spent a decade imagining myself as the local talent scout extraordinaire, and I never even noticed David." She put her hand around Sarah's shoulder and gave an awkward squeeze. "Some of these are really good, you know. I've kept five of the best ones for myself. I'm going to take them to my Georgetown gallery in December."

Sarah raised her eyebrows. Exposure in Washington was a compliment granted only to Judith's favorites. It was typical of her not to ask permission; Judith preferred announcements over inquiries. But Sarah nodded her approval. "I was wondering where that charcoal sketch of myself had gone."

"I didn't think you'd want to bare your breasts in such a small town."

"Yes. Much better to show them off to strangers."

An electric bell chimed, and Judith glanced at the door. "My, my, what have we here?"

Nate was standing in the entrance, pinching at the fingertips of his dark leather gloves. Sarah walked over and gave him a quick kiss on the cheek. "I didn't know you were coming."

"I wanted to see the exhibit without the crowds." He stuffed his gloves into the pocket of his navy overcoat. "It's hard to appreciate art at an opening, with all the people and the conversation."

"You're absolutely right." Judith came forward with her hand outstretched.

"This is Judith Keen. She owns the gallery." Sarah helped Nate out of his coat. "This is David's brother, Nate."

"The resemblance is striking." Judith shook Nate's hand. "It's like having the artist himself walk into the room."

Not quite, Sarah thought as she hung Nate's coat in the closet. David had never inspired the sort of fawning attention that Judith now lavished on Nate. She was steering him to the best paintings, speaking with a knowledgeable flirtatiousness, "Of *course,* watercolors aren't in *vogue,* but look at *this* one." Each time Nate leaned toward a canvas, Sarah could see Judith's curatorial eyes assess his silhouette. There was something almost chemical about her brother-in-law; when he entered a room, women changed their posture.

Sarah walked into the foyer, where a polished walnut table held a silver-framed photograph of David. He was leaning against a poplar tree, wearing a white collared shirt rolled up at the elbows. She had chosen the photo as his most characteristic pose, arms crossed and eyes intent. When she held it in the light he seemed to grin at her. What was he doing now? Fishing? Drawing?

She hadn't visited the cabin in the past two weeks, and the time and distance had transformed David back into a shadowy figure. Once again she wondered about her husband's spiritual and physical state. The river had transfigured him beyond the mental rebirth that he acknowledged. Something material and essential had changed.

But wasn't that to be expected? Sarah examined the lines on

David's two-dimensional face. What would Eurydice have been like, if Orpheus had managed to lead her into daylight? Would she still have been so fragile as to disappear at a wayward glance? And what about Lazarus? What was he like after Jesus left? Did his sisters notice an unsettling change?

Behind her, Nate and Judith were inching past the oils. Nate looked back and held up a finger, mouthing the words "Wait for me."

She placed David's photo back on the table. What was missing? Here was the gold-trimmed guest register, with a ballpoint pen in a velvet case. And here was a small brass lamp, amber beads dangling from its shade. She stared at the table for another three minutes before she heard Nate's voice nearby.

"It looks like a terrific show."

"You were wise to see it early." Judith's fingers had migrated into the crook of Nate's elbow.

"This also gives me a chance to take you out to lunch." He smiled at Sarah. "If you're free?"

She glanced again at David's picture. "I'm always free."

"Take him to Il Trattoria," Judith insisted as she withdrew her fingers from Nate's arm. "It's the *only* place for lunch." She opened the closet and handed Sarah her long coat, then held Nate's open at the collar, momentarily resting her hands on his shoulders as he stepped into the silk lining. "I'll see you both on Friday."

"Judith." Sarah turned back at the door. "Some flowers for this table?"

"Of course. I'll take care of it."

* * *

Twenty minutes later Sarah was sitting over a plate of chicken piccata, sorting the capers with the tines of a silver fork. She had made a polite remark about the economy, and now Nate was mulling the possibility of a market rebound. His words were distant, as if he sat two booths away, while in her own mind she wondered whether to tell him the truth.

As David's closest living relative, Nate had certain rights. He had a right to know whether his brother was alive or dead, a right to be spared unnecessary grief. But David had rights as well, a claim to his own secrets, and although he had not solicited any promises of silence, Sarah felt inclined to grant him this chance at a new life. Besides, she doubted whether Nate would believe her, if she told him about the cabin, and the ghost in the basement.

"What are you thinking?" Nate asked.

"I was admiring your skill with the spaghetti. David always got a drop of sauce on his tie when we came here."

"David could get away with it. I never could."

True. Beauty entailed responsibilities—an obligation not to disappoint.

As Nate reached for his wineglass, Sarah was surprised to see his father's wedding ring on his right hand. She hadn't expected such a sentimental gesture. Beneath that placid face, was he mourning his lost family?

She had witnessed Nate's grief only once, at Helen's burial in Vermont. As the casket descended into the grave, he had given way to convulsive sobs, his head drooping like a wilted rose. He might have sunk to his knees, had David not wrapped his arm around his brother's shoulder, pressing him to his side.

After the ceremony she and Nate had left David at the grave

with a shovel in hand. David always fought sorrow with physical labor, and he insisted that his mother's burial should not be left to strangers. Nate wanted to help, but though the soul was willing, the flesh was weak. On their return to Helen's house, riding in the funeral home's silver Buick, she had held Nate's head against her bare throat. It was the most maternal experience of her life; his sobs muffled against her skin sounded like a nursing baby.

"Do you want dessert?" she asked when he put down his fork.

"Will you share something with me?"

"A slice of tiramisu?"

"With coffee?"

"Tea for me."

"Of course."

She could not recall a moment since David's disappearance when Nate had seemed distraught. On the morning after the flood, when he arrived at her door, his hair was uncombed and his face unshaven, but his voice had remained calm. She remembered sitting on her couch while he held her head steady against his collarbone. There, with the beat of his heart murmuring in her ear, she had told him everything. How she had waited for an hour by the muddy river, standing under an umbrella while the branches and leaves swirled by. How she had driven to the Jackson police station and filed a missing-persons report. With two girls already drowned that day, and less than two hours of daylight left, the police had dispatched a helicopter to scan the river. They had also alerted the volunteer rescue squads—mostly local boys in pickup trucks with flashing lights on their dashboards—to search the riverbanks for whatever washed ashore.

She had telephoned Margaret from the station, ensuring that a pot of tea would be waiting when she got home, and together they had held vigil at the kitchen table until a police officer arrived at the door. It was David's friend Carver Petty, come to say that a yellow kayak had been spotted upside down in a tangle of branches. There was no sign of David.

Sarah's blood had registered the news before her mind, going suddenly cold, her teeth chattering so hard she could only reply to Carver with a low, animal moan. She remembered experiencing the initial stages of shock, her tongue all thick and fuzzy, her body bending double. Margaret was instantly at her side, settling her on the couch with a down comforter, raising her feet and rubbing her hands and answering the phone calls that came every fifteen minutes. David's cell phone had been found . . . his water bottle . . . his paddle. The objects from his journey were returning one by one, all except his body. By ten o'clock the police had given up for the night, and Margaret had begun the round of calls to family and friends, which had brought Nate to her couch that morning, listening silently to every word, never altering the even rhythm of his breath.

That afternoon he had gone with them to see the motorboats drag the river. While she stood arm in arm with Margaret, watching the divers emerge, circle, and submerge, he had paced the bank like a retriever, eager to fetch. Then, as now, there was no aura of tragedy about him. Resignation perhaps, and loss, but no sign of acute sorrow. Apparently his tears had all been spent on Helen—*after the first death there is no other*.

Now, as Sarah studied him from across the table, she looked for telltale signs of grief—worry lines, thinning cheeks, eyes glassing over. If she sensed that he was in pain she would have to tell him everything; David had no right to cause suffering. But Nate's fingernails on his silver fork were so clean, misery seemed incompatible with such impeccable grooming.

She flagged down the waitress and asked for the check, then turned back to Nate. "After the show Judith wants a group of us to celebrate at a local bar. There's going to be a zydeco band, visiting from out of town. You should come."

"Thanks."

"And you're welcome to spend the night. There's liable to be a lot of drinking, and you won't want to be driving back over the mountains at midnight."

Nate nodded. "How about if I leave my bag at your house on Friday evening and we drive to the opening together?"

"Fine," Sarah agreed. "Friday it is."

• 18 •

Friday came with Sarah sitting in Margaret's kitchen, squeezing a quartered lemon over a cold salmon fillet. The salmon lay on a silver platter, framed with cherry tomatoes carved like miniature tulip heads, that were stuffed with cream cheese and minced black olives. Margaret stood watch at the stove, stirring a pot of peanut sauce while she sipped a glass of Pinot Noir. "Can you check the grill?" she asked, and Sarah lifted a plate from the counter and walked out onto the deck.

November had taken hold of Virginia; the trees were bare and the air smelled of burning leaves. She raised the lid from the grill and leaned forward to warm her face. Inside were two dozen small skewers of chicken, lightly charred for satay. She flipped them with pincers hanging at the side of the grill, removing the finished ones and replacing them with raw strips from a nearby tray. They sizzled and spat as they touched the grill. Carrying the plate into the kitchen, she dumped the skewers into a large wooden salad bowl.

"How many do you think we have?" asked Margaret.

"About forty-five."

"We'll need twice that many."

Sarah poured herself a glass of wine, then leaned against the sink as she surveyed the room. Yesterday she had joined Margaret for an afternoon of baking with a few mutual friends, and now the counters were overflowing with dozens of mint brownies, chocolate-dipped strawberries, and key-lime tarts.

"This is more elaborate than my wedding." She swirled a sip of wine across her gums.

Margaret walked over and toasted Sarah's glass. "I wouldn't do this for just anyone."

"You are a star." Sarah rested her head against Margaret's neck.

"The show is going to be brilliant," Margaret said. "I stopped by the gallery yesterday to check on their kitchen, and I chose a painting for myself, a landscape with stormy clouds over a barn. You'll have to help me decide where to hang it."

"You should get a nicer frame for that one. David just hammered some black wood around the edges."

Margaret shrugged. "Frames can be distracting."

She returned to the stove while Sarah finished her wine. "Tell me what to do next," Sarah said as she poured herself another glass.

"If you could slice the baguettes, I think we'll be in good shape." Margaret put a chopping block on the table and placed three large bakery bags next to it. "I bought a dozen of these."

From a drawer beneath the microwave Sarah removed a serrated knife. She knew where to find every item in this kitchen—the pots, the peelers, the decades-old sippy-cups that Margaret kept in anticipation of grandchildren.

Margaret transferred her peanut sauce into a Tupperware bowl, then sat down at the table. "Have you seen David recently?"

Sarah hesitated with the knife poised above the bread. How nice it would be to tell the truth, to let the weight of the last few weeks unravel in one long sentence.

"I saw him on Halloween night," she began, "in a dream. He sat at my kitchen table and told me all about his kayaking trip. He said that he was all right, and that I shouldn't worry. He's become a sort of naturalist, a friend to the birds and the trees. And he's painting again. His heaven is full of paint."

Margaret nodded as she poured herself another glass of wine. "I still have dreams about Ethan. Usually he's outside, and it's spring, and the crab tree is blooming. Sometimes we lie down together and look up through the branches. But whenever I try to touch him, I wake up chilled."

The front door opened and Judith came bustling in. "Well, ladies, I've bought all of the Table Water crackers in Jackson." She nodded at their wineglasses. "I see you've started the party already."

"Would you like a glass?" Margaret held up the bottle.

"No thanks. Too much to do. Everything you asked for is in the back of my car. I've got student bartenders setting up the drinks. What can I take right now?"

Margaret opened the refrigerator and loaded Judith's arms with freezer bags full of baby asparagus. Judith and Sarah began making trips to the car, carrying tubs of crab dip, spinach dip, sour cream mixed with lemon and dill. Margaret gave them silver serving spoons, ceramic bowls, and two embroidered tablecloths, ironed and folded on hangers.

"This is the best spread we've ever had at an opening." Judith smiled as Margaret handed her an almond-covered wheel of Brie. "You should think about catering. You're much better than the usual folks I hire, and I pay them a fortune."

Margaret attached a handwritten note to the Brie, with instructions for heating. "Cooking is an act of love. I don't do it for strangers."

Sarah held the car door as Judith placed a final tray of shrimp on her passenger seat. "Tell Margaret I'll be back for the rest of the food in about twenty minutes. And, Sarah, you must get dressed. You're the guest of honor."

Sarah stepped back and watched Judith's Lexus disappear down the street, then she returned to the kitchen and rinsed her wineglass in the sink. "Do you need anything else?" Margaret was sprinkling confectioners' sugar on the desserts; a gentle snowfall drifted down from her sifter.

"I'm fine. You get going."

Back at her house Sarah entered the guest room, where the mirrors still rested on the bed. Walking to the edge of the covers, she stared into the collage of glass and saw three angles of her face, eyes shaded behind falling hair. She lifted a narrow, full-length mirror and propped it against the bed. This was the first time in several months that she had examined a complete reflection of herself, and she seemed to have lost weight. Her cheekbones were more pronounced than usual, her shoulders more fragile. Mealtimes had become haphazard in recent weeks. There were days when she didn't eat at all until three or four in the afternoon, settling for a bowl of soup and slices of buttered toast. On other mornings she feasted with such indiscriminate gluttony, the aftermath repulsed her. There were so many crumbs in her sofa, she felt as if she was leaving a trail to find her way home.

Sarah carried the mirror into her bedroom, leaned it against the wall, and began to undress. For days she had fretted over what to wear to the opening, remembering the widowed Scarlett O'Hara in her bloodred gown. Back then, black was required for the first year of mourning; next came the grays, the mauves, the whites, the necklaces made of dead men's teeth and lockets filled with children's hair. She admired the Victorians' flair for the morbid, and would have liked to pay them homage with a touch of crepe or bombazine. But she had no cap or veil, only an ivory willow comb that resembled a tree at her family home. She retrieved it from her jewelry box and walked into the bathroom. Two inches of hair gel, rubbed in her hands, was enough to twist her hair into a bun, pinned tight with a crisscrossed pair of Chinese needles. Leaning her head to the left, she pushed the teeth of the bone-white comb into her hair, and set the willow to weep above her right ear.

The real question was her clothes. She owned two black cocktail dresses, both cut higher above the knee than seemed appropriate for a widow. But she was not a widow, only a dark pretender. She spread the dresses across her bed and stepped back to consider them. Spaghetti straps would not do. The faux widow required, at a minimum, a bra. The second dress was tight, with elbow-length sleeves that hung from the ends of her shoulders. With black stockings and high heels she would look more seductive than sorrowful, but her only alternatives were ankle-length tea dresses in floral cotton.

Nate's Mercedes pulled into the driveway as she held the dress against her breasts. Wrapping herself in a towel, she knocked on the window and waved at him to come inside. Black lace underwear suited the dress, and a necklace of glass rubies with matching earrings that hung like drops of glittering blood. She held her perfume bottles up, allowing lamplight to shine through the gold and sapphire glass. Allure, Obsession, Tender Poison. She sprayed Vanity on her throat and wrists and into her hair, and walked into the bathroom, where she opened the wall cabinet.

Here were the Prozac and Lunesta, waiting for their time to come. Sarah pushed them aside and revealed a silver case untouched for almost a year. Placing it on the counter, she lifted the lid and began thumbing through mascara, eyebrow pencils, and old lipstick. A dusting of Smoky Glow seemed best for her cheeks, a layer of Auburn Mist for her eyelids. She highlighted her brow bones with a subtle gold glitter, used a crimson pencil to outline her lips, and colored between the lines with Beaujolais Nouveau.

Inside her bedroom, she shuffled through her chest of drawers and found a black velvet purse. Some tissue, a comb, forty dollars, and she snapped the golden clasp. Looking into the mirror, she rubbed her cheeks with the heel of her palms and sighed. It would have to do.

Nate was waiting on the sofa, absorbed in a coffee table book of Kandinsky paintings. He wore a white-ribbed turtleneck and a dark sport jacket, looking very much like a stylish sea captain.

"Ahoy there," she said as she walked into the room.

"Wow." Nate closed the book and rose to his feet. "You look terrific." He reached inside his jacket. "I have something for you." His fingers opened to reveal a red rosebud backed with a tip of fern.

"How sweet." She laughed as he pinned the flower above her left breast. "I feel like I'm going to the prom."

Nate took her coat from the closet and held it as she slid her arms through. Then he opened the front door and bowed his head. "After you."

They arrived fifteen minutes into the opening and found the gallery already packed; a wave of noise greeted them when they opened the door. Sarah hadn't been near a crowd since the memorial service, and the presence of so many bodies in one space seemed unnatural, but retreat was not an option. Heads had turned; friends were converging.

The first to reach her was the English department chair, a grandfatherly man who took her hand within his two warm palms. "My dear, such a beautiful exhibit. It's marvelous." Next came a pair of nurses who raved about the paintings and insisted on how much they missed David. Behind them Sarah saw the Fosters, the Warrens, the Doves, Carver and his little girl, and the red-haired sociologist from Margaret's widows group.

When Nate pulled her coat from her shoulders she felt completely exposed. Her dress was too short, her heels too high, her throat too pale and bare. But Judith, God bless her, emerged from the crowd in a see-through chemise that revealed a black lace bra and freckled breasts.

"What a stunning entrance! You two light up the room."

While Nate left for the closet, Judith took Sarah by the arm. "The turnout is amazing, and they love the work."

Sarah scanned the room. These were the people from the memorial service, whose repetitive condolences had filled her with contempt. Then, she had been absorbed in the isolation of mourning, wanting nothing more than her bed, her cat, and an oversize bottle of Chardonnay. But now there was comfort in this return of the faithful. The electric friction of so much silk and cashmere gave an odd impression of life's continuity.

Sarah tilted her head. "Is that Bach?"

"That's my surprise." Judith led her by the elbow. "Come and see."

Beside the bay window overlooking the garden, Judith had arranged a flute-and-guitar duet. Sarah recognized the guitarist as their student housesitter from the previous summer. The girl smiled and nodded before turning back to her fingers, which tapped at the frets in a percussive accompaniment.

"Margaret deserves the credit," Judith explained. "She told me you played flute all through college, and that you and David always liked classical music."

Sarah nodded as she listened to the layer of breath that hovered above the flautist's melody.

"Can I get you both a drink?" Nate was back at her side.

"Another white wine for me." Judith handed him her glass.

He smiled at Sarah. "Vodka tonic with lime?"

"How did you know?"

"Seventeen years of family functions." He disappeared into the crowd.

"President Wilson is here with his wife." Judith steered Sarah away from the music. "You must speak to him. He's thinking about getting something for the lobby in Cabot Hall."

A tall, gray-haired man stood in one corner, orbited by a small cluster of faculty. Beside him stood a woman in a red dress with gold buttons, looking perfect for a Republican tea. Two female students in black neckties offered hors d'oeuvres on silver platters, and the gold-buttoned woman was gushing over a piece of coconut shrimp. She turned as Sarah and Judith approached.

"Oh, Sarah." She reached out with ring-laden fingers. "This is such a lovely tribute. We miss David so much."

Sarah wondered if Myra Wilson could even recall David's face; the only time she had ever spoken to him was to ask advice about tennis elbow. Meanwhile, Jim Wilson stood six inches above his wife, his perpetually rigid posture an apparent job requirement.

"I didn't know David was an artist." His eyes scanned the walls. "When did he have the time?"

Sarah detected the slightest hint of accusation in the words, the tone of an obsessive boss who has just discovered a shirker. "Twenty years of spare hours," she said. "A few of these paintings go back to his medical school days."

"Beautiful work. I'm considering one of the bigger landscapes for our commerce school. That winter scene in the woods reminds me of Robert Frost. 'The woods are lovely, dark and—' "

"Tell us," interrupted his wife, "who was that man who came with you?"

"Yes." One of the professors joined in. "We were just saying how strange it was to see the two of you arrive. It looked as if David was your escort."

Sarah gestured toward the bar. "That's David's brother, Nate. He's an investment adviser in Charlottesville. Very successful. Here, he's coming."

Nate edged through the crowd with a wineglass and two cocktails triangled in his fingers.

"What did you get for yourself?" Sarah uncurled her vodka from his grasp while Judith took her wine.

"Chivas Regal on ice."

"Nate, this is Jim Wilson and his wife, Myra. Jim is the president of the college."

"Of course." Nate gave the slightest of bows. "David appreciated your support for the new student health center."

Well done. Sarah smiled. She hadn't imagined that Nate paid attention to David's work.

"I hope we can break ground in the next year," the president replied. "Our endowment has taken a hit in this economy. I understand that's your line of work."

"Yes, we are all trying to weather the storm." Nate flashed Myra a clever grin as he lifted his sparkling Scotch. "What doesn't kill us makes us stronger."

Sarah excused herself to get some food, confident that Nate was in his element. He always knew how to handle the rich; by the end of the conversation they would be asking for his business card.

She small-talked her way to the middle of the room, where a noisy group was milling around a twelve-foot table. A fountain of flowers spilled from the center, and seemed to have strewn the food with edible pansies and Johnny-jump-ups. Sarah dipped a skewer of chicken into the peanut sauce, and sprinkled it with fresh cilantro.

"Hello, love, don't you look smashing." Margaret emerged from the crowd and slipped her arm around Sarah's waist.

"The food is wonderful," Sarah said. "Everyone loves it."

"They love the paintings. Have you noticed, they're almost all taken." A gold sticker-star on the corner of a frame indicated when a painting had sold, and as Sarah glanced around she saw that the room was a sparkling galaxy.

She shrugged. "Everyone wants their memento mori." But inwardly she was pleased. She had never been to a show where more than half of the paintings sold on opening night. David would be delighted.

"By the way . . ." She took a long sip of vodka. "Judith wants to go out for a celebration after the show. You're welcome to come."

"Thanks, but Judith is a bit much for me. Anyway, this is all the celebration I need." Margaret raised her glass.

"Would you like a refill?" Nate was at Sarah's side, taking the half-empty glass from her hand. "I'm getting to know the bartender very well." He nodded toward Margaret's glass. "Would you like another?"

"No thanks, I'm all right." She raised an eyebrow as Nate walked away. "Well, well. Isn't he helpful?"

"He's been very kind."

"Has he?" Margaret eyed him across the room, chatting with the wives at the bar. "He is a beauty, isn't he?"

"Yes." Sarah focused on a plate of bruschetta. "It's his vocation."

The chiming of a wineglass drew all eyes to the middle of the room, where a student waiter had set a small footstool at Judith's feet. As she stepped up, Judith spread her arms to embrace the entire crowd.

"Thank you all so much for coming. I think I speak for everyone when I say that the one thing that would make this evening complete is if David could be here to share in his triumph." She raised her glass. "A toast to our friend, our physician, and one of the most amazing hidden talents in our community, David McConnell."

"Here, here." Glasses flashed around the room.

"I know that you are all as impressed as I am with these beautiful paintings. For those of you who want to get one and haven't had a chance, there are just a few left." She gestured toward some of the larger oil paintings, then pointed vaguely in the direction of the sketches. "I myself have been so impressed with David's work that I have decided to display a few of his best pieces at my gallery in Washington. So if any of you are coming to D.C. in December, I hope you'll stop by Wisconsin Avenue and see the exhibit. It will feature some of the finest new artists from across the South."

Another round of applause.

"And now I want to propose one more toast for David's family members who are with us tonight. You all know our Sarah." Glasses shimmered in her direction. "And if you haven't met David's charming brother, Nate, please take some time to introduce yourself. Where are you, Nate?"

Nate waved from the bar, and Judith pointed one of her long red fingernails. "A toast to Sarah and Nate McConnell."

Sarah blushed as the glasses rose.

"Sounds like she's married you off," Margaret whispered.

Seeing Nate approach with more drinks, Margaret left Sarah with a kiss on the cheek.

Two hours and three drinks later, Sarah and Nate were standing in the foyer, saying good-bye to the last few guests. Nate had been entertaining Sarah with childhood memories, old stories that took on new colors when seen from the younger brother's eyes, and for the first time in a year, she felt content. Part of it was the alcohol; the room tipped like a ship's deck whenever she crossed the floor. But she was also high on happy adrenaline. Every work had sold, every visitor seemed buoyant. Glancing around at the star-touched art, Sarah felt that perhaps David had done the right thing; in death, he had transformed himself from doctor to artist.

Judith was tallying profits on a pocket-size calculator. "Why don't you go ahead to the bar, I'll meet you there." She flicked her wrist toward the front table. "And take the roses with you. It's your night."

They left the vase in Nate's car, then walked two blocks down the street to a noisy bar, where a large crowd was celebrating at a corner table. The group applauded as Sarah and Nate entered, gesturing toward two open chairs, and Sarah sat down beside a young Asian woman whom she recognized as the new physician at the college. Sarah liked the idea of a female doctor for the students.

"Mei-li, isn't it?"

"Yes." The woman smiled. "The next round is on me. What would you two like?"

"Kahlúa and cream on ice," Sarah said.

"Same for me." Nate nodded.

The room was loud and smoky; Sarah couldn't distinguish the separate voices fanning out around her. Faces spoke in her direction, offering a mixture of congratulations and condolence, and all the while she smiled and nodded, sliding into her own thoughts, where the scent of tobacco mingled with Royal Copenhagen.

When Judith arrived she sat opposite Sarah and Nate. Leaning across the table, she took both of their hands into her own thin fingers and practically shouted: "I want you both to come to Washington when the exhibit opens. I have a tab at the Mayflower for visiting artists. You can stay for the whole weekend."

Sarah continued to nod and smile, savoring the cold and sweet Kahlúa. She imagined the Capitol in December, white columns cold as the ice at the bottom of her glass.

"Would you like another?" Nate asked, and she smiled in reply.

Sarah remembered laughing as she walked into her house that night. Nate placed the roses on the living-room coffee table, then spread her coat and his jacket over the back of a chair while she collapsed on the sofa.

"You should drink some water." Nate headed for the kitchen and was back in a moment with two tall glasses.

Just like his brother, Sarah thought, always tending to the body's needs. She drank the first one dutifully, two-thirds down, then he gave her his own.

"Thank you for being so sweet." Sarah rested her hand on Nate's kneecap, and he lifted her fingers to kiss them.

What happened next she couldn't say. Was it her own hand that reached back behind his ear, stroking his hair? Or was it Nate who pulled her forward, placing her fingers at the back of his skull and shutting his eyes? Either way, she found his head cradled in her palm, her mouth inches away from his beautiful eyelashes. It was a pity, she thought, for a man to have such lovely lashes when so many women were doomed to mascara. They were like butterfly wings, opening and shutting.

She remembered next the taste of his lips—Kahlúa and Scotch and wine—and the lingering smell of smoke as he pulled his shirt over his head. His chest was smooth as a boy's, and she could feel his heart beating against her lips, her tongue, her breasts. He lowered his mouth to her neck, and the flowers on the upholstery merged with the table of roses. The room was an immense, fragrant garden, full of butterflies, and she smiled as the petals melted into liquid.

• 19 •

Sarah woke the next morning in her bedroom. From the angle of sunlight she guessed that it was early dawn, and images from the previous night came rushing back in broken pieces. Her temples were throbbing, and as she lifted her fingers to rub them, they brushed against an arm.

"Oh, shit." Her right hand settled on her face and covered her eyes.

Nate was asleep, lying on his stomach, his naked thigh pressed against her hip. Slowly she pulled her body away from him, lifted the comforter, and placed her feet on the carpet. A trail of clothes extended from the door to the bed—her stockings, underpants, dress, bra. One by one she gathered them, whispering "Hell, hell, hell." She entered her closet and dropped the evidence into the laundry hamper, then chose some jeans, a sweater, and sneakers. Back in her room, she opened her dresser and flinched at the scrape of the wood, but Nate's breath remained steady. She grabbed some underwear and socks, then walked to the door and pushed it open with her shoulder. Before exiting, she took one last look at Nate. His arm extended down her side of the bed, empty fingers inviting her back.

She dressed in the kitchen, still cursing her stupidity. What had happened to her life, that she could have slept with her brother-in-law? She pictured Vivien Leigh in the arms of Marlon Brando—the lonely, drunkard widow, with her madness and desire. All life was a repetition of the archetypal stories.

But Nate hadn't forced her. He hadn't even "taken advantage." The images now racing back were all too consensual.

She couldn't stay for breakfast, couldn't fix Nate pancakes. Not at the table once occupied by David's ghost. Instead, she took down the memo pad hanging by the telephone:

Sorry I had to leave so early. Help yourself to breakfast.

She slipped the note on the table beneath a bag of bagels, clutched her pocketbook, and headed for the door. On the living-room coffee table, two sweating glasses were making gray water rings, but she did not stop to pick them up. The damage was already done.

Sarah was grateful for the empty streets at seven on a Saturday. With her mind wrestling between recriminations and delight, she was scarcely conscious of the lines between the lanes. Around the college track, the early risers were out walking, old men with elbows flapping like chicken wings. Run, she thought. Run away from death. And what was she running from? From life, from sex?

In the back of her mind she had a small fear that last night might have been an act of reprisal, her semiconscious revenge against the brother who had abandoned her. But there was no longer any need for revenge. Yesterday, when the gallery was filled with David's friends, each painting starred with a kiss of acceptance, she had felt a profound sense of forgiveness. These people with their stories of how David had healed them—sometimes with medicine, sometimes with kindness—reminded her of why she had married him, and why she wanted to see him again.

The bridge was now humming beneath her tires. One more right turn and she joined the river, winding with the bend of its lazy current, the fallen woman following the serpentine path. The farther she drove from Nate's warm body, the calmer her mind became, because what did it matter, if at thirty-nine, she had enjoyed one night of physical pleasure? It was best not to analyze a drunken romp. Better to let the memory fade. Nate was the forbidden fruit, only to be tasted once. *Nunca más,* she told herself. Never, never again.

An hour later, when she pulled up at the cabin, she had the old sensation of arriving at an empty house. No lights shone in the windows; the grass was still unmowed. When she unlocked the door, an immense stillness confronted her. She turned the thermostat up from sixty and laid her pocketbook on the table.

David was probably asleep—probably sprawled like Nate, his arm reaching for her across empty sheets. She let the image settle into her brain, and when she opened the bedroom door all was as she had imagined. He was lying on his stomach, his head turned to the right, one arm extended down the mattress, resting on the empty half. Her lovely doppelgänger.

At the edge of the bed Sarah gazed down on her husband, noticing the details that distinguished him from Nate. The gray hairs, the extra pounds, the dirt in his fingernails. Quietly, she removed her coat, untied her shoes, and unzipped her pants. She crawled into bed without touching his skin, pulled the covers up to her shoulders, and with deep, deep breaths, she washed away the morning's shock until Nate had dissipated with the early fog. A different bed, a different brother; her mistake had been corrected. Soon she would fall asleep, and could begin the day again.

• 20 •

Two hours later Sarah woke alone in an empty room. She shivered as she sat up against the headboard, pulling the comforter around her shoulders. It took several minutes for her mind to reconstruct the situation—how she had run away from Nate, coming here to seek out her husband and regain her sense of balance. As she thought of David's hands and eyes and hair, the smell of bacon came floating from the kitchen, and he appeared in the doorway with a cup of tea.

"Breakfast is almost ready. How would you like your eggs?"

"Over easy." He approached, and she lifted the cup from his hand, letting the steam rise into the curve of her palm.

"I'm glad you've come," David said.

"I had to tell you about the show. It was a huge success." She described the lights and the flute and the flowers, Judith's chemise and Margaret's bruschetta, and President Wilson's poetic mood.

"Everything sold. And you could see that the people weren't buying just to be polite—they were really impressed with your work." She took a sip of tea. "Jim Wilson bought the biggest painting of all—that winter landscape you did five years ago. It's going to hang in the lobby of Cabot Hall."

David smiled. "Come and tell me everything. I have to check the stove."

When he was gone Sarah opened the dresser and fingered the extra scraps of clothing that they left for occasional weekend visits—a few T-shirts, some cut-off shorts, one pair of blue jeans, and an extra-large sweatshirt that she pulled over her head.

"Do you have any other clothes?" she asked as she entered the main room.

David shook his head. "I've been wearing this shirt for seven days. Usually I wash my clothes in the bathroom sink and hang them on the deck, but it's getting too cold for anything to dry quickly."

"I'll have to bring you some things." She was surprised by her own words. Was it guilt or love that inspired this generosity?

David brought plates of bacon and toast to the table, then watched as Sarah dipped her knife into a stick of butter. "Tell me more about last night."

"Margaret set up a four-tiered silver dessert server. She covered it with lemon bars and macaroons and key-lime tarts, and there was a bouquet of lilies at the top that hung down in tendrils, so that it looked like a giant wedding cake."

He returned to the stove, coming back with the frying pan in one hand, an egg-laden spatula in the other. She touched her buttered toast with the tip of her knife, and he slid the egg on top.

"Everyone was talking about how much they miss you, and

what a great doctor you were. And listen, here's the big news." She paused for effect. "Judith is going to show some of your paintings at her gallery in Washington."

She watched David's eyes widen, his mouth open slightly. He returned the frying pan to the stove, then walked across the room to the wall behind his easel, where he lifted an oil painting that was leaning against the window. "You should show her this one."

A gray heron was wading at the river's edge, surrounded by cattails and misty-blue chicory. Black Egyptian trim marked the corner of the bird's eye, and its wet breast feathers hung down like porcupine quills. Sarah assessed it skeptically.

"I suppose I could tell Judith that I found more paintings in the attic."

"Yes." David examined his work at arm's length. "I think you'll be finding lots of things in the attic over the next few months." He leaned the canvas against the couch and rejoined her at the table.

"So. I've been promoted to the big leagues." He bit into his toast. "It never would have happened if they knew I was alive."

"You don't know that. Judith doesn't take paintings to Washington out of pity. No one in D.C. will care whether you are alive or dead."

The words were more harsh than Sarah had intended, but David merely nodded.

"It's a beautiful day," he said. "We should go for a walk. Can you stay?"

She thought back to her own house. By now Nate would be rising, looking for her, reading her note. He would probably eat a bagel, take a shower, turn on the TV. He might settle on the couch and decide to wait. "Yes," she answered. "I can stay."

* * *

Twenty minutes later, as they exited the cabin, David lifted a long-handled ax from the woodpile by the hearth. It had been propped like a bookend against the volumes of firewood, and now its curve of polished pine leaned into his shoulder.

"Is that the Paul Bunyan look?" Sarah asked.

"It comes in handy."

The last crickets of the season leaped from blade to blade as they walked down the yard, Sarah trailing her fingers over the tips of the grass. "Do you ever plan to mow this?"

"It's not supposed to look like anyone's been here, and the way sound travels, I was afraid a lawn mower would attract attention. But you could do it whenever you come."

"Yes, I suppose I could."

He stopped at a small tree, barely four feet tall, with a trunk no wider than Sarah's wrist. "You remember this Japanese tulipwood that I planted a few years ago?"

"You bought it because Jefferson liked them. We saw them at Monticello."

"Right. And you know how it would never grow?" He pointed to a ring of scratches at the base of the trunk. "If you look closely you can see where a groundhog has been chewing at the bark."

Sarah knelt to touch the scars. "At Monticello they wrapped their seedlings in chicken wire."

"Exactly. It's obvious. But I never paid attention before. That's the sort of thing you notice when you slow your life down."

Sarah ran her fingers along the bark, thinking that her own life was slow enough already. She liked this little tree with its stunted limbs and tiny branches reaching toward a vast, untouchable sky. What it needed was acceleration, a midlife growth spurt. Sunshine and water and the care of loving hands.

She stood and pointed toward the river. "The dock needs fixing."

David nodded. "I need some two-by-fours."

"You need a car."

"No. I don't want a car. Not yet."

Bushes rustled across the water, and a flock of large birds scurried uphill into the woods. They looked like thin gray pheasants with skinny necks, leaning forward at a sharp angle, wings tight at their sides.

"These woods are full of wild turkeys," David explained as the last bird disappeared into the undergrowth. Turning downstream, he walked to the edge of the clearing, where the tall grass met a line of taller trees. "Let's follow the river." He glanced back at Sarah, tipped his head in invitation, then stepped into the darkness.

Strange, how fully he vanished, as if he existed only when her eyes could discern him. She moved to the line of trees, where a fallen pine branch marked the boundary between sunlight and shade. Ten yards ahead a shadow passed behind a group of tall boulders, but she hesitated to follow. Her misgivings were indefinable; partly it was the woods with their hint of threat—foxes and snakes and dead men with sharp axes. But more than that, she sensed that she should not be forever trailing after David.

For seventeen years she had followed him, from New York to Jackson, and now into this foggy new existence at the cabin. And it wasn't right, to be always shadowing a man. When, if not by age forty, was she going to be independent—let David go off on his own adventure, while she sought out a journey equally transformative?

"Come along." David's voice rose from the darkness, and she pushed aside a branch and stepped into the shadows. David paralleled the river downstream, pausing to hack an occasional path through brambles and spiderwebs. She reached him at a calm eddy where a glossy bronze grackle had stopped to bathe, dipping its head into the cold water and shivering its feathers dry. Above them a red-tailed hawk stood sentinel in a barren oak.

"Beautiful birds," Sarah said.

"They are my best company. Let's keep going. I want to show you something."

He led the way at a brisk pace, the ax like a shining pendulum that rocked back and forth on his shoulder. Once she called for him to slow down, but always he continued, stopping only at a sunny opening, where the river divided briefly into two branches, wide and thin.

"We can rest here." He led her to a grove of young trees along the bank, pointing out a few saplings that poked from the ground in chewed-off spear tips two feet tall. They formed the outposts of a Lilliputian village, stakes whittled to pencil points to impale the heads of tiny enemies.

"Beaver?"

"Yes." He pointed downstream to a pile of sticks and leaves and mud that might have been mistaken for the washed-out remnants of a flood. Crouching down, he gestured for her to do the same. When she whispered a question he replied with a finger raised to his lips.

Above them, dozens of starlings rose en masse from a sycamore. They moved like a cloud of locusts, zigzagging south from tree to tree. She watched their swerving progress until they disappeared from view, then turned her eyes to the water, where a beaver's nose twitched just above the surface. He circled and submerged, reminding her of the last divers she had seen in this river. Another minute passed and the beaver reemerged and slid onto a rock, poised erect and glistening. She could see the orange tint of the creature's teeth, his tiny paws curved in humility, alert for a friend who approached and floated past, soundlessly cutting across the surface. The rock dweller scurried back into the water, followed his companion, then dove.

"In the evening, the whole family comes out," David explained. "I've seen at least five." They knelt for a few more minutes, watching the unbroken water, until David stood and pointed to a ridge downstream, where the riverbank rose up a fifty-foot rock face. "I'd like to climb that. I want to show you the view."

Sarah assessed the jutting rocks and thin, diagonal pines. How typical of David, to challenge her like this. He was never satisfied with an easy stroll, never content to meander on a riverbank, skipping stones. David was always pushing toward higher peaks, urging her to follow when she would have been happy to walk for miles beside the water.

She sighed as she considered the jagged cliff. "I make no promises."

The initial climb was easy, with the ridge ascending in a crooked staircase of limestone. But as the cliff became sheer, pebbles rolled away beneath her tennis shoes and she slowed to a stop, her arms raised against the rock in surrender. She bent her right ear to the cliff as if listening for the mountain's pulse, then looked down, guessing it was a thirty-foot drop.

She lifted her eyes toward the ledge above, beyond which David had already disappeared.

"David?" she called, but he did not come.

"David!" Still no sign of him.

He had abandoned her, the son of a bitch. Probably lured her there on purpose with the idea that she might fall. That was what the dead always wanted—company. And how easy it would be, to let go of these rocks, lean backward and allow gravity to have its way. After all, a woman should not outlive her husband. A widow was, by historical standards, an abomination. Sarah closed her eyes and thought of Shakespeare's Juliet with her bloody dagger, of Japanese and Roman widows falling on their husbands' swords, and of all the poor widows in India, burned alive on their husbands' funeral pyres.

But she was not the type of woman to sacrifice herself. Sarah raised her foot and placed it on the trunk of a pine sapling. She was a graduate of Barnard, for Christ's sake. She reached for the next handhold, then another, and another. A few feet from the top, she stopped to catch her breath, and only then did David reappear.

"Would you like a hand?"

"No. I can do it myself." She pulled herself over the rim, brushed off her pants, and stood up. "Lead on."

She followed David to the summit, where a flat-topped boulder offered a clear view in every direction. Sarah climbed up beside him on that broad rock, the woods rolling up and down the surrounding foothills while the river appeared and disappeared in silvery threads.

"It's an amazing view," she granted.

"All-encompassing." He spread his arms and rotated slowly, north, northeast.

"Look down there." David pointed south toward two stone towers, reduced to the height of toothpicks, rising from the water like chimneys in a burned-out ruin. She recognized the structures as canal locks.

"That's the place where I flipped over."

She stared at the spot, imagining David's face gazing up from the riverbed—*those are pearls that were his eyes.*

"It changed me," he said, and Sarah nodded.

Nothing of his that remains
But hath suffered a sea change
Into something rich and strange.

A gunshot pierced the quiet. Instinctively they crouched while the air reverberated.

"Deer season," David said. Another shot cracked to the north, and they both jumped down from the rock.

Sarah turned upriver. "We'd better get back before someone kills us."

On the return they spoke in deliberately loud voices, tromping through the undergrowth with a clatter that sent squirrels rushing to the treetops. Sarah gathered kindling while David hacked at a huge dead limb that dangled from a maple tree. He dragged it through the woods, slicing a path whenever the approach was narrow. When they reached the cabin he stopped at a wide oak stump, the remnant of a beautiful tree split by lightning years ago. He pulled the thinnest branches across this chopping block, sheared off the leaves and twigs, and began to cut the wood into foot-long sections. Meanwhile Sarah went inside, stretched on the couch, and settled into the opening chapters of *War and Peace*.

By four-thirty, when the sun had dipped below the treetops, she knew that she would spend the night. Her own house still seemed forbidding, and the cabin was warmed by a large fire that David had built. She prepared an early supper, opening a can of baked beans and a jar of applesauce. Some ground meat from the refrigerator was enough for three hamburgers, and she cooked them in the frying pan, cutting off a sliver to see if they were done.

"Yuck." She spat into the sink. "Your hamburger is rotten."

"It's not hamburger." David spoke from behind his easel. "It's ground venison. The owner of the general store is a hunter. You don't like it?"

"It's not what I was expecting." But perhaps that was a blessing. Her expectations had sunk so low in the past few years. "Venison is fine." She pulled a bottle of red wine from the kitchen rack. "We should celebrate your show's success, and your debut in Washington." She brought two glasses and a corkscrew to the table.

"Let's drink to Judith," David said, "and all of her new discoveries."

Midway through dinner David made a request: "I was hoping you might join me on Thursday for Thanksgiving. It's lonely out here, with winter coming on. The nights are getting colder, and the birds are flying south, and they are the only living things that I've been speaking to."

It was odd, how David's life had become an echo of her own. They were both alone in their separate quarters, equally plagued by silence and the need for closer human contact. "I'll come," she said. "I'll do the shopping, you can help with the cooking." She rose from the table, took a piece of paper and pencil from a kitchen drawer, and began to write.

"What are you doing?"

"Making a list of things to bring on Thursday."

"Like what?"

"Clothes, shoes, hats, gloves. Your winter jacket. A snow shovel. Chicken wire for your tulipwood tree." She had become his accomplice, planning months ahead, anticipating his needs. Perhaps it was only a selfish gesture; she didn't want her dead husband discovered buying wool socks at Wal-Mart. But there was also some comfort in writing down her traditional Thanksgiving menu: turkey and cranberries, sausage, celery, mushrooms, onions and stuffing, sweet potatoes and green beans, sourdough rolls.

"What would you like me to get for you?" she asked.

"I want fresh fruit." David replied without hesitation. "And imported beer. And some good steaks . . . I want clean sheets for my bed, and Woolite, and a clothesline with clothespins. Books, and magazines, and a Sunday *New York Times*. More canvases, more paint, and a lot more toilet paper." She scribbled a list of abbreviations, until he reached his last request.

"And try to see how Nate is doing. You know how depressed he was when Mom died. Maybe you can cheer him up."

"Yes," she answered. "Maybe I can."

* * *

That evening they gathered comforters and pillows from the chilly bedrooms and spread them across the braided rug in front of the fire.

"It's like a winter picnic," Sarah said as they opened another bottle of wine. By the second glass, she had pulled off her sweater. By the third, she had unbuttoned her blouse. David lifted his shirt over his head, revealing a chest neither so smooth nor muscular as Nate's, but still the body of an attractive man.

So, thought Sarah. It was time to touch her husband—to place her hands upon him and feel the depth of his change. She put down her glass, reached out her right-hand fingers, and pressed them to his chest.

What she touched was cold, very cold. Cold as the bottom of the river. It's natural, she assured herself. The air in the cabin was freezing. But still she shivered as she pulled her hand away.

"You're like ice," she murmured, and he nodded.

"Warm me up."

PART THREE

Resurrection

• 21 •

Arriving home on Sunday morning, Sarah opened her front door and was struck with a vision of spring. Lilies graced the hall table and chrysanthemums bloomed in the kitchen. The living room's red roses now mingled with pink and white, and yellow snapdragons fanned out from the top of the piano. Each room was a kaleidoscope of petals, which she took to be Nate's version of an exit, until she saw Judith's card lying on the hall table. *The flowers are for you, left over from the show. Enjoy the moment.*

Sarah crumpled the card. Enjoy the moment indeed. She could imagine Judith's lilting smile, the arch of her penciled brows when greeted at the door on Saturday morning by a bleary-eyed Nate. So be it. She walked into the kitchen and tossed the card into the trash. The gods will have their little jokes.

On the refrigerator, Nate had left a note as laconic as her own farewell.

Sorry I missed you. Give me a call.

Yes, she would call him. She would telephone during work hours and explain to his home machine that she was oh, so busy. Maybe they could get together after Thanksgiving.

Inside her room, Nate had made the bed with precise, hospital corners. She lifted a pillow and inhaled the lingering scent of his hair, then stripped the pillowcases, bundled the top sheet in her arms, and paused at the sight of the fitted sheet, with its Rorschach test of wet spots. The memory of Nate's soft lips made her dizzy, and she lay down on the bed with the linens hugged to her chest. Five minutes—that was all she would allow herself. Five minutes to absorb his sweet narcotic, to slide backward forty hours into the care of his warm hands.

Red numbers clicked by on her digital clock: ten, eleven, twelve minutes. Sighing, she stood and pulled off the fitted sheet, carrying the guilty linens into the basement. As the washer filled with water, she poured in a cup of Tide, and when the load was almost swimming, she added another. Upstairs, she opened the linen closet and took out a set of flannel sheets, soft and innocent as the lining of children's sleeping bags.

Resting on her newly made bed, she pressed the blinking button on her answering machine.

"Hello, love." Margaret's voice was a ray of sunlight. "My refrigerator is full of leftovers from the show. Judith brought them all this morning. I want you to come for dinner and help me make a dent."

Next came Nate, calling on Saturday night. "Hi, Sarah. Just checking in. Call me when you're back."

Then Margaret spoke again, repeating yesterday's invitation. "Where are you, my dear? I can't eat all this alone."

And so, at five o'clock Sarah found herself in Margaret's kitchen, bracketed by granite counters arranged in a cold smorgasbord—cream cheese with red pepper jelly, salmon with dill sauce, a bowl of spinach dip circled with torn chunks of bread.

"You're looking well." Margaret admired the color in Sarah's cheeks. "Did you finally get some sleep?"

"Yes." Sarah smiled. She had never before appreciated the tranquilizing effect of sex.

Margaret poured two glasses of red wine. "I hope you were pleased with the show. Everyone I've seen this weekend has been going on about it. Judith was still excited when she came yesterday. She was wondering where you were."

Sarah stirred a slice of bread in the bowl of spinach dip. "The weather was so nice, I went for a long walk by the river."

"Well, be sure to call her. She's got some questions for you."

"Sure. How are your daughters doing? Are they coming for Thanksgiving?" Sarah was adept at subject changes—*No, she had lost the baby, but weren't the cherry trees looking lovely?*

"Beth is coming on Wednesday to help me bake our usual pies, pecan and pumpkin and apple. We always make extras so that each girl can take one home. And Kate will be here Thursday with her boyfriend."

"The one who works at the music store?"

"Yes, the budding disc jockey."

"You don't like him?"

"It's not a question of liking. I suppose he's very likable. But he's one of those sweet types who's always at loose ends." Margaret dipped a chicken skewer into a plate of mango chutney. "Can you join us for Thanksgiving dinner?"

"Thanks"—Sarah stared into her wine—"but I'm going to visit Anne."

"Oh, good. How is she?"

"She's busy with all of her daughters' activities. Dance class and music lessons and that sort of stuff."

"I remember it well." Margaret spooned a pile of blueberries onto her plate. "And what are you doing for the next few days?"

"I'm in charge of the campus food drive, so I'll be carting lots of boxes over to St. Francis's."

"Do you need a hand?"

"No." Sarah balanced a slice of salmon with a trio of capers on a Table Water cracker. "Some fraternity brother is supposed to do the lifting."

"Men do serve their purpose," Margaret said.

"Yes." Sarah blushed. "They do." Her fingers shook ever so slightly, causing a caper to roll off onto the floor. She leaned over to pick it up, and when she lifted her eyes again to Margaret, Sarah detected a smile in the corner of her friend's lips.

"Clumsy of me."

"It's not that." Margaret laughed. "It's your expression. I can always tell when you're hiding something. Your eyes are so obvious."

Sarah dropped her gaze to the bottom of her wineglass, where the stem formed a dark pupil. "Yes," she murmured. "I do have a secret. A *big* secret."

She envisioned David, thigh-deep in the river, water dripping over the rim of his hip boots. His fly rod hissed across the water's surface, and as she listened for its words, Sarah opened her mouth and let the syllables fall.

"I slept with Nate. It happened after the show. We were drunk and I could barely remember what happened the next morning. But there he was, lying beside me." She laughed. Saying it aloud made it seem almost comical. "I was so embarrassed I fled the scene. I haven't answered his calls since. It was a stupid thing to do . . . It won't happen again."

Margaret remained quiet until at last Sarah flinched.

"*What?*"

Margaret smiled. "Methinks the lady doth protest too much."

"Wouldn't you protest, if you had slept with your brother-in-law?"

"*My* brother-in-law"—Margaret laughed—"is bald, fat, and gay . . . Anyway, it's not surprising, the way Nate was doting on you all night. And with Judith there, playing the panderer. It's sort of natural, isn't it? You've lost your husband, he's lost his girlfriend and his brother. Maybe you two could do each other some good."

"You don't sound convinced."

"Well . . ." Margaret hesitated. "He's not the sort I would have chosen for you. Nate's a little too sleek for my tastes. I prefer men with more obvious imperfections."

"Nate has imperfections."

"Ah." Margaret nodded. "There you go." She took a sip of

wine. "My only question is whether you really like Nate, or whether he's just a way of holding on to David."

Once again Sarah's eyes turned to her wineglass. "I think I'm holding on to David in all kinds of ways . . . But to tell you the truth, I've always had a little crush on Nate. Purely physical, never an emotional attraction. It's hard to have a brother-in-law who's so damn handsome."

Against the nearest window a dying leaf had pressed its yellow face, black-veined and dotted with age spots. Sarah watched the wind peel it away from the glass. "Our neighbors would be so appalled if they knew that I had slept with my brother-in-law. And David only gone three months."

"Christ." Margaret planted her glass on the table, causing a tiny red tidal wave to splash over the rim. "We are both too old to give a damn about what the neighbors think. The question is, what do *you* think?"

Sarah shrugged. "I think I'm going to hide from Nate."

"Right. Good plan." Margaret rolled her eyes as she dabbed a sponge at the puddle of wine. "Can I ask you something very personal?"

"Since when have you ever asked permission?"

"All right, then. When was the last time you and David had sex?"

Sarah almost laughed. She thought to say "yesterday" just to watch Margaret's expression, but instead her mind traveled back over the last year of her marriage, in all of its dull grays and muted browns—the bitter politeness, the numbing routine, the occasional kiss on the cheek. After her third miscarriage she and David had stopped having sex. The act had become tainted, love and death intertwined just as the poets always said. Still, on David's forty-third birthday she had imagined her body as a gift, a bit worn and faded, but nevertheless a three-dimensional object that might be dressed up with a bow.

"Four months before he disappeared." Sarah flashed Margaret a biting smile. "You think I'm in need of some sexual healing?"

Margaret did not flinch. "I think you've been in mourning for a long time. Long before David died. And I think you are entitled to a little joy in your life, wherever it comes from."

When Sarah did not respond, Margaret lifted a silver platter from the counter to her right. "Enough of this . . . Have a tart."

• 22 •

The next morning, as she drove a blue campus van down fraternity row, Sarah mulled over Margaret's words. It was true that she had been in mourning for a long time, and for her, mourning took the form of hibernation, a retreat into dreams in her Victorian cave. She supposed it was high time to rejoin the living, to set aside her brooding and find some pleasure in the world. After all, if David could be resurrected, transformed according to some lost vision from his youth, then why not her? She certainly had the time and the money, and enough years ahead to make a new life possible. But it would take a mighty effort to wake from these past few months. She imagined Rip Van Winkle rising from his mountain knoll—the calcified limbs unfolding, the eyes still cloudy with dreams. What force of nature broke that character's long siesta?

Nate had roused her body with the pressure of his lips. That was the role of the handsome prince, to wake the cursed woman from her hundred years' sleep. But even his expert fingers had not managed to touch her heart. That was her own task, she told herself. The goal to which she must consecrate her life. From this day forward—Sarah pledged to the traffic—she must resurrect her own dormant spirit.

And perhaps this was a start, she thought as she parked at the PKE house. This was how widows had repaired their broken lives for centuries, by stepping out of their houses, out of their own thin skins, and into the lives of strangers. There were always other people whose situations were more desperate, people open to the charity of lonely women. The only danger Sarah foresaw in her middling philanthropy was that she might measure her life by the scale of local suffering and end up taking solace in the misery of others.

But there was no misery on fraternity row, where the white pickets gleamed like well-tended teeth. The PKE house had symmetrical staircases that curled in vast parentheses up to a wide verandah. Sarah's fingers trailed along the railing as she approached the double doors—twelve panels of solid oak, and a half-moon glowing above the transom. She lifted the brass knocker and dropped it once, enough to beckon a sixties-ish housemother whose pleated tennis skirt matched her wrinkled cheeks. Sarah explained that she had come to meet an unnamed senior who was supposed to help with the campus food drive. The woman pointed toward the living room.

"Have a seat in the parlor while I check upstairs."

The "parlor" was a thirty-foot room with high ceilings, wood floors, and a vast Oriental rug. Its intricate weave of reds and blues seemed perfect for hiding decades of mud, beer, and vomit, but the furniture was less forgiving, with stains on the chintz upholstery and nicks in the legs of the walnut chairs. So much careless wealth—plastic lawn furniture would have been more appropriate.

She remembered standing in a room like this seventeen years ago, when she and David were still dating. They had come to visit Nate in his senior year of college, to attend a Halloween party his fraternity was hosting. David was dressed as Frankenstein and she was his terrible bride—a parody of the undead even in their early days—she with a beehive perched on her skull like a giant Brillo pad. Together they had walked from room to room in search of the too-beautiful brother, finding him in a space like this, with Persian rugs and French doors and leather couches with white creases.

Nate was a young Count Dracula; black circles framed his blue eyes. He was lounging on a sofa, bowing his mouth to the neck of any girl who ventured within reach, and all of them ventured, his ever-willing victims, as if Nate were a bishop offering Communion. He marked each throat with a slimy gel that squirted from the tip of his fangs.

Sarah's neck alone remained untouched, for when he spotted his brother Nate popped the fangs from his mouth and rose with a benign grin.

"You don't want to suck my blood?" she had asked when Nate shook her hand.

She still remembered his reply: "Some other time."

Sarah piveted at a noise in the hallway. The housemother was back, followed by a lanky boy in wrinkled khakis whose hair poked east and west.

"What's your name?" Sarah asked.

"This is Zack," the woman answered. "He should be very helpful." She addressed these last words to the yawning student, heaving a cardboard box full of tin cans into his arms.

Outside, as they descended the curving staircase, Sarah admired the spring in Zack's legs, and the effortless way he slid the box into the back of the van. When he turned and looked at her, she blushed. "I appreciate your help."

Zack shrugged with one shoulder and flung his hair back from his eyes. "Our house is on probation. We've each got to do five hours of community service before we can have another party."

"I see." She smiled. "You are a paragon of altruism."

Together they walked fraternity row from door to door, along sidewalks barely shaded by skeletal trees. Most of the houses were immense brick structures with round white columns and covered porches. Respectable facades, she thought, for havens of debauchery. Often when they entered, they discovered an empty box waiting in the foyer where Sarah had deposited it three weeks ago. Zack was especially useful then, buttonholing anyone found lounging in front of a television.

"Hey!" He waved the empty box like a cardboard manifesto. "You assholes didn't leave any food for the poor! Get off your lazy butts and find something in the kitchen!" And when a sheepish boy returned with a few cans: "Don't give them that crap! Nobody wants to eat that."

"You have a flair," Sarah said, which made Zack grin.

At the Sigma Nu house, while Zack was off corralling sophomores, Sarah stood in an alcove and stared out the window. Nate had danced in a space like this on Halloween night—a wood floor, a bay window, stereo speakers three feet tall. She had expected him to gravitate to the most beautiful girls, to reserve himself for partners who approached his own perfection. But no, Nate danced with a pink-haired clown whose waist was twice his size. He danced with fairies, danced with ghosts, danced with a red-lipped Elvira in fishnet stockings. Dark skin, pale skin, freckled and rouged—he was utterly catholic in his taste in partners, bowing to a trio of witches who circled their wands above his head.

But he never danced with Sarah. And now, as she looked out at the leaves crushed beneath the wheels of passing cars, she remembered how she had felt on that distant Halloween, how she had wanted Nate to cross the room and extend his hand—to lead her to the dance floor with the tips of his long, plastic nails. Somehow David's presence had always rendered her untouchable. She had been waiting seventeen years for her dance with Nate.

"Are you ready?" Zack stood in the doorway with a tower of pasta boxes.

Together they visited sorority houses, administrative buildings, and academic offices. They packed the van so full, it sank down like a low-rider, then they drove to the basement entrance of the local Catholic church, where red double doors opened upon a library of food, thousands of tin cans stacked row after row. There were shelves of tomato paste, shelves of green beans, shelves of peas and corn and beets. A complete Dewey Decimal System of vegetables, and a reference section of cereal.

Here was the practical counterpoint to the world of libraries that Sarah had occupied since high school. She smiled at Zack's open mouth, and pointed to a gray-haired woman at the top of a stepladder.

"Molly was a middle school librarian before she retired."

Zack nodded. "Cool."

The woman examined them through half-moon glasses. "Hello, Sarah. Let's see what you've got for me."

Outside, when they opened the van's back doors, a white Lincoln town car pulled up beside them and a bald man in his fifties stepped out of the driver's side. He opened the passenger door and extracted an elderly woman in a long purple coat and red sequined hat. Sarah recognized Adele, from Margaret's widows group.

"You're looking wonderful," Molly said as Adele smoothed her coat.

"I'm meeting my red-hatted ladies," Adele explained.

Her driver opened the trunk, revealing rows of cardboard boxes filled with mason jars, each one topped with green-checkered cloth and a red ribbon.

"This one is for you." Adele handed a jar to Molly.

"Adele makes the best strawberry jam," Molly explained.

"Raspberry this year." Adele winked at Sarah. "I'm full of surprises." She gave Sarah a jar, then nodded at her driver. "This is my nephew Fred. This is Molly, and this is Sarah."

Fred tipped his hat, lifted two boxes from the trunk, and carried them inside.

"Come with me, dear." Adele took Sarah's elbow. "We should leave the lifting to the men."

In a back room with fluorescent lights and wood paneling, one hundred and twenty Thanksgiving dinners waited in cardboard boxes on rows of folding tables. Sarah surveyed the water-packed turkey breasts and stiff cylinders of cranberry sauce, generic cans of sweet potatoes and twenty-cent cartons of macaroni and cheese.

Fred settled the boxes of preserves on a table against the wall, and Adele began unloading the jars one by one, packing them carefully inside each dinner.

Sarah paused to admire the handwritten label on one jar. "You made all of these yourself?"

"Oh no." Adele chuckled. "There are six of us. We go berry picking together, with plenty of grandchildren to help, and we play bridge while the preserves simmer."

"You do this every Thanksgiving?"

Adele nodded. "We like to add a personal touch to the dinners. Canned green beans can get so depressing."

Sarah wedged a jar between boxes of stuffing. "I was thinking that I should do more volunteer work. Get out of the house more, out of my own thoughts."

Adele held a jar to the light and straightened its checkered cloth. "It took me four months after Edward died—to get out of my house, back into town. And it's important. Otherwise you just get stuck in the past." She smiled at Sarah. "You should come here at Christmas. We have three times as many meals then, and we need lots of drivers. I can't drive." She nodded at Fred as he carried in another box. "My vision is too cloudy."

When Fred was gone Adele placed her arthritic fingers, glittering with rings, on Sarah's hand.

"Have you seen your husband lately?"

Sarah had been expecting the question. "I saw him on Halloween . . . He showed up at the house and talked for a long time . . . And I imagine that I might see him tomorrow, on Thanksgiving."

"Oh yes." Adele smiled. "They always come on the holidays.

My Edward makes an annual appearance around Christmastime. Last year I only caught a glimpse of him, walking through the hallway. But usually he stops for conversation, and I can see the stitching in his uniform, and the expression in his eyes."

Sarah contemplated Adele's foggy pupils. "Do you ever think it's just a dream?"

"Of course. At my age, anything is possible. But I also saw him when I was younger. He would come when I was feeling most desperate. We had a son who died in Vietnam, you know."

Sarah shook her head. "I didn't know."

"I have a daughter in Charlotte and a son in Richmond. Five grandchildren and one great-grandson. But our youngest boy was killed in 1969, and once, when I was miserable, sitting in my kitchen, I felt Edward standing behind me. He wrapped his arms around me like this big, warm necklace." Adele pressed her crooked fingers to her throat. "I've read that when a person is emotionally vulnerable, that's when they're most likely to feel the spirits. And that's how it was for me. I couldn't see him that day, but I could feel the weight of his arms, and it was as if my whole body was being heated. I felt completely reassured."

She stood there with her hands poised around her neck—like she's strangling herself, Sarah thought. What a pair they made, two solitary widows, nurturing their private lunacies.

"Everything with me is still confused," she murmured.

"You're newly widowed, my dear." Adele patted her hand. "Give it time."

• 23 •

The next day Sarah prepared her own donations, clothes and books and music for her newly needy husband. She had reserved eight cardboard boxes when organizing the food drive, expecting to take most of David's belongings to Goodwill. Now the boxes lay on her bed like a nest of gaping baby birds.

Inside David's closet, she ignored his slacks and jackets, linen shirts and silk ties—all the accoutrements of his medical career. What he needed now were flannel shirts, blue jeans, and long underwear. Much of his winter wardrobe was an homage to L.L. Bean, Polartec pullovers and fleece vests, a Teflon-coated anorak. In the back of the closet she found a yellow Gore-Tex parka with matching yellow pants. The outfit had made her wince when Helen sent it as a Christmas present; it seemed like an oversize version of a child's duckling rainwear. But now the color struck her as a shield against hunters. She stuffed it into an empty box, then added all of the woolen souvenirs from David's youth—socks, caps, and scarves, some hand-knitted by his mother. She regretted that Nate had taken David's favorite Scottish sweater, but she compensated with a bulky Nepalese pullover thick as a buffalo hide.

Downstairs in the basement she packed David's art supplies—paints and chalk and charcoal and a multitude of brushes. She found a few blank canvases stapled to wooden frames, wrapped them inside his sweatshirts, and carried them to her wagon. Finally, she rummaged through the tools in the garage.

The chain saw was the first to go; she would never dare to use it. Next went the Weedwacker, on loan for a few weeks. The staple gun caused her to pause for a few seconds before she stacked it next to the blowtorch. She filled half of a cardboard box with wrenches, hammers, nails and screws, sandpaper and Spackle. A not-so-subtle hint that the cabin needed work.

Upstairs she stood before her living-room shelves, formulating a reading list for David's long winter. Dante's sojourn into the underworld seemed fitting for a dead man; Thoreau, Ammons, and Dickey were good companions for the woods; Thurber might lighten a dark winter evening, and Ruth Rendell was always welcome. She topped the pile with *The Complete Poems of Robert Frost,* before turning toward the stereo.

Sarah chose CDs as if arranging a wine tasting—a drop of fusion, a splash of blues, a hint of Oscar Peterson. In keeping with the nature theme, she chose Beethoven's *Pastoral* Symphony, Vivaldi's *Four Seasons*, and Copland's *Appalachian Spring*. She packed them in a box with a portable CD player and carried everything to the car, congratulating herself on her thematic wit. But when she stood before the open hatch, admiring the boxes full of books and music, she realized that all she had managed was to gather her own favorites. This was not an offering for the dead, it was a collection to carry her through her own dark season, with David nothing more than a peripheral thought.

Early on Thanksgiving morning she returned to the Food Lion for the first time since her episode with David. She was afraid to shop at the local Safeway, where Margaret might appear and see the turkey in her cart. Here, on the outskirts of town, she had no fear of detection; her only question was whether the manager with the patriotic name tag would remember her face.

Winding through the store aisle by aisle, she bought piles of bananas, apples and pears, sweet potatoes, zucchini, and broccoli. She stocked up on cheeses, nuts, and bagels, frozen shrimp, fresh sirloins, and a sixteen-pound turkey, enough leftovers to feed David for weeks.

Gathering these objects made her feel that she was giving substance to his life. He was the merest outline of a man, a blank page that she was coloring in with red potatoes and green beans, yellow squash and blue tortilla chips, all of which she unloaded into the backseat of her car. Driving through the woods with her edible bounty, she imagined herself as an early Santa, bringing Christmas in November, and at the cabin, David greeted her with the joy of a child.

"This is fantastic." He laughed, placing bags of fruit on boxes of fleece and lugging them all inside. While Sarah unpacked groceries he carried the clothing and art supplies into the corner of the spare bedroom.

"Tell me what to do," he said when the last box was stored.

"Choose a jazz CD. And open a bottle of wine." Even before noon, a glass of Chardonnay was a prerequisite for her cooking.

When David handed her the glass, she gave him a bag of apples. "Peel and core and slice these. I'm making an apple pie."

His paring knife made long red-and-white spirals that dangled in twelve-inch strips before falling into the trash can. "Do you remember our first Thanksgiving?"

"At your parents' house?"

"Yes. When we got engaged."

She remembered it well—the Vermont college town with its boutiques and galleries framing a gently sloping green. The church with a tall white steeple, not Presbyterian or Methodist, but Unitarian Universalist.

"I remember your mother's church, and seeing your house for the first time."

She had never before seen black window trim. Something about those dark rectangles reminded her of Nathaniel Hawthorne.

"Your father kept the thermostat at a constant sixty-two, and I wore thick socks and stayed in a chair by the living-room fire."

Sarah didn't say what she remembered most—standing at the kitchen window that overlooked the backyard, watching Nate throw a Frisbee to their black Lab, Pilgrim. Four weeks had passed since the Halloween party, and in that time she had often thought of David's younger brother. It was partly David's fault; he told so many stories about Nate, so many recollections of how girls flocked to his brother but never made him happy. Nate was always seeking something unexplained, the handsome prince with his impossible glass slipper.

Watching Nate from the window, Sarah had tried to define his appeal. *Beautiful* was not the right word. Neither was *cute,* an adjective for dogs and teddy bears. *Handsome* would not apply for a few more decades. Perhaps *lovely* was the best word. Nate had a face that inspired love, the face of Helen's son.

When he came inside, his cheeks were flushed.

"Your hair," he said to Sarah, "looks much better without the lightning bolt."

"And yours looks better without the Vitalis."

She was pleased that she could speak to him without a tremor in her voice, that she could slide her hand around David's waist and gaze upon Nate with something akin to defiance. She told herself that her fascination with this bright-eyed fraternity boy was purely aesthetic, but still she couldn't quell the ache in her chest every time he looked at her.

That Thanksgiving evening, as she and David sat opposite Nate, with the parents flanking them at the table ends, the ache had pressed against her lungs like a fist of pneumonia. When the family raised their glasses to toast the holiday, David had announced their engagement, prompting Helen to rise from her seat and approach Sarah with arms outstretched. Next came David's father, and finally Nate, who slid his chair back slowly and walked to Sarah's side. With one hand in her hair and the other in the small of her back, he had held her against his warm body. When he pulled away, it was like the disconnection of an electric current.

Now, as Sarah looked out the kitchen window, those memories seemed tied to another life. Nate's face had changed in the past decade. Two years in business school and ten on Wall Street had robbed his expression of its vulnerability. He was more polished now, a shining stone, and she wondered if she could have spared him that hardening—if the right woman could have softened his edges. But she had never been the right woman. Not then, not now.

"Here." She handed a bag of sweet potatoes to David. "Peel these."

When she and David sat down to dinner, the meal was so excessive it seemed almost grotesque—the turkey basted to a sweaty perfection, the marshmallows oozing across her yams like a seven-day mold. Sarah envisioned Jackson's poorest families opening their tin cans, cutting their cranberry sauce into slices thick as hockey pucks.

"Shall we say what we are thankful for?" David asked.

Sarah had not felt thankful for the past three years.

"I am thankful for your paintings," she said, "and for Margaret's cooking."

David laughed. "Fair enough."

"And what about you?" she asked.

"I'm thankful that you haven't given up on me."

"Not yet." Sarah poured a stream of gravy across her plate, then stared at her food, wondering why she held herself so aloof from her husband. "There's something else," she said after a moment. "I'm thankful to have been given this second chance with you, just for a little while." Once she had spoken she felt relieved, as if the glacier in her chest was beginning to melt. She looked into David's face and saw that he was smiling at her in the old way, the way they both had smiled in the earliest years of their marriage, when they had been able to look at each other and feel—what was it? Delight. Sarah reached across the table and for a few seconds she rested her warm palm over David's hand.

Then she lifted her fork. "Let's eat."

After dinner David carved the turkey down to its skeleton, segregating the white meat from the dark and wrapping it all in plastic. He wiped the wishbone with a paper towel before handing one end to Sarah, and she snapped it with a twist. Looking at the large, splintered piece in her hand, she realized that she had automatically wished the same wish for the past five years, the one desire lavished on every coin thrown in a fountain, every eyelash blown from her fingertips. She had wished for a child.

"I have a request," David said.

"What is it?"

"I was wondering if you would model for me? I'd like to paint you."

Sarah winced. She hadn't posed for David since the earliest years of their marriage, and she wondered if it wasn't better that way. Perhaps she should leave him with the idealized vision of his charcoal nude, so wistful and compliant. What might he see now if he stared at her for too long?

"What did you have in mind?"

David surveyed the room. "Why don't you sit in the rocking chair, by the hearth?"

She obeyed, folding her hands in her lap.

"Look into the fire," he said, and she turned her face to the flames. Inside the coals, she heard the hissing of a dozen cats.

"It's too dark," he said. "Could you stand at the window?"

"Which one?"

He wasn't sure. She moved from window to window, looking north, east, south. One view was too shady, another too bright. The multiple panes on the doors to the deck cast shadows across her face.

"Would you mind coming into the bedroom?" She followed his hand, which pointed down the hall to the room that faced the river. There, the four-paned window was covered by thin lace curtains that hung to the floor, filtering the afternoon sunlight. As she walked to the window she reached up and pulled the lace aside, as if brushing a child's hair out of his eyes. Beyond the tall grass she could see a flock of Canada geese, floating by the dock.

"That's perfect. Don't move."

"I can't hold my arm like this for long."

"I'll sketch your arm first."

He retrieved his drawing pad from the living room, along with a jar of pencils and charcoal, and a chair from the table. Spreading his supplies across the foot of the bed, he propped the pad on his knee, then watched Sarah for a long time without lifting his pencil.

"I have one more request."

"Tell me."

"Your sweater doesn't look quite right; it's too bulky. Would you mind changing into your nightgown and robe?" He pointed toward the opposite corner, where her suitcase lay open on a chair, her gown folded on top, and her robe visible beneath.

She hadn't worn that white cotton nightgown in years; its collar of forget-me-nots seemed too childish. Neither had she worn the white silk robe that David bought her ten years ago for Christmas. It was a remnant of their early marriage, when she still cared about looking pretty. Of late, she had cared more about the dry-cleaning bill.

But why had she packed them for this visit, except as an act of contrition? An apology for all the months that she had padded around their house in T-shirts and underwear, wrapped in a thick green terry-cloth robe designed for a man. It was warm, she had explained whenever David flinched. It was soft, it was comfortable, she could throw it in the wash. But in recent weeks she had seen the robe's hideous message, the sluggish hausfrau's flag of surrender.

How strange it seemed to undress in front of David. He had seen so many women's bodies—young, collegiate girls with firm thighs, cherry lipstick, and painted toenails. Variations on herself twenty years earlier. Now, as she covered her skin in white silk, she felt that she was becoming insubstantial, the pale counterpoint to her spectral husband.

When she returned to the window, the sun was setting to her right. Her robe was untied, and as she pushed the curtain aside the sunset fell upon her throat with an orange light that shed no warmth. The room was cold without a fire nearby, and she felt melancholy staring at the river, alone in her nightgown. David was so quiet that she hesitated to move, thinking that if she looked back, he would fade into the walls.

After ten minutes of raising her arm, shaking it out, and raising it again, he told her that she could leave it down. David pulled a shoelace from one of his sneakers, tied the curtain to the side, then watched her for fifteen minutes more, until the sky had faded to a purple bruise.

"That's enough for now," he said. "Thanks."

She walked over to his shoulder and saw three sketches of her hand—fingers curled, fingers spread, one with her index finger extended lackadaisically like Michelangelo's Adam, so bored with God's gift of life. David had attended to the curve of her fingernails, the angle of her knuckles, and the glint of sapphires on her right-hand ring, a gift from their tenth anniversary. He had also focused on fabrics—ivory silk gathered in folds a few inches past her elbow, and the intricate lace curtains, a tapestry of spiderwebs. This painting would take weeks, but she would not stay for more than a day or two.

The next morning they hiked upstream, where the ice had formed a white froth at the river's edge, and by midafternoon Sarah had returned to her nightgown, staring out the window at the tulipwood tree, no more than a few groping sticks. She remembered her yard in South Carolina, its towering willow a perennial green, except for one cold winter, when the leaves faded to a spotted yellow. She thought also of Vermont, with its reds and golds and coppery browns, and the blue of Nate's bright eyes.

On the third day Sarah woke early and packed her bag. She placed a kiss on David's forehead, then left while the sun was still making its way up the pines. Two nights at the cabin were enough; she recognized the danger of being lulled into this dreamy world, becoming nothing more than a painted silhouette. Driving home, she felt that she was emerging from a deep lake, gradually coming up for air.

• 24 •

She was home for less than an hour when a knock came at the door. Margaret stood on the porch, looking quizzical.

"I saw your car in the driveway and I thought I'd stop by. Are you all right?"

"I'm fine. Why do you ask?"

Margaret glanced behind Sarah, into the house, as if she were expecting someone. "Anne called on Thursday to wish you a nice Thanksgiving. She somehow had the impression that you were eating with us. I didn't know what to say."

Of course, thought Sarah. How stupid of her. Caught like a pathetic rat in a trap. She stepped back from the door. "Come in."

"I told her that you couldn't come to the phone." Margaret spoke as she walked into the living room. "I said you'd call her back."

"Have a seat." Sarah pointed toward the sofa and had a brief flashback of Nate, pulling the white turtleneck over his head. She wondered if Margaret would smell his aftershave in the cushions, or notice the gray water rings paired on the table.

"I came over the next day to see if you were home," Margaret said. "But your car hasn't been here, so I was starting to get worried."

Sarah took a seat across the room and stared into her hands, noticing how the lifelines branched into multiple children before curving down her wrists. Promises, promises.

"I spent Thanksgiving at the cabin," she said. "I wanted to get away someplace quiet for the holiday." With an effort, she raised her eyes to Margaret's. "I told you I was going to Anne's because I didn't want you to worry. I thought you might think it was a bad idea."

From the furrow in Margaret's brow Sarah knew she had been right; Margaret's disapproval formed a little cloud above her eyes. There was something unhealthy about a widow alone in the woods, sleeping in the last bed her husband had occupied. Perhaps in the summer, with the green grass and warm air, but not among the late fall's barren trees and early darkness.

"What did you do out there?" Margaret asked.

"I walked. I read. Mostly I daydreamed."

"Did you eat anything?"

"Yes," Sarah answered. "I'm well fed."

"And have you been able to sleep?"

Sarah smiled, sensing that the cloud was lifting. "I still ramble sometimes at night. I wake up disoriented, and it takes a while to bring things into focus. But it's getting better.

"I'm sorry I lied," she added. "I didn't want to bother you with explanations."

"Well, you should call Anne and say hello. You can stick with the story that you were at my house."

"Thanks."

"And I was thinking . . ." Margaret paused, looking around the room at all of its dusty furniture. "Ever since David died, it's seemed kind of silly for both of us to live alone in such big houses . . . You mentioned that you've been thinking about getting a smaller place, and I thought that maybe you should consider moving in with me for a little while?" She settled her eyes on Sarah's face. "My girls only come to visit a couple of weekends each year. Most of the time the house is empty. You could have the guest suite with the sitting room and the private bath."

"The one with the bay window and the doors out onto the porch?"

"Exactly. We could try it for a few months—bring some of your furniture and put the rest into storage. Put up wallpaper and curtains—whatever you like. And you could think of it as temporary lodging between selling your house and finding a new one."

How sweet, thought Sarah. This was Margaret's antidote to her isolation. The safe house for the woman on the edge.

"I would want to help pay the mortgage."

"Sure," said Margaret, "and I would clear out some kitchen cupboards and refrigerator shelves."

"We'd get a second telephone line?"

"And another cable for your computer."

"You wouldn't mind Grace?"

"I wouldn't mind any creature that came with you."

Sarah smiled. Margaret had no idea of the creatures that came with her.

She walked around the table and sat beside Margaret on the couch. Placing her hand around her friend's shoulder, she inhaled the soothing scent of chamomile shampoo. "You are a sweetheart," she said. "I'll think about it."

Two days later when the telephone rang, Sarah was greeted by Nate's calm tenor: "I'd like to talk to you." For eight days she had been screening all calls, avoiding the siren song of his voice.

"Can I come to your house?" he asked.

No. She couldn't sit with him on the sofa newly exorcised by Margaret. Nor could he sit at the kitchen table where David's ghost had lingered. Her bedroom was the only space where Nate seemed to fit, and that was a temptation she wanted to resist.

"There's a nice coffee shop on Main Street, across from the post office," she said.

"Perfect. I could be there tomorrow at nine, and be back in Charlottesville in time for lunch."

"Fine."

The next morning she arrived at the coffee shop fifteen minutes early. She didn't want to stand shoulder to shoulder with Nate at the counter, and make small talk with acquaintances who would expect to be introduced. The extra minutes allowed her time to claim an inconspicuous table in the back and nurse her cappuccino slowly, scooping whipped cream with the tip of her plastic spoon. Every so often she lifted her eyes to the upper walls of exposed brick, where burlap sacks were branded with the names of foreign countries—Costa Rica, Ecuador, Guatemala, Mexico. So many places she would rather be.

She waved when Nate entered, a brief flick of her fingers, trying not to look like a woman who had been waiting for fifteen minutes. It seemed that the counter girl smiled a little too brightly at Nate, and he smiled back, the constant Casanova. He ordered a cup of the house blend—black, with no cream, no sugar, no froth. Nate was not the type for froth.

"How was your Thanksgiving?" he asked when he came to Sarah's table.

"Nice. How was yours?"

"Uneventful." He put down his coffee and folded his coat over the back of a chair. "I went out to dinner with a fellow bachelor and we ordered lobster."

It occurred to Sarah that she was Nate's only immediate family, his only link to turkey dinners and a Christmas stocking. Last year he had spent Thanksgiving with Jenny's family in North Carolina, but usually he came to her house, with Anne's daughters providing the family atmosphere.

Nate blew into his coffee while he glanced around the room. When he spoke, his voice was low, barely above a whisper. "I know you've been avoiding me." He gave a small laugh. "It's the first time in my life that a woman hasn't answered my calls . . . I suppose you think we've made some terrible mistake."

"Don't you?" Sarah asked.

"Of course not. I regret nothing."

"No"—she shook her head—"you wouldn't." There was something Nietzschean about Nate, a trace of the *Übermensch* who could survey the entire breadth of his life and declare "Thus I willed it."

She had willed nothing. All her life she had floated with the current, a lingering Ophelia.

"David would want us to be happy." Nate had fallen into platitudes.

"Happy in our separate lives."

Sarah knew what few people recognized—that David, the calm doctor, was capable of rage. Not often, and not for long. His anger came in thunderstorms trailing with rainbows. But oh, how the sky would split if he knew she had slept with Nate.

"You know, I was always a little jealous of David." Nate smiled into her eyes. "Which doesn't mean that I'm in love with you, or that I want you to love me. I'm just saying that so long as we enjoy each other's company, we might as well make the most of it."

"What does that mean?" Sarah asked.

"Just this." He paused. "Judith called me about the exhibit in Washington. The show opens this Friday, and she wants us both to come for the whole weekend and put it on her tab at the Mayflower—two separate rooms. I know it's short notice, but I think we should do it."

Sarah looked up at the burlap bags with their promises of new landscapes, new streets, new faces.

"And here's the great thing," Nate went on. "I called the Kennedy Center, and this Saturday night the National Symphony and the Robert Shaw Chorale are combining to do the *Carmina Burana*. The concert is sold out, but I have a friend who can still get tickets if I call right away."

God, he knew her well. The *Carmina Burana* was one of Sarah's favorite pieces of music. She liked to play it on her stereo at a pounding fortissimo whenever she folded loads of laundry.

Of course he was manipulating her. But why use such an ugly word? Why not call it "wooing," or "courtship," or "temptation"?

Nate covered her hand with his warm fingers and she felt the smooth metal of his father's wedding band. "We can ride up together on Friday afternoon, check into the hotel, and eat a late dinner at some really nice restaurant before going to the exhibit. On Saturday we can sightsee and shop all day before the concert . . . Come on, Sarah. Live a little."

Sarah let her hand lie curled beneath his own. He was right; she needed to live, more than a little. And perhaps Nate could help her. Perhaps, as Margaret had said, they could do each other some good.

"Yes," she said to Nate. "I'd like that."

• 25 •

On Friday afternoon shortly before four, Sarah arrived at Nate's Charlottesville condominium. The outside resembled a Santa Fe villa framed with Southern shrubbery, but the interior was all New York. So many angles and polished surfaces, so much black and tan and brown. What was the word—chic? sleek? Art deco, or art nouveau? Her own house reeked of Laura Ashley, with floral curtains, pastel walls, and piles of pillows. But this space was a monument to domestic technology—the security system, the remote-controlled lighting, the stereo speakers and televisions in the living room, kitchen, and bedroom. She ran her finger across the stainless steel of his Jenn Air stove, then pondered her reflection in the sheen of his black refrigerator.

"Your place is immaculate," she said when Nate entered with a garment bag.

"I have a maid who comes once a week."

Of course. A life full of women waiting on him.

"Have you ever thought of getting a pet?" The perfection of it all was a little unnerving. She would have appreciated a chew toy on the carpet.

"I wouldn't mind a dog. But I travel so much, it wouldn't make sense."

"What about a cat?"

Nate shuddered. "I hate cats. They give me the creeps."

Sarah felt a little sad for Grace, as if the poor creature had been given a kick.

"Would you like a drink for the road?" Nate opened his spotless refrigerator. "I've got bottled water, and soda, and tomato juice."

"Some water, thanks."

While he programmed his security system, she examined the photographs on his hall table—his parents in Vermont, David at Christmas, Jenny in a bikini on a tropical beach, with turquoise water and dazzling sand. It seemed strange for an ex-girlfriend to maintain such a prominent place among the family photos. Sarah took it as a sign that Nate still cared for Jenny, which was just as well; it made the coming weekend all the more innocuous, to think that Nate's heart might be elsewhere.

Nate held the front door. "Your car or mine?"

Sarah rolled her eyes. "Don't toy with me."

Inside his Mercedes she leaned back and absorbed the scent of new leather. Luxury was a wonderful thing when someone else was paying. Nate started the ignition and a screen above the CD player mapped the route from his garage to the Mayflower hotel. She needed one of those for her life, something to show her how to get from point A to point B.

When Nate put on a jazz CD, Sarah closed her eyes. "Sleep if you'd like," he said. "We'll be there in two hours."

At six P.M. Sarah stood in the Mayflower lobby, admiring a fountain with copper lights, where the water resembled a shower of newly minted pennies. Nate had checked them in and was now walking toward her, holding up the plastic room keys like a pair of aces. He thinks he's going to get lucky, she told herself, and she resolved to disappoint him.

Together they rode the brass elevators to the seventh floor, and walked down a carpet covered in fleur-de-lis. Sarah's room was a junior suite with a king-size bed, a whirlpool bath, and a sitting area with a sofa and two Queen Anne chairs. A note on the minibar said that everything was free, compliments of Judith.

"Look." Nate walked to the desk, where a crystal vase held a dozen red roses. "The card's from Judith. She says that dinner tonight is on her. We should keep the receipt."

Sarah came over and lowered her face to the petals. They reminded her of the roses from the night of the Jackson opening; once again Judith was setting the mood.

Nate spread the curtains and looked at the view. "There's a restaurant three blocks from here called the Desert Inn. They have an excellent menu. Kind of a gourmet Tex-Mex. I've made reservations for seven o'clock. Of course we don't have to eat there. We can go anywhere you like."

"That sounds fine," Sarah replied. It felt good to let someone else make the reservations, drive the car, pay the bills.

"We have half an hour before we'll need to leave for dinner."

He crossed the threshold between their adjoining rooms. "I'll let you change."

When he was gone, she stretched out on her bed, picked up the remote, and turned to the weather. A winter storm was blanketing Chicago, burying abandoned cars in four-foot drifts. Across the nation's map, the white strip covering the Midwest was an ominous void, but for now the Eastern states shone fluorescent green, and she watched New Yorkers ice-skating sleeveless at Rockefeller Center.

Ten minutes later she rose and removed the ironing board from the closet. From the top of her suitcase she lifted a black spaghetti-strap cocktail dress. It was the only thing she owned that seemed right for a Georgetown gallery, but she didn't want to look too pretty, as if she were trying to impress Nate. It would be best to leave her hair down and color her face with only the slightest hint of makeup. She would wear small earrings and a simple necklace, nothing dramatic or expensive. One spray of perfume—no more—and her lips would have no gloss.

She was pulling the heated dress over her skin when Nate knocked. He, too, seemed deliberately casual, unshaven and underdressed, in a dark sport jacket with a light blue shirt.

"I forgot to bring a purse," she said as she folded the ironing board and switched off the television. "Do you mind if I put a few things in your pocket?"

Into the silk lining of his jacket she dropped a comb, her room key, a credit card, and sixty dollars. It was a married woman's gesture, this proprietary attitude toward a man's pockets, but Sarah thought that it made Nate less intimidating, to treat him with familiarity.

She opened the door to the hallway. "Let us go then, you and I."

* * *

The restaurant was a blaze of color and conversation, its walls striped with Navajo rugs, the floor a loud mosaic of burnt orange and cranberry tile. They sat at a window table sipping margaritas while Nate watched the passersby, coatless in December.

"Winter hasn't arrived yet," he said.

"Winter is a state of mind," Sarah replied.

"Not if you live in Vermont."

"Do you miss New England?"

Nate shrugged. "I miss the life I had in Vermont, but not the state itself. It was too cold and too liberal for me, a lot of spoiled bohemians building their log cabins in the woods."

Sarah smiled. She and David had often thought of joining those bohemians, escaping the conservative tide of southwest Virginia. But her Southern blood had balked at the thought of those long winters.

"Do you think you'll stay in Charlottesville?"

"I don't know. New York has a certain attraction. I still have a lot of friends up there. But I'd be paying a fortune for a one-bedroom apartment with a closet for a kitchen. What about you? Have you ever thought of moving to the city?"

"People move to Jackson to escape the city."

"But is it a mistake?"

"Not if you have a family." She stopped short, feeling the old acid of misery rise in her stomach. *A woman without a child is an empty shell, a woman alone lives a broken life.*

"You could go anywhere in the world," Nate continued. "Paris, London, Rome. They always need English teachers in China, if you're feeling virtuous."

"Traveling isn't half as much fun when you're alone," Sarah said.

"You wouldn't have to be alone."

She looked up, wondering if Nate was referring to himself. Would Nate abandon his clients to be her traveling companion for a year? Of course not. He probably envisioned her as a Peace Corps volunteer.

"I'll have to see what happens." She licked the salt from the rim of her glass. "Right now I have no concrete plans."

After dinner they drove to Georgetown in search of "Studio Four." The cab deposited them at a three-story brownstone that resembled a private residence, except for the small brass plaque to the right of the door. Inside, the living room, dining room, and study had been converted into a gallery with white walls, refinished floors, and a collection of Afghan rugs. Two swinging doors in the back led into a small kitchen, which wafted occasional scents of pastry and focaccia.

Judith met them with kisses and a jingling of bracelets. "David's paintings are in the dining room. Two have already sold . . . Let me introduce you to William Reed. He's a sculptor from North Carolina who works with red clay." A tall, bearded man extended a rouge-tinted hand. Beside him stood a female painter who specialized in transforming Tennessee barns into geometric marvels—triangles and trapezoids, red and green and purple. Her body was as angular as her art.

"I like your husband's work," the woman said in a low drawl. "There's something dreamy about it."

Sarah wasn't quite sure what the woman meant until she stepped into the dining room, and there, above the fireplace, was the charcoal drawing of herself, rising from tousled sheets, gray shadows gathering under her breasts. She had forgotten about that one. How ironic. Just when she was resolved to keep her clothes on around Nate, here she was, on display, nipples puckered like a pair of Hershey's Kisses.

"It's a nice piece," Nate said.

"You're *not* going to buy it."

"Not if it would make you uncomfortable."

A thin man in silver spectacles seemed to connect the drawing with Sarah. He stared at her face, her breasts, her face. "Let's get out of here," she said, and retreated to the study.

"How long do you want to stay?" Nate spoke across the head of a small clay child, who reached out to Sarah with a tiny soccer ball.

"Twenty minutes. Do you like this crowd?"

Nate looked around at the sea of black clothing. "They seem to be poised between pretension and desperation."

Sarah smiled. "Aren't we all?"

Another fifteen minutes and they said good-bye to Judith, apologizing for their haste. "Of *course*." Judith kissed them twice, Parisian style. "It's *stifling* in here. You two go and have some fun."

Outside, a current of college students was flowing along the sidewalks, wearing chinos and flip-flops. Nate glanced down the street. "Would you like to go into one of these bars?"

"With all that free liquor at our hotel?" Sarah shook her head. "What I'd really enjoy is a walk around the monuments."

Nate hailed a cab and bowed as he opened the door. "Your wish is my command."

Together they rode past the lights and music of Georgetown, winding through the poured concrete of the Foggy Bottom district and emerging at the Potomac's edge, beside the Lincoln Memorial. Handfuls of tourists were out walking, their voices muted by the vast proportions of the glowing columns, while inside the memorial an unseen flautist played something slow and mournful. "Erik Satie," Sarah murmured as they ascended the white stone stairs.

They stopped at the foot of the statue, where the toe of Lincoln's boot jutted over their heads. Sarah examined the shadows carved into the sculpture's eyes, and considered the surrounding words: . . . *that this nation under God shall have a new birth of freedom*. She turned her back and looked to the other side of the reflecting pool, where the Washington Monument stood circled with unmoving flags. It seemed so small, a spotlit pin piercing the sky, with red serpent eyes that blinked as she watched them. Behind her, the flautist's last breath faded into a few seconds of quiet, shattered by the crescendo of a jet, descending over the Potomac.

"The World War Two memorial is straight ahead." Nate pointed. "Korea's to the right and Vietnam's to the left. What would you like to see?"

Sarah hesitated, trying to choose a war. "None of them," she said, because it had suddenly occurred to her that this was the wrong place to be. Tranquil as the setting was, she didn't need to stand in this quadrangle of memorials. Memory of the dead was the one human compulsion that she had mastered. The last thing she needed was to walk downhill past a wall of dead men's names, thousands upon thousands, the list growing deeper until it was over her head, and all the flowers at the base, and the children with their rubbings, and the veterans with their black-and-white POW flags. Washington was little more than a giant mausoleum—the Holocaust Museum with its depressing shoes; the Pentagon hatching its shameless plans; the National Museum of the American Indian, a government's weak apology for genocide. Even the teary-eyed mammals in the Natural History Museum, which she had enjoyed so much as a child, now struck her as an exercise in morbid illusion. Every corner of the city was saturated in death, and for the first time in four months she felt ready to scream, scream at all the lives thrown away.

"Are you all right?" Nate wrapped his jacket around her shoulders.

"Let's go back to the room," she said. "I want to raid the minibar."

Back at the hotel they drank vodka and watched TV long past midnight. Nate kept her laughing with a running commentary on the idiocy of reality shows, and when she saw his face lit by the flashing screen, she remembered David years ago, watching *Tales from the Crypt*.

She was grateful for Nate's company, grateful for his willingness to take her to art exhibits and trendy restaurants. He was the perfect companion for this juncture in her life. But she didn't love him; so she kept reminding herself. How could she love the quintessential capitalist, a man whose happiness was tied to the Standard & Poor 500, who went through cars and women as if they were glasses of water? Nate's appeal was the appeal of all vices, a momentary pleasure followed by weeks of guilt. And yet, when she tried to classify him along with chocolate truffles, as just another sweet to be given up for Lent, she could not dismiss him so easily. He had been kind to her, more than generous with his time, and she liked him for it.

"Shall we have breakfast in the morning?" he asked when they turned off the TV.

"Not early."

"No, not early. I'll probably go down to the fitness center when I first wake up. I'll take a shower and maybe we could have brunch after that?"

She nodded and Nate leaned forward briefly, as if he were inclined to kiss her cheek. But he thought better of it.

"Well, good night, Sarah."

"Good night."

The next morning, after an elaborate breakfast buffet, they went for a walk around the hotel. The neighborhood was full of clothing stores and restaurants in the ground floors of dull, rectangular office buildings. Sarah followed Nate into Burberry, where an older gentleman in a gray suit offered his assistance. While she admired the Christmas ties, Nate and his attendant strolled the labyrinth of racks, speaking a language of cuffs and collars and thread counts. What was it that gave her brother-in-law the unmistakable aura of a spender? Was it only the cut of his hair, or the leather in his shoes? She glanced at the other women in the store, with their skirts and boots and expensive jackets, then looked down at her own meager blue jeans and sneakers.

When Nate was finished they continued down the street.

"I can't believe that you spent one hundred and eighty dollars on a shirt."

"Do you think it's immoral?" Nate smiled.

"I think you could have gotten something just as nice for half the price."

"But every time I put it on I would feel the difference."

"That sounds like a line from 'The Princess and the Pea.' " Sarah shrugged. "But never mind. Please yourself."

Nate stopped at a window where a trio of mannequins glittered in sequined snow. "When was the last time you pleased yourself?" He took her hand and led her inside. There, they were greeted by a wave of potpourri and a saleswoman who looked to be about twenty-two. Nate flashed her a charming grin. "My sister-in-law is looking for a new evening dress."

"No," Sarah said. "I'm not."

Nate smiled again at the young woman, then tilted his head toward Sarah. "What are you wearing tonight?"

"The same dress that I wore to the show in Jackson."

"You look terrific in that dress, but how long have you owned it?"

She hesitated. "Eleven years."

Nate exchanged knowing glances with the saleswoman, then turned and looked directly into Sarah's eyes.

"Indulge yourself," he said. "Indulge me."

Twenty minutes and five dresses later she was rotating before a semi-octagon of mirrors, wearing a sleeveless silk affair with a beaded skirt, looking like a Gypsy soaked in Merlot. She glanced over her shoulder at the back, where gentle oval folds rippled beneath her shoulder blades. Why had she been wearing jeans and sweatshirts for the past ten years? Was it a habit from graduate school, her preference for thrift stores? Now she was only satisfied when wearing a bargain.

But perhaps this was a bargain. She watched the beads shimmer as she swayed from side to side. So what if the price tag made Nate's shirt look like a Target special? If a woman had a chance to buy a little happiness, wasn't that money well spent?

When she stepped out of the dressing room Nate's smile confirmed her thoughts.

"Perfect."

The saleswoman nodded. "Have you got shoes to go with it? There's a wonderful shoe store on the next block north."

By noon Sarah found herself walking toward Dupont Circle with two shopping bags on her arm.

"I've never worn heels that high in my life."

"That's because you've spent your life in Birkenstocks."

"I'll probably never wear them again, after tonight."

"Then you have a very limited view of your future."

"So." She stopped to consider the bookstores and restaurants. "Where to now?"

Nate surveyed the street. "I have an idea." He hailed a cab and opened the door.

"Where are we going?"

"It's a surprise."

They drove into Georgetown and emerged from the cab at a sign that read ROMAN HOLIDAY.

"A spa?" Sarah laughed.

"Why not? It'll be my treat."

The last time Sarah had tried a spa was early in her first pregnancy. Then, she had understood the old adage of the body as a temple, something to be polished and painted and filled with edible offerings. But with each new miscarriage the deities had abandoned her, until she felt that her unproductive flesh didn't deserve to be pampered.

"I've signed you up for a Swedish massage and a manicure." Nate spoke from the counter, holding up a leather-bound menu that resembled a wine list. "Is that okay?"

"I guess."

"Try to have fun," he called as an assistant led Sarah away.

She felt embarrassed, lying naked beneath a cotton sheet, her face pressed into a crushed-velvet halo while her eyes wandered a maze of purple veins along the marble floor. Beside her, an Asian woman with a cartful of bottles folded the sheet down to Sarah's hips, and she felt the woman's fingers run lightly across her sides and arms, tracing the form that was about to be filled in. Then she heard a tinkling of unstoppered glass, smelled a wave of lavender, and experienced the full pressure of the woman's palms, oily smooth, kneading her neck in symmetric swirls. The hands worked one by one, progressing in a seamless spiral, so that Sarah couldn't tell where one hand ended and the other began. From the base of her neck the waves pushed down, puddling at the small of her back and spilling onto the floor, until, unexpectedly, she found herself smiling. Let it all fall away, she thought. All the sadness and the guilt, the puritanical repressions. Fall, fall on the floor and disappear into the purple maze. She would enjoy this hour of peace, this entire decadent day. She would enjoy the dress and the shoes and the brother, her rewards for just being alive. Nate was a brilliant man; he had a genius for pleasure. She must remember to thank him.

Ninety minutes more and she was sipping an Evian, her right hand spread on a piece of cloth while a manicurist rubbed oil into her cuticles.

"How was your massage?" Nate asked from behind a copy of *Fortune*.

"Heavenly. I feel like I could slide right into the floor. Did you have one?"

"Yes."

"A beautiful girl with a cartful of bottles?"

"No. A big thug who pounded the crap out of me. I feel like a pulverized steak."

"You requested that?"

"Absolutely."

"I thought you would have chosen an Asian woman with eucalyptus oil."

Nate smiled. "That doesn't relax me. That arouses me."

"Ah." Sarah watched her thumbnail disappear beneath a layer of crimson. "Enough said."

That night, they arrived at the Kennedy Center five minutes before the downbeat. Inside the concert hall, their seats were midway down the tenth row.

"So close," Sarah murmured. "The one time David and I came, we sat in the cheap seats."

The mention of David's name left a silence between them, and Sarah opened her program in search of a prompt.

"Oh, look! Colleen Britain is singing soprano."

"Wonderful." Nate rested his program on his knees. "A feast for the eyes, as well as the ears."

"She has the perfect voice for this. Sweet and clear and young."

"Good," said Nate. "I hate listening to hefty, fortysomething sopranos belting out the lines of adolescent virgins."

The concert began with a few orchestral preludes from the twentieth century. Then, with a rustle of fabric and footsteps, the chorus flowed in from the right and left—a choir of young boys in the middle, surrounded by altos and tenors who spread sideways, while the sopranos and basses rose to the top. A round of applause marked the soloists' entrance. First came Colleen, sweeping across the stage in purple velvet that shimmered against her coffee-colored skin. She was followed by an alto in an ankle-length golden dress, and a tenor and bass in modest tuxedos. All smiled and nodded. They stood before their chairs as the young conductor trotted on stage, his arms spread wide toward the musicians. Spinning around to the audience, he fell into a low bow, long black hair brushing at his cheeks. He jerked upward and stepped onto the podium, while the chorus opened their folders and the soloists took their seats.

The conductor lifted his baton, and at stage left, in a mirror image, the timpanist raised his mallet to an equal height. A moment of exquisite silence followed, as the two arms remained frozen, then the baton and mallet fell simultaneously, the deep boom of the timpani sounding at the bottom of the conductor's stroke, and on the upbeat of his arm, the full chorus and orchestra exploded in a fortissimo chord:

O Fortuna
velut Luna
statu variabilis.

They held the last note while the conductor stood with both arms raised, his hands shaking, until the sound ended as abruptly as it had begun. The brasses and percussion fell silent, the hall still ringing with the aftershock, while the chorus and strings launched into a hissing pianissimo. They whispered about the cruelty of fate, the whirling wheel, how happiness melts into misery as the moon waxes and wanes. The bassoons and cellos maintained one low pulse, letting the violins press forward in an agitated pizzicato, and at the third verse the music erupted again, with a gong crashing into each measure. As the chorus held the last note there was a brief orchestral frenzy—a crash of cymbals, a roll of timpani, and the trumpets double-tongued a staccato pattern that landed on one long exhale, cut off by the flick of the conductor's baton.

That was the first song. There were twenty-two to go. Sarah settled her mind into a medieval frame, imagining a time of lords and ladies wandering dark castles. A baritone sang in a boyish voice, *Omnia sol temperat*, and she opened her program notes: "The sun warms everything/pure and gentle . . . the soul of man/is urged towards love." Now the chorus echoed the call, "A wretched soul is he/who does not live/or lust/under summer's rule," and soon the music began to dance, the language changing from Latin to German: "*Wol dir Werlt,/daz du bist/Also freudenriche!*" Two hundred singers hailed the joyous world, pledging their faith to all its pleasures, and Sarah was ready to join them. But first she listened to the baritone's cautionary despair:

I am eager for the pleasures of the flesh
More than for salvation,
My soul is dead,
So I shall look after the flesh.

The first section ended in a tavern, with a male chorus singing in praise of Bacchus:

The old lady drinks, the mother drinks,
This woman drinks, that man drinks,
A hundred drink, a thousand drink.

"I think I want a beer," Nate whispered at her cheek, but Sarah was lost in a mute state of sublimity. It seemed that every line was written expressly for her—the arbitrariness of fate, the solace of alcohol, the desperate need for companionship. Especially in the Court of Love, when Colleen sang with a choir of boys, her voice high and sweet:

The girl without a lover
Misses out on all pleasures
She keeps the dark night
Hidden
In the depth of her heart;
It is a most bitter fate.

How well Sarah knew that sense of missed pleasures, the dark night of the soul, extended, in her case, into three years of festering gall. And now the soprano was lost in an ecstatic vision: "*Stetit puella/rufa tunica,*"

A girl stood
in a red tunic;
if anyone touched it,
the tunic rustled.
Eia!

Each exclamation was a sweetly descending melody. The baritone was wooing her, "Come, come, come," and Colleen was giving way in a quiet lullaby: "I submit my neck to the yoke;/I yield to the sweet yoke."

Colleen lifted her voice two octaves for the climactic "*Dulcissime!*"—winding the line down a small flight of tonal stairs. Then suddenly she leaped to an even higher pitch—"Ah! I give myself to you totally!"—and in a few more minutes the music came to its conclusion, ending with a return to the crashing gong, the wheel of fate, and the clatter of the audience's applause.

Sarah remained seated when the crowd rose to leave. She wondered if Nate was familiar with the text; he hadn't been reading the translation. She wondered if he knew that this entire piece was an extended call to love, building toward a woman's high-pitched orgasm. But of course he must know. For what else was this day, except one long, elaborate seduction?

She didn't care. It felt good to sit in a concert hall with a handsome man, her bare arm pressed against his jacket's soft cashmere.

It felt good, in the lobby, to slip her arms into her coat while Nate held the collar. It felt even better, after the concert, to take a cab to a Georgetown café and share a chocolate mousse, their silver spoons clicking as they leaned over the table.

The girl without a lover/Misses out on all pleasures, she thought as they walked arm in arm across the Mayflower lobby. *She keeps the dark night/Hidden/In the depth of her heart.* When Nate thanked her for the evening and turned toward his adjoining door, she took both of his hands and placed them in the small of her back. Lifting her crimson fingernails, she undid his necktie, letting it dangle from his collar. Slowly she unbuttoned his $180 shirt, placing a kiss on his throat, his chest, his stomach. An end to restraint, she told herself. An end to renunciation. She would dedicate herself to the pleasures of the moment. *I submit my neck to the yoke,* she thought. *I yield to the sweet yoke.*

• 26 •

Hedonism was easy in a hotel room, in a city with ten thousand Sarahs, where no one knew her history or her husband. Within this modern-day Mayflower Sarah imagined that she could sail to a New World. She could become a different woman, a fertile woman, a woman with a lover who dwelled upon her fingers, her belly and lips with infinite tenderness. And after all, wasn't Nate the brother she had always wanted? Or was it only that this room, with its neutral carpet, beige walls, and anonymous art, made all identity fade into a blessed haze?

Early Sunday morning, when the sun began to filter down Connecticut Avenue, Sarah rose and pulled the curtains tight. She wanted to prolong the time before their noon checkout. Twelve o'clock loomed like Cinderella's midnight, but for the next five hours she was determined to be happy.

"What time is it?" Nate murmured from the bed.

"Not morning yet," she lied, and returned to his arms.

That evening, when she arrived at her house and turned on the lights, every picture of David was a silent rebuke. She walked from room to room, pulling photos off the piano, the refrigerator, and her bedside table. She didn't want to face his accusing eyes, or to detect, on his lips, the slightest hint of a threat. In taking Nate as her lover she had crossed an unforgivable line, and there would be a reckoning. There was always a reckoning.

Sarah tucked the pictures away in a dresser drawer inside the guest room. It was time to concentrate on herself, not on images of David. One by one she lifted the mirrors from the guest bed and returned them to their empty walls in the hallway and bedrooms. Last of all she found a screwdriver and reassembled her vanity, then sat in front of its dusty glass and assessed her face. For the first time in many months, she liked what she saw. When she smiled she looked younger; she would have to smile more.

As she stared into the glass, Sarah tried to construct a twelve-step plan for her happiness—something to lift her spirits when Nate wasn't around. The first step was obvious: food, glorious food. For months she had dined at home on granola bars and bowls of cereal. Balanced meals came only in mixed company, as if a solitary woman did not merit a full stomach. But now she craved red meat, fresh vegetables, and creamy sauces. She wanted to layer her ribs in Oreo sundaes.

Early the next morning she headed for the Safeway, where the bulk foods waited in tall, plastic towers. She turned a silver faucet and a pound of basmati rice spilled into her bag. Then almonds, then walnuts, then honey-roasted sunflower seeds. She twisted, tied, and weighed them all, settling them into a row in the back of her cart.

Next came the pasta aisle, where she shunned the mundane seashells and elbows from her childhood—body parts and bow ties offered in blunt English. Beside them lay an unexplored world—campanelle, cavatappi, cellentani, conchiglie. A feast of exotic syllables, like the names of Tuscan villages. Here the spaghetti did not dwindle into angel hair; it fattened into perciatelli, thick as stereo wires. She lifted a bag of orechiette, just to admire the concave circles shaped like contact lenses. Into her cart it went, along with other unpronounceables, topped with a little bag of stars—tiny specks of semolina, to be sprinkled like glitter on soups and salads.

From there she moved to the pickle section, with its prosaic strains of English. Here were midgets and babies and bread and butter, in shapes like spears and rings and chips, flavored with a dash of American sensationalism—zingers, snackers, and munchers.

She placed a jar of baby dills beside her orechiette, thinking that in twelve years she had sampled only the tiniest fraction of this store's inventory. She had never tasted olives stuffed with hot deviled chili peppers, never bought star fruit or blood oranges. Grocery shopping had always been a matter of routine, with success measured in speed. But now she resolved to buy something new at every visit.

At home, she took twenty minutes to unload her trunk. Can by can her cupboards filled to the top, and shelf by shelf her refrigerator filled to the bottom. She topped off her dried-goods canisters with flour, rice, and sugar, until the whole kitchen swelled with promises. Then she stretched out on the couch with her old friends Ben & Jerry, and considered her next step.

This, too, was an easy choice; she would embark on a budgetless shopping spree. After all, it was Christmas, and the town was filled with wreaths and lights and giddy, red-nosed Santas on fraternity lawns. Consumerism was the American recipe for joy, and who was she to criticize the national pastime? That very afternoon she walked one mile to the local coffeehouse and ordered a pound of Colombian Supreme for Nate, wrapped with a golden bow. For Margaret, she examined the rows of carved cedar boxes with tea bags lying on squares of felt, like pairs of precious earrings. Much too fancy for a Brit who kept her loose tea in a Tupperware bowl.

She bought a cappuccino and went next door to the bakery, where gingerbread men with peppermint buttons lay side by side with chocolate-death bars. For Friday—her next date with Nate—she ordered a double-layer carrot cake with nuts and raisins and cream-cheese icing. In the past, she had ordered cakes only once or twice a year, sometimes for David's birthday, or for a Christmas party. But why not once a month? Or at least five times a year?

She bought a loaf of sourdough bread and tore chunks from its warm center as she walked three blocks to the kitchen store. Here, among the ladles and linens, were all the items she usually reserved for wedding presents—a salad bowl of smooth teak, with matching serving spoons carved into thin brown giraffes—perfect for Anne. And for Margaret—a casserole dish, hand-painted in Poland, with flowers of royal blue and bright sunflower yellow. She chose a hand-embroidered tablecloth for herself, ignoring the price tag with its ominous zeroes, then stood outside on the curb and adjusted her scarf before the long walk home. There was something about red shopping bags with white twine handles that made her feel like a woman of means.

Day two was devoted to clothing. Out of habit she began at the local consignment store, filled with college students' once-worn cocktail dresses. The names on the tags—Liz Claiborne, Donna Karan—were like a circle of wealthy friends whose parties she had never attended. She thought of how in preschool, children's own names were written in black marker on their coat tags. Now all the boys were named Eddie and Ralph and Giorgio.

An hour later she left the shop with a rayon blouse and a tea-length skirt, slacks and scarves and thick gold bracelets, and walked two doors down to a store decorated with tutus and nutcrackers. A large basket of handmade gloves lay just inside the threshold, the fingertips knitted into faces of sheep and cows and frogs. She tucked her fingers into a litter of puppies and watched their ears wiggle. How quickly these woolen smiles would be grimy and torn, with children's fingers gripping at trees and rocks. But she liked the concept and chose a planetary theme for her nieces, silver stars and blue moons and gold, blazing comets.

Beside them hung the babies' after-bath wrappers, followed by matching bibs, matching caps, matching socks. Two months ago these racks of frog-strewn onesies would have gnawed at her empty stomach, but now her world was open to endless possibilities. She stroked a pair of tiny slippers stuffed with llama's wool, before moving on to the jewelry counter for her nieces.

Finally, she walked to the body shop and purchased basketfuls of bubble bath—sweet pea and hibiscus, vanilla and peppermint.

At home that afternoon, she surrounded her tub with scented candles and bowls of inhalation beads, then watched as the windows faded into fog.

On the third day she rose slowly. It was time to shop for the men in her life, to leave the bath and baby stores and enter a darker world. She knew what she wanted for David, something to keep him company on lonely afternoons, but Nate was a challenge, having already indulged himself in everything a man could desire.

She drove to Best Buy, thirty minutes away in a larger town, and spent an hour wandering the aisles of cell phones, digital cameras, and iPod accessories. Only one item caught her attention, a lightweight video camcorder. She had never seen Nate using one; these were toys for couples with children, always trying to capture the moment. Sarah cupped it in her palm, lifted it to her eye, and thought that yes, this would do.

On Saturday morning she and Margaret met briefly to exchange gifts. In two days Margaret was off to England for her annual Christmas visit. She would be back in the New Year with a sharpened accent and a taste for clotted cream.

"My my, aren't we fancy." Margaret laughed as she pulled the hand-painted casserole from its gift-wrapped box. "I'm afraid your present isn't half as impressive."

Sarah unwrapped a pair of hand-knitted wool socks, navy blue with green stripes. "They're perfect."

"I made them for my girls as well. It gives me something to do while watching TV."

"You'll have to teach me. I need a hobby."

"We'll make it a New Year's resolution." Margaret placed her casserole back into its tissue paper. "Are you going to be all right over Christmas?"

"Yes, I'm going to Anne's house." Sarah blushed at Margaret's arching brow. "This time I really *am* going. Nate's coming, too."

"Oh, really? Isn't that a risk, taking your new beau to meet the family?"

"Nate *is* the family." Sarah smiled. "Besides, he already knows Anne well, and he doesn't have anywhere else to go."

"So this is an act of charity?"

"Oh yes, I'm full of charity."

"You're full of it all right." Margaret laughed. "So, are we falling in love?"

"I wouldn't call it love." Sarah ran her finger along the edge of the table. "When you were growing up, wasn't there ever a boy in school who liked all the girls?"

"Sure. They called him Georgie Porgie."

"Very clever. I'm talking about someone who all the girls liked back. Someone who dated a lot of people. Someone *you* liked."

Margaret shook her head. "I was never attracted to the popular crowd."

"I was." Sarah sighed. "At least a little. And now I feel like I'm having my time with the popular boy. Like it's my turn."

"You make Nate sound like an amusement-park ride. Just a little spin through the Tunnel of Love?"

Sarah shrugged. "It's better than the Haunted Mansion."

By three-thirty that afternoon she was unlocking the door to Nate's condominium, a cake box balanced in her left hand. He wasn't scheduled to come home from work for another two hours, but she liked the sensation of wandering alone through his empty rooms. They were so clean, so cool, like a luxury hotel. She poured a glass of Zinfandel from a bottle in the refrigerator, then turned on his wide-screen TV and watched sleet falling in the mountains of West Virginia. Inside Nate's master bathroom, where the brass fixtures blended with golden brown walls, she filled the Jacuzzi and opened Nate's cabinets in a futile search for bubble bath—*there* was the gift for the man who had everything. With her wineglass perched on the tile rim, she stacked her clothes by the sink and settled into the steaming water.

An hour passed before she heard the telephone ring. Nate's voice rose from the bedroom, asking if she had arrived. He would pick up some dinner on his way home. Once his voice had faded she lifted a towel from the rack, pressed the drain, and left a trail of wet footprints leading into the bedroom. Inside Nate's closet she found a long terry-cloth robe, and she wrapped herself within it and crawled into his bed.

He arrived at six o'clock with a bag of take-out Thai, and laughed when he saw Sarah in his robe, reading on the living-room couch.

"Make yourself comfortable."

They ate in the kitchen, opening another bottle of wine as Nate told her about his day. It seemed that the Fed was likely to hold interest rates steady for another few months. The market was climbing again, and the risks of inflation and deflation were balancing each other out. Sarah tried not to listen. It was all too mundane, this man coming home from the office, recounting his day to the woman waiting with her carrot cake. She opened the white bakery box just to silence him.

The top of the cake was rimmed with bright orange and lime-green icing, a garland of tiny carrots reminiscent of Peter Rabbit. She cut two slices, then watched Nate's clean fingernails as he untied the golden bow on his pound of coffee beans.

"Colombian Supreme." He smiled. "My favorite."

"Wait." She walked into the living room and came back with a box wrapped in silver.

"I wanted to give you your Christmas present early, without Anne and the kids watching."

"Good idea." He laughed when he tore off the paper. "I've never owned one of these."

Nate pulled the camera from its foam packing, plugged the battery into the wall, and examined all the buttons while Sarah ate her cake. Over the next ten minutes he showed her the zoom and the focus, explaining how the images could be broadcast on the Internet.

"Don't you dare," she murmured.

He inserted the battery and began to film her as she rinsed the plates in the sink.

"Leave the dishes for a while." Nate lowered the lens and disappeared down the hall. "I've got something for you, too."

He came back with a small red gift in one hand and the camera in the other, still filming.

"This is Sarah, a week before Christmas, opening her present."

The camera watched as she unwrapped the red paper, lifted the lid from a small white box and stared inside at Nate's gift, lying on its cottony bed. A ring of gold, coated with diamonds, but not for her finger. It was a bracelet shaped in a perfect circle; the diamonds sparkled as she raised it from the box. Normally she would have refused anything so extravagant. This was a gift for a twentieth anniversary, not a one-month affair. But the stones were so beautiful and the craftsmanship so delicate, she felt subdued. Her spree at the grocery store, her enthusiasm for casseroles, tablecloths, and teak, seemed suddenly foolish. They represented only the tiniest taste of luxury, while here, cupped in her fingers, was the definition of self-indulgence.

"Do you like it?" Nate asked.

She looked into the dark eye of the lens. "Yes."

When he clipped the bracelet around her wrist she felt that she had been claimed. This circle could not fit over her hand, just as her wedding ring could no longer slip past her knuckle, and they were the only two objects that remained on her body that evening, when she lay down on Nate's bed.

In the dark morning hours she remained awake with the bracelet suspended above her eyes, turning her wrist clockwise, then counterclockwise. Her mind was preoccupied, pondering Nate's motivations, wondering why he wasn't lying beside a different woman, someone younger and more beautiful, someone like Jenny. She supposed there was a victory in sleeping with his brother's wife. She supposed, too, that she was the first woman available after his breakup. He was probably the sort of man who didn't do well alone, who needed a woman's admiration to feel good about himself. Especially now, with his brother dead, she imagined that their affair was an outgrowth of his mourning, a way of holding on to the last member of his family.

But she hoped that there was more to it, for there was something she hadn't told Nate back at the Mayflower, a key detail that had nagged at her thoughts all through dinner, and was keeping her awake at this late hour. She had never told Nate, point-blank, that she hadn't used birth control for the past five years.

Of course Nate was not some irresponsible teenager, oblivious to consequences. A man in his midthirties must understand that for a woman like her, sexuality and fertility were one and the same. He must know what was at stake, just as he had known about every miscarriage, calling with condolences after each little death, saying how sorry he was, how he wished there was something that he could do. And now he was doing it. With David gone, Nate was performing the biblical function, sleeping with the widowed sister-in-law, so that the family might live on.

She couldn't say *that* out loud. It would sound too crass, too calculating and incestuous. But she viewed it as the unspoken agreement that lay between them in this bed. Nate was playing the role of Kevin Kline in *The Big Chill*, the handsome sperm donor, sharing his excellent gene pool. Which didn't mean that he could spare her another miscarriage; that specter always loomed. But so long as she was sexually active there was a glimmer of hope, and that was Nate's greatest gift to her this Christmas season—more than the bracelet, which winked at her as she rotated it in the moonlight.

• 27 •

Daylight had a way of exposing the flaws in Sarah's reasoning, and by the next afternoon she was torn between self-satisfaction and self-loathing. She knew that she should speak to Nate, to make sure that they were operating on the same plane, but she sensed that their affair relied upon its unspoken, uninterrogated nature. It was as if she were Psyche, sleeping with Cupid, and if she could maintain the secrecy and darkness, their love might result in the birth of Pleasure. But if she exposed it to light, Nate would flee, leaving her trailing behind, clinging to his feet.

Driving home late Sunday morning, she envisioned the churchgoers of Jackson, arriving at the houses of worship that lined the town's main street. Presbyterian, Methodist, Baptist, Episcopalian—no synagogues, no mosques, no Unitarians with their ambiguous creeds. How would her secrets ruffle such homogeneous morality? She pictured Margaret, flying over the Atlantic Ocean, then thought of her own crossings from brother to brother, bridging the gap between the living and the dead. She could not sustain this bizarre routine; eventually it would all implode under the weight of her silences. But for now, her secrets were the most compelling part of her life.

Three days later she was off to see David, driving to the cabin with two poinsettias in her backseat and a devil's food cake in the front. When she arrived, the fireplace was a pile of ashes and David nowhere to be found. Out on the deck she listened for footsteps in the woods, but heard only the thin whisper of wind in pine needles. Stepping back inside, she hung her coat by the door and took a plastic trash can from underneath the kitchen sink. She knelt beside the hearth and lifted the charred logs with the tips of her fingers, dropping them one by one into the trash before she scooped out the rest of the ashes with a dustpan and poured them on top of the logs, sending up smoky clouds of soot. A wicker basket beside the hearth contained leftover copies of *The Washington Post*, and she crumpled the news of war and famine and stuffed each ball of misery under the grate.

Around this she built a lean-to of kindling, topping it off with a small pine log. It wasn't Boy Scout quality, but it would suffice. She lit the fire in three places, then stared into the spreading flames while her mind tried to summon David back from the river. She imagined that their nervous systems were intertwined, that she could jolt his limbs into motion with the force of her thoughts, just as his unspoken wishes had prompted her to action so many times in their marriage. But twenty minutes passed before she heard his steps on the deck stairs. When she turned toward the French doors he was standing on the other side, his face pale as the sky. It occurred to her that as her own life gained color, his was fading. The two of them seemed to exist in inverse proportions.

He came inside with an armful of wood and stacked it along the wall, then sat beside her with his coat still on.

"I'm glad you've come," he said. "I've been so bored."

He hadn't shaved in at least a week, and when she raised her hand to his cheek, his skin was even colder than usual.

"Winter has muted everything." He spoke toward the fire. "The colors are dull, the birds have flown. It gets dark by five o'clock."

"I have something that might help." She leaned over and kissed him quickly. "Come out to the car."

Inside her trunk she showed David an enormous box, wrapped in shiny gold paper. Beside it lay a thinner box that she lifted.

"I thought we'd have Christmas today. I'll be leaving for Anne's at the end of the week."

"Good." David hoisted the larger box into his arms. "I have something for you, too."

Inside the cabin, he placed the box on the floor and walked to the bedroom. When he came back he was holding a homemade Christmas wreath, stuffed with branches of fir and cedar, and colored at the top with sprigs of holly berries and two small pinecones.

"My gosh." She took it from his hands and admired it at arm's length. "You made this yourself?"

He nodded. "I walked through the woods and gathered branches from all of the evergreens that I could find. Some of them were shrubs that we planted years ago. I pulled dried honeysuckle vines from the trees by the river, and curled them into a wreath. The rest was just a matter of experimentation, stuffing in lots of different colors and textures, and tying it all down in the back with wire. I made another one, too." He opened the hall closet and pulled out a wreath of bare vines twisted into a shamrock, with a bouquet of spruce and elderberries shooting from its center.

Sarah closed her eyes and inhaled the clean scent of cedar. One way or another, David always managed to outdo her. His Christmas gifts were always a little more thoughtful, his taste in films and wine and furniture a little more sophisticated. She supposed that was why she had sympathized with Nate for so many years, because he knew how it felt to be the lesser half of a pair, locked in competition with a relentless perfectionist. And how would Nate feel now, if he knew that he was still competing with David, that his ring of diamonds had been matched by this circle of greenery?

"My gift is much less original," she apologized when David took off the bow.

"Well, size counts for something." He tore at the paper. "Wow. A television!"

"An *Ultravision* HD flat-screen TV."

"But I don't have a satellite dish."

"It's not for that. Open the other present."

Inside the slimmer box David found a DVD player.

"I've got a dozen DVDs in the car," Sarah said. "Some of them are your favorites from our house, and a few are new ones. I also saw that your general store rents movies."

"Yes." David smiled. "Mostly adult movies."

"I thought that the images of other people might help when it gets too quiet out here."

He nodded. "I suppose it's a sign of failure. If I were a better man I would be able to entertain myself all day with books and paint and long walks in the woods. But the truth is, I've been dying for a little technology."

"Would you like to watch something now?"

"What have you got?"

"*The Lord of the Rings* trilogy, *Young Frankenstein, The Truman Show,* some recent comedies."

For the rest of the day they shared the cabin with hobbits and wizards and elves, watching Tolkien's characters begin their slow descent into hell. The voices seemed to comfort David; he fed disc after disc into the machine with a zeal almost disturbing. At night, as the two of them walked from lamp to lamp turning out lights, the last glimmer in the room came from the television, which spread blue shadows across the walls. David seemed reluctant to turn it off. When the screen blacked out, the darkness in the cabin was complete.

The next afternoon they agreed to decorate a Christmas tree.

"Not inside," David insisted. It seemed such a waste to cut one down, while the small cedar at the foot of the deck cried out so pitifully for a makeover. Together they sat in front of the television stringing wreaths of popcorn dotted with cranberries left over from Thanksgiving. Sarah cut stars and crescent moons from the television's empty cardboard box and covered them in aluminum foil. She poked little holes into their tops with the tip of a steak knife, and looped them with fishing line. Then they went outside and walked through the woods, gathering pinecones to spread with peanut butter and birdseed. When it was time to decorate the tree, they wore gloves to protect their fingers from the cedar's prickly touch.

"What shall we put at the top?" Sarah asked as she hung the last thin star.

David picked up his shamrock wreath, and from a perch high on the deck he leaned over and pushed it down into the top of the tree.

"Too bad we have no lights," Sarah said. "Only the sun and moon."

That afternoon she agreed to pose again in her robe and nightgown. She had left them at the cabin, thinking David might want to study the weave of the fabric. Now, as she looked out toward the river, her mind traveled across the Blue Ridge, down the meadows and rolling hills of Albemarle County, and into the city limits of Charlottesville. At this hour Nate was probably meeting with a client, or checking stock quotes at his computer. A telephone headset would be poised at his lips, his fingers brushing over a keyboard, hitting return, return, return.

From the corner of her eye she saw David pause. Could he tell what she was thinking? Could he smell Nate in her hair? So be it. Let him guess. Let him paint her as Emma Bovary, the doomed wife of a country doctor, planning her next escape to her lover's arms.

This business of modeling was a tedious annoyance. It reminded her of what had always bothered her about David—his habit of watching. It was a doctor's job, to look, to peer, to examine other people's bodies for the slightest of clues. So, too, for the painter, absorbed in observation, trying to see beyond the veil of the average human eye. Dissection, portraiture, what was the difference? David was doubly bound to stare.

"Let's stop this," she said, and he released her.

As she changed back into her sweater and jeans, she glanced at David's canvas. Strange, how the edges of her body were not merely softened in his usual way; they seemed to melt into the window, her nightgown merging with the curtains. His other recent paintings showed the same confusion—trees and water and birds in motion, each one growing more amorphous than the last. She wondered if the cabin was getting to his mind—all this isolation, and the darkness of the winter woods.

"You seem to be entering a new artistic phase."

"A new mental phase, maybe. I'm seeing things in a different way."

"A blurry way?"

He shrugged. "The world is not so clear as it seems."

The next morning, while she stood in the bedroom packing her bag, David thanked her for the visit. "I'll miss you over the holidays. You've made the place brighter with the decorations, and the movies."

"I have one more surprise before I go." She reached into the bottom of her overnight bag and handed him a manila envelope. When he dipped his fingers inside, they emerged with a handful of one-hundred-dollar bills.

"It's the money from the Jackson exhibit." She hoisted her bag onto her shoulder. "Judith sent me the check last week. Eight thousand dollars. The other half went to the gallery. You've also got some money coming from the Washington show. I know Judith sold at least two of your paintings, and the prices she put on those were twice as high as in Jackson."

David poured the bills onto the bed and ran his index finger across Benjamin Franklin's broad forehead.

"You can give the ATM a rest for a while." She kissed him on the cheek. "Merry Christmas."

• 28 •

Christmas Eve arrived with Sarah sitting beside Anne in a Presbyterian church, while Nate and Anne's husband, Ben, bracketed the sisters like a pair of bookends. They had come for the children's pageant, and the pews were filled with girls and boys decked in red velvet and green corduroy. The littlest girls colored their programs with crayons tucked beside the hymnals, while the boys spied through programs rolled periscope-style.

"When's the last time you were at church?" Sarah asked Nate.

"Does David's memorial service count?"

She shook her head.

"Then probably last Easter. Jenny used to take me to her church sometimes, but I've never gone without a woman's prodding. I'm not a believer."

Sarah was a little surprised; she knew few people who would admit to being unbelievers. Most of her friends were fuzzy Deists, with faith in a Creator but not a Christ. Even David had maintained a vague belief in intelligent design, saying that if Albert Einstein believed in God, who were they to doubt? And yet Sarah doubted, though not in the traditional sense. She didn't doubt the existence of God so much as the ability of human beings to inspire a god's love.

But here, in this clean white church, where the minister read from the Gospel of Luke while little girls in angel wings and boys with shepherds' crooks performed a silent tableau, she could imagine a reason for grace freely given. These children merited divine intervention; before adolescence most children still bore traces of heaven. How did Wordsworth put it? *Trailing clouds of glory do we come from God.*

The minister's brief sermon seemed to recognize as much. Christmas, he said, was a time to treasure children, to remember that each life was sacred, every infant touched with the Holy Spirit. He invited all of the children present to come forward in single file, and gave each one a red carnation, offering words of blessing as he passed the stems to the small, smooth fists.

This was a communion that Sarah could admire—no wine, no wafer, no savior to be devoured, only a small gift of nature given with a prayer. She felt chastened by its simplicity. For eight days she had been seeking joy in her credit cards, discovering what measure of contentment could be derived from plastic. And there was some consolation in her "flexible friends," with all their promises of silk suits and luxury hotels. But ultimately her happiness could not stem from a bank account. Looking at the children, she knew that any hope for a new life would have to grow within her.

She glanced at Nate, wondering if he felt as she did, that children were the only consolation in this world, the only recompense for so much suffering. She still hadn't talked to him about birth control, trying to gauge the opportune moment. And perhaps now, if Nate would give her a reassuring sign, some remark about how sweet the children looked, or a conspiratorial squeeze of her hand—instead he sat with lowered eyes, staring at his program.

"It was a lovely pageant," she said as they were leaving.

Nate shrugged. "Same show we did when I was a boy."

Sarah studied him again on Christmas morning, while her nieces negotiated a hill of presents. Anne and Ben went overboard every year; most of these toys and gadgets would be ignored or broken within a few months. But for one blissful hour, the children were absolutely happy, and she wondered if Nate appreciated the rarity of it.

He had seemed restless for the past two days, probably, as Margaret predicted, bored by all this domesticity—the eggnog and iced cookies and Anne's Hummel collection. Even Sarah felt a little embarrassed by her sister's naive hospitality; Anne appeared oblivious to any change between Sarah and Nate. She had housed Nate in the guest room while Sarah slept upstairs in the bed of her younger niece, the girl lying on the floor in a *Little Mermaid* sleeping bag, forming a boundary that Nate would never cross. Throughout the entire visit he did not so much as brush Sarah's hand with his fingers. He seemed at ease only after Christmas dinner, when he went sledding with the two girls just before sunset, helping them to drag silver saucers up their subdivision's undeveloped lots, and spinning down with them to the base of the old fire pond.

The girls' laughter filtered through the thermopane windows as

Sarah watched from the dining room. When Nate came inside his cheeks were red, just as she remembered them in Vermont.

"You're good with kids," she said as he hung his coat by the door.

"I like playing games," he replied.

"You'll make a good father, someday."

Nate laughed. "I guess." He dropped his voice to a whisper as he unwrapped his scarf. "If you want to know the truth, I've never met a couple who didn't have ten years taken off their lives by the time their kids were two. It saps the energy right out of you."

"I've always thought of children as a beginning," Sarah suggested.

Nate ran his fingers through his hair. "The beginning of the end."

Sarah stood motionless as he walked into the living room and joined Ben in front of a football game.

"I think I'll lie down for a while," she said, and she retreated upstairs to her niece's lavender room. There, she stared at all the trappings of a child's life—the Hogwarts posters scotchtaped to the walls, the dresser cluttered with lip gloss and nail polish and snow globes and pictures of Orlando Bloom tucked into the mirror's frame. She had never expected Nate to care about such things, never imagined that he would want to play house. Nor had she thought that he would marry her, or make child support payments, or hold her hand in a delivery room. But she *had* envisioned him as a devoted uncle, the sort who would bring lavish gifts on every holiday. And she had assumed, at a minimum, that he would be happy for her, if she could ever make another life take firm hold in her body.

But now she knew the truth, that if she told him she hadn't been using birth control he would be appalled. And why not? She was appalled. Appalled at her own capacity for self-delusion.

Of course a man like Nate would have no thought of consequences. That was a woman's job, to deal with the awkward mess of contraception. All his life Nate had probably hopped from one bed to another without ever laying eyes on a birth control pill. For all she knew he might have fathered a child already; he might have peopled the entire East Coast with little dark-haired boys.

Sarah glanced over at the window ledge, where her niece's American Girl dolls were seated like a panel of reproachful judges, assessing her from their vantage of wholesome sterility. Oh, what a mess she was making of her life.

• 29 •

The next morning she packed her suitcase and stood outside on the porch while Nate carried it to his trunk.

"I wish you would stay for a few more days." Anne plucked small pieces of lint from the shoulders of Sarah's coat. "The girls don't go back to school for another week."

"Thanks," Sarah replied. "But Nate's got work to do, and I've left Grace long enough."

"You know," Anne chided, "you can't spend all your time with a cat."

Sarah smiled. "Don't worry. I'll get a fish, too."

How could she tell her sister that the normality of her world made Sarah feel ashamed of her own bizarre existence? This house, this holiday, Anne's earnest face—it was all a cold reality check. As she waved good-bye to her nieces, huddled in pajamas inside the glass door, Sarah thought that it was wrong to live as she had, nurturing love affairs too secret and strange to share with her closest family.

Back in Virginia, within the safety of her house, Nate carried her bag to the bedroom and asked if he should stay.

"No thanks." She kissed him on the cheek. "I'm going to take a nap."

When his car was out of sight she headed straight for her master bathroom and opened the wooden cabinet that hung above the toilet. There, she pulled out a white rectangular box with a purple swirl of color: e.p.t., early pregnancy test, Easy to Read Results, 99% accurate. It was a remnant from four years ago, when she had first tried to get pregnant. Back then she had been the company's most faithful customer, taking a test every month, the perpetual student, still at the mercy of a plus-and-minus grading system.

How she had hated those little blue minuses, every one like a flatlined EKG. She had experienced each blue hyphen as a painful subtraction, as if something was being wrested away from her body. What she hadn't realized was that even after her first success, her first glorious plus, the victory could be removed, the plus returned to minus as if some arbitrary teacher had changed his mind.

Now she reached into the box and pulled out a tester, wrapped in foil like a Nutri-Grain bar. Inside the shiny paper lay a strip of white-and-lavender plastic, resembling a cross between a thermometer and a tongue depresser. The words on the instruction pamphlet were all too familiar: *Place the absorbent tip in the urine flow for just 5 seconds*. When she was done, she lay the tester on the counter and washed her hands.

The oval window on the white plastic contained a small circle, the size of a scrap of paper left over from a hole puncher. Across that circle she watched a faint wisp of blue emerge, spreading horizontally in a perfect diameter, unmistakably negative. She was not pregnant.

Sarah took a deep breath and braced herself for the coming misery, the tidal wave of disappointment that always emerged in the wake of these little blue failures. But as she stood there taut and expectant, the emotion that surfaced was oddly surprising. She felt buoyant, elated. She looked into the mirror and laughed out loud, because for the first time in her life she was relieved to see that minus sign, an indicator not of failure but of liberation.

What a wonderful feeling, not to want to be pregnant, to be content with the single life within her body. Only now did she realize how obsessively she had pursued the dream of a healthy pregnancy. It had become the driving force of her world over the past few years, crowding out all other thoughts, until the rest of her life had seemed insignificant. She had been wrong to base her happiness on something which she could not control. It had made her passive, all this waiting—passive and angry, and much too hard on David.

Of course she still wanted a child—that desire would not go away. But there were better ways to go about it, ways that did not involve using her brother-in-law as an unwitting sperm bank. In the meantime, there were other things that might grow within her. Things like generosity and ambition and joy. Sarah tossed the plastic tester into the trash, thinking that now, at last, she was awake.

Two days later Nate called from his office. "What are you doing for New Year's Eve?"

"Going to bed early."

"You should come to a party with me."

She leaned back into her pillows. "I'm not much of a New Year's Eve person."

"Come on, Sarah." His voice slipped into the cajoling tone that she had just begun to notice in recent days. "I think you'd like this. It's become my annual ritual for starting the year."

"Who's hosting the party?"

"It's a surprise."

Sarah didn't like surprises; there had been too many in the past few months. She pictured David, alone at the cabin, staring at another movie. By all rights, she should spend New Year's Eve with him. She had planned to maintain a balance between the brothers, to give her life some sense of equilibrium. But here was Nate, warm and alive and promising a party, and perhaps this would be the best way to end their affair.

Because it couldn't go on; she had felt that concretely in the last forty-eight hours. Lovely as Nate might be, the two of them were very different people, and their affair was nothing more than a temporary shelter. Soon she would have to say good-bye to her beautiful brother-in-law, and this party might be a nice send-off, a fitting culmination of the past six weeks.

"Okay," she said. "Why not?"

At three o'clock on December 31, Sarah pulled up at Nate's condominium. Her overnight bag was filled with jewelry, perfume, and lace underwear, a pair of rhinestone-studded heels, the burgundy dress from Washington, and, tucked inside her bathroom kit, her old diaphragm.

Nate greeted her at the curb and transferred her bag into his trunk.

"We're leaving right away?"

"Yes. We've got a plane to catch."

He did not see the color drain from Sarah's face as he walked inside. He did not notice how she braced her arm against his car, trying to breathe deeply. This was her punishment for choosing the wrong brother. David would have known how she hated to fly, how she dreaded being strapped into a metal shell and hurled across the sky. Ever since childhood she had suffered the doubts of the unscientific, dumbstruck in the face of radio waves and roaring jet engines. God in heaven was more conceivable than her television set.

An airplane flight was a miracle only to be attempted after weeks of mental adjustment. Faced with an impending trip, she always took time to reconcile herself to the possibility of death. Now, with only a few hours before takeoff, she felt as if she were going to hyperventilate. Breathe, she told herself, bending forward almost to her knees. Breathe deeply; spontaneity was a gift.

"Are you all right?" Nate asked when he came outside.

"Sure." She straightened up. "Just a cramp."

The Charlottesville airport had six gates and one tiny lounge, where Sarah ordered two vodka tonics. Nate laid a plane ticket on the bar before her: Nassau, Bahamas.

"I didn't pack a swimsuit," she said as she squeezed a lime into her drink.

"You can buy one at the hotel."

"And I didn't bring my passport."

Nate pulled it from his jacket and placed it beside the ticket. "I got it from your desk drawer when I dropped you off after Christmas. I've been planning this for a while."

I bet you have, Sarah thought. The McConnell brothers were

always so damn confident, so certain that she would follow their lead. And why not? She had never given them reason to expect otherwise. Maybe this was the time to walk away, to tell Nate that he assumed too much. Their affair had been nice while it lasted, but she must learn to stand alone, without substituting one brother for another.

Sarah stared into the bottom of her drink. It would be wise to turn back, but her soul craved sunshine, and outside the terminal's plate-glass windows Virginia remained locked in a wintry gray.

Thirty minutes later Nate held her elbow as they climbed the metal stairs onto a twenty-seat plane. He gestured toward the front row, and Sarah smiled weakly: "First class?" She sat down and stretched her legs, her toes touching the curtain that separated cabin from cockpit. When the propellers roared to life, she whispered the only prayer that came to mind: "If I should die before I wake I pray the Lord my soul to take." Halfway through the third recitation the wheels left the ground, and she felt the sickening sensation of dipping, as if the plane's tail was going to scrape and spark, but outside her window, the world shrank into a soft patchwork of farmers' fields, and the squares of green and gold soothed her mind with the illusion of many gentle landings. She closed her eyes and the blur of vodka merged with the buzzing of metal.

Late that evening she sat beside a wall of glass in a restaurant perched on a latter-day pyramid. The hotel balconies zigzagged down in concrete steps, and Sarah's eyes followed them to the edge of the palm-ringed pool.

"No one could leap to their death from here. You could only break your ankles, jumping from floor to floor."

"A charming thought," said Nate. "How about a bottle of wine?"

Far below they could hear the music of a steel-drum band, calling to them as they ordered scallop croquettes and Caesar salads. Its song continued all the way into dessert, a reggae Pied Piper that coaxed the diners to come outside and join the party. Eventually Sarah and Nate rode a glass elevator down to the mezzanine level, where a vast, red-carpeted casino stood between them and the doors out to the beach.

"I'm going to stop by the bathroom." Sarah turned left, and by the time she had returned Nate was sitting at a roulette table, stacking little towers of chips on multiple numbers. He had lost three thousand dollars in six minutes, a fact which Sarah found staggering. If David had gambled away that sort of money she would have strangled him, but she realized that she had no control over Nate. He was her date, her dance partner, her alternative to Zoloft. He was her brother-in-law, and this was his element, this world of casinos and five-star resorts and weekend getaways. It was all very pretty, Sarah thought. Very comfortable. And in the end, it had nothing to do with her.

Nate dismissed the table with a flick of his wrist, and together they walked out to the free-form pool, with its waterfalls and swim-up bars and tipsy tourists slopping rum punch into the chlorine. At the poolside buffet, a woman with a fan of ostrich feathers waved buzzing flies away from mounds of mango and papaya. Nate led Sarah beyond a line of palm trees, onto the beach where a bonfire exhaled thousands of sparks into the night sky.

"I like these fireworks," she said, watching how the smooth water mirrored the glow; women in cocktail dresses waded through the flames. She took off her shoes and followed Nate down the beach, away from the fire and food and laughter, deep into the shadows, where he put his right hand behind her back, twined her fingers with his left, and rested his cheek in her hair. And there, in the cool sand, they began to dance, the dance that had been overdue for seventeen years. It was hardly even a dance, that slow shuffle, but Sarah felt that a circle was completing itself, their unfinished business was being put to rest.

Something about the sand and the water and the palm trees seemed oddly familiar, until it came to her.

"You've been here with Jenny."

Nate stepped back and looked into her eyes. "Yes. Twice. How did you know?"

"The picture on your hall table."

Sarah marveled at how she felt nothing, no disappointment or betrayal. It seemed completely natural.

"Why did you two break up?" she asked as they continued their shuffling steps.

"She wanted to get married . . . And more than that. She wanted to have children right away. You know how I feel about children."

"Yes, I know. How old is Jenny?"

"Twenty-nine."

"She's young, then."

"Sure, but she doesn't appreciate it."

Sarah leaned her cheek on Nate's shoulder. "The two of you seemed well matched."

"And you and I, Sarah? Are we well matched?"

She smiled, thinking that nothing could be further from the truth.

"For this one night," she said, "in this one winter, we are perfect."

PART FOUR

Resolutions

• 30 •

"What did you do for New Year's Eve?"

David was standing over a chopping board, spreading mayonnaise on a thin slice of honey-wheat bread. It was the fourth of January and Sarah had come as an act of penitence.

She sat at the table, staring out toward the icy river. "I watched some fireworks. How about you?"

"I went to bed before midnight. But in the morning I got dressed early and walked outside. The first snow of the year had fallen, and I've never seen the world so quiet." He washed his hands and came to the table with a plate of ham sandwiches.

"There were deer tracks leading into the woods, and I followed them for a hundred yards, but I didn't find anything. The river was frozen in the flat sections, so I walked out onto the water about three yards from the bank, until bubbles came up under my boots.

Then I stepped back to where the ice was thick, and I stood there on the river, looking up at the cliffs."

His voice was unemotional, which made Sarah turn to face him. "It sounds nice."

He shook his head. "It was too quiet. I've decided that this is the only winter I'll spend here at the cabin."

"Where will you go?"

"I don't know. I'll have to think about it."

David took a sandwich to the couch and turned on the same *Lord of the Rings* film that he had been staring at all morning. As Sarah watched him, she supposed that she had made a mistake, to have introduced a television into the cabin's peaceful quiet. David had never been a screen addict back in Jackson; he had been too busy with patients and painting and dinner parties. But now his mind was filled with two-dimensional worlds. She sighed as she turned away from him, thinking that he was right; David should not stay here for another winter.

She pulled on his hiking boots and Gore-Tex jacket and walked toward the door. "I'm going for a walk, want to come?" He didn't answer.

Outside the snow was melting, leaving puddles covered in thin layers of ice. She pressed one with the ball of her foot, and the surface cracked into a broad white web, reminding her of a traffic accident she and David had experienced years ago. For some reason she hadn't been wearing a seat belt, and when a car rear-ended them at a red light, her body had lurched forward, the front of her scalp burrowing into the windshield. White cracks had spread like electric currents.

She remembered how gently David had touched her as they

stood outside the car, waiting for the police. He had lifted her eyelids with the tips of his thumbs, examining her pupils for signs of concussion, and then, with equal softness, he had traced the bones of her brow and cheek, running his fingers across her jaw and pressing at the back of her neck.

"Does it hurt here? Or here?"

No, the only pain was beneath her bangs, where a bruise the size of a golf ball had swollen outward, lavender and lime and royal blue.

"The body is fragile," he had said as he brushed her hair away from her forehead. "You must take care of yourself."

His words came back as she stood beside the river, hugging her arms tightly around her waist. She had loved him for his tenderness in those days, especially after her parents died, when she had wanted to be guided and pampered and soothed; she had loved his almost paternal care. It was only in recent years that his authority had begun to grate, and that her unhappiness with her own life had manifested itself in dissatisfaction with him. Then she had understood how it was possible for a man to *do* nothing wrong, and still to *be* wrong, day after day.

Now it was decision time, because if David was leaving then she must choose whether to follow him—to give up the house, the college, the town, and most of all, Margaret. The only New Year's resolution she had made thus far was to say good-bye to Nate, a feat she hadn't managed while they were in the Bahamas. It had seemed ungracious, to call things off after he had spent so much money, and she had wanted to enjoy the beach and the rum without any wounded feelings hovering between them.

But now there were no excuses. Sarah lobbed a stone high into the air, onto the opposite bank. She would have to end the affair with Nate, then decide what to do about David.

Over the next few weeks procrastination set in. Winter drained all impetus for change, and she resumed her old habit of staying in bed until noon, padding through the house in thick socks and terry cloth. Her few active hours passed in the kitchen, as she experimented with an ever-increasing bounty from the grocery store. For dinner she fixed pad thai and coconut-ginger soup; for breakfast she baked zucchini bread topped with pineapple cream cheese.

"I mean to get fat and sassy," she explained to Margaret when she arrived at Friday tea with a platter of chocolate muffins.

"Instead of thin and bitter?" Margaret asked with a smile.

"You know me too well."

She had made one resolution to which she managed to cling: she would no longer drive to Charlottesville. Passivity was almost a strategy; if she initiated nothing, Nate would eventually tire of the drive. The mountains formed a natural barrier, encouraging the two of them to blend back into their separate valleys.

But when Nate asked to come to her, she did not resist. He visited twice in January, first at midmonth, when he called from his office on a Friday, offering to bring a take-out Indian dinner. Sarah could never refuse a man bearing food, and for the first time that year she wore earrings and a necklace.

Nate wooed her with pakoras, garlic naan, and vindaloo. The spices made them sweat, and after dinner they showered together, washing each other's body until they felt mutually spotless. For a moment she forgot about Jenny and David and all of the shadows that lingered between them. So long as she and Nate remained within a private universe, she thought she might enjoy his company for a little while longer.

But on his second visit the outside world intruded. They had agreed to see a movie, something mindless yet sufficient to get Sarah out of the house. Unfortunately she hadn't considered how many acquaintances she would meet in a town the size of Jackson, and outside the ticket booth two of her former students eyed Nate and giggled.

"Let's sit in back," Sarah said when they entered the theater.

"But the seats are much better up here." Nate kept on walking.

Midway down the aisle she spotted a trio of teachers from the elementary school. Margaret was at the far end, and she acknowledged Sarah with a slight nod. Sarah tried to be casual, waving back as she and Nate sat down four rows ahead. But halfway through the movie, when he put his arm around her shoulder, she could feel the women's eyes following his fingers, and each stroke through her hair was another public lashing. She remained immovable until the end of the credits, when a teenage boy approached with a mop and a trash bag.

Her visits to the cabin weren't much better. The absence of color in the landscape seemed to drain David's spirit. He painted little, and instead spent hours chopping wood with a fanatical concentration, arms swinging up and down, implacable as an oil drill. It looked as if he were trying to kill something, battling against winter, or perhaps clearing a path to see his way ahead. When he rested in front of the television, the ax leaned against its bounty—a three-foot high-water mark, ominously rising. *The center cannot hold,*

Sarah thought as she watched him from across the room. *Things fall apart.*

Outside, her walks grew longer and more solitary. She saw the pine trees crusted with snow, the junipers shagged with ice, and heard a misery in the sound of the wind. *One must have a mind of winter,* she recited to the air, and when she returned to the cabin she saw, for the first time, *Nothing that is not there and the nothing that is.*

• 31 •

At home, on her kitchen calendar, Sarah colored February 14 with a red question mark. All month she dreaded the date, debating the proper etiquette for a woman with two lovers, and when the afternoon finally arrived, she bought a bottle of Royal Copenhagen and took it to her kitchen table, where she tied a red bow around the silver box, then sat and stared at it. She and David had always spent Valentine's Day together; no patients or students were allowed to interrupt their annual dinner, and she supposed that nothing, not even death, should break that tradition. If she left for the cabin by five-thirty, she could stop on the way for pizza and drugstore chocolates.

The doorbell rang just as she was searching for her car keys, but when she opened the front door, she found no one outside. The porch, the steps, the walkway—all were empty. She crossed to the porch railing and peered down into the magnolia's shade, where

David had been waiting on Halloween night; no one was there. Shrugging, she stepped back, turned around, and gasped.

"Surprise." Nate was standing in her hallway in his business suit, brandishing two lobsters like a pair of pistols.

"Work was slow today, so I thought I'd leave early and make dinner for us. I parked down the street so you wouldn't hear me coming, and I let myself in through the back." He smiled at her stare. "I'm sorry, I didn't mean to frighten you."

"I was just going out."

"Where?"

"To get some pizza."

"This will be much better than pizza, don't you think?"

He walked into the kitchen and settled the lobsters in the twin basins of her sink. Then he reached into a brown bag on the counter and pulled out a bundle of fresh asparagus and a bottle of Chardonnay.

"You have rice, don't you?"

"Yes." Sarah followed him in. "But I really don't think—"

"Oh, how sweet." He lifted the bottle of cologne from the kitchen table.

While Nate untied the bow, Sarah imagined David alone with his near-empty cupboards. She had never seen a calendar at the cabin, and she hoped that he wasn't keeping track of dates. Tomorrow she would make it all up to him.

"Just sit down." Nate poured her a glass of wine, and she took a small sip.

"Put on some music," Nate said. "And try to relax."

When dinner was ready he set the dining-room table with candles and her new embroidered tablecloth. He tied a plastic bib from the seafood store around Sarah's neck, brought her one plate with a still-steaming lobster, and another with asparagus, rice pilaf, and bread. When her nutcracker punctured the lobster's claw, Sarah cringed at the pale, stringy liquid that ran across her plate. But Nate flinched at nothing. He tore the tail off Sarah's lobster, sliced it open with a serrated knife, and presented her with the unscathed meat. After dinner he poured Kahlúa into small cups of coffee, and they sat on the living-room couch, warm and full.

"I have a gift for you." Nate returned to the kitchen one last time, and came back with a small red box topped with a silver bow.

More jewelry, thought Sarah. More diamonds. But when she unwrapped the box she lifted a glass jar with a gold label. "Chocolate body paint," she read. "This is a gift for *you*."

"For both of us. Wait for me in the bedroom. I'll go and heat it up."

She remained on the couch for a long time, tracing the flowers in the upholstery with the tip of her finger. This should have been David's night; she should have been insistent. Should have, should have. She sighed and rose to her feet. Tomorrow she would try to slow this train down, but for now it was Valentine's Day, and Nate made a lovely Eros. She pulled her sweater over her head as she walked down the hall.

When Nate came into the bedroom, stirring the chocolate with a long red paintbrush, she lifted the covers up to her chin. He placed the jar on the dresser, took off his shoes and socks, then unbuttoned his shirt and laid it on Sarah's vanity. She admired the muscles in his back, so many beautiful lines all moving in unison. He left his pants on as he climbed across the bedspread, straddling her hips, and with the jar in his left hand, he reached forward with his right and pulled the covers down to her breasts, smoothing them in a ridge just above her nipples.

"Lift your chin," he said, and she obeyed.

When the chocolate touched her skin it was hot, almost burning. She could smell the sugar as the thin edge of the brush ran down her neck and into the hollow of her throat, where Nate drew a perfect circle. Dipping the brush back into the jar, he started at the right edge of the circle and traced her collarbone west, ending at her right shoulder. He painted a small star, then followed the same pattern east, a stripe along her collarbone and a star at her shoulder. From the lower half of the circle he painted radiant sunbeams down her breasts, connecting the end points with one long arc so that the lines became the rectangular segments of an Egyptian necklace.

He dipped the brush back into the paint, and used his free hand to pull the covers down to her waist. With a thick-coated brush, he transformed her breasts into swirls of chocolate, sculpting the curling tips with a flick of his wrist. They looked like Dairy Queen dipped cones, and Sarah laughed at the idea, her stomach convulsing as Nate decorated it with hearts and flowers. He rolled off her waist, slid the sheet down to her knees, and lying beside her, he painted wavy arrows from the tops of her kneecaps to the insides of her thighs, coating her inside and out.

When she was thoroughly warm and sticky, he lowered the brush into the jar and surveyed her painted body. "My masterpiece." Placing the jar on her vanity, he finished undressing at the foot of the bed and lay down beside her.

Nate ran his finger across her right kneecap and tasted the chocolate, then lowered his mouth to her left thigh and began following the arrows. She closed her eyes as his lips moved higher, and when his tongue dipped between her legs she pressed her head back deep into her pillow. Nate climbed above her, his mouth moving up her belly and breasts, sucking on flowers and circles and stars. He was kissing her neck as he slid his arms beneath her knees, and pulled her to him. When their bodies came together, she turned her head to the side, opened her eyes wide, and gasped.

David was at the window, pale and staring. His eyes had the impact of a blade, and she was gasping, gasping with horror and pleasure. She lifted her hand to push Nate away and block out the vision of David's eyes, but her fingers sank into Nate's chest as he pushed forward. Two universes were colliding, matter and antimatter, and she leaned back, closed her eyes, and let David watch.

When Nate lay quiet, Sarah rose and walked into the bathroom.

"Where are you going?" he mumbled from the pillows.

"To take a shower."

Nate rolled over, turning his back.

The chocolate ran down her skin like blood as Sarah sat on the floor of the shower, holding her face in her hands. The brown streaks reminded her of her second miscarriage, and she instinctively lowered her palms and cradled her stomach. She should have said good-bye to Nate weeks ago, should have had the self-discipline to walk away. Then she could have avoided this undignified mess, the glare of her self-righteous husband, the peeping son of a bitch.

Once all the chocolate had swirled down the drain, she dried herself and returned to her room. With Nate still sleeping, she closed the door, walked into the kitchen, and began her slow descent into the basement. At first the room seemed empty; the only light was a dim lamp and her eyes took several seconds to adjust. But after a while she saw David's image forming in the corner, his back toward her. When he turned around his face was twisted, as if he had suffered a stroke. He took a few steps forward, his right hand groping blindly, then he stopped and lowered his arm.

"God damn you." His voice was an icy whisper. "God damn you both."

She was prepared to feel guilty, to offer apologies, but his anger triggered a backlash. From the pit of her stomach six months of bile came spilling out.

"Damn yourself," she hissed. "What the hell did you expect? That I would sit here alone for months and wait for you to figure out what to do with your life? You're the one who left *me,* remember? You're the one who's been hiding out in the woods. Don't you *dare* curse me, you selfish bastard."

He staggered as if slapped. "I thought we would have dinner. I brought groceries in my knapsack. But I saw Nate walking up the street, going around back. I watched him cook for you, and serve you, and paint you." He broke off. When he lifted his head again his voice was quiet. "I never said you couldn't have your own life. But Jesus, Sarah, it's *Nate.* You're fucking my brother."

And then the shame kicked in, weighing down her shoulders. "You abandoned him, too."

It was the wrong thing to say. "Oh, right! So now I'm supposed to feel sorry for Nate? He looks to me like he's really suffering!" David slammed around the room, kicking at the furniture. "Do you think that he loves you? Or that he even gives a damn? You know he's doing it just to get at me."

"Everything is not about you. *You* are a dead man."

"I'm more alive now than I was for the past two years."

"Alive in your own mind, but dead to the world."

He stopped pacing and stared into her eyes. "And am I dead to you, Sarah?"

She slumped on the couch and shrugged her shoulders. "I don't know what you are."

David walked to the door, opening it wide so that the icy air came rushing in.

"Maybe you should figure it out." He disappeared up the stairs, leaving the door ajar while Sarah leaned forward and pressed her head to her knees, letting the cold spread deep into her body.

• 32 •

Later that night Sarah returned to her bed, but not to Nate's arms. She lay at the edge of the mattress, five inches between her thighs and his fingers. For half an hour she watched the window, imagining David outside, her monstrous creation haunting the winter woods. Her mind was full of Mary Shelley, and that seemed fitting—another widow of a drowned man, whose imagination was haunted with images of dead things brought to life.

All night dreams came in fits and starts, until, in the first blue glow of sunrise, Nate began to stir. Sarah pretended to be asleep as he stumbled around the bed, picking up clothes and carrying them into the bathroom. The shower ran for ten minutes, and when he came back and leaned over her pillow, smelling of soap and cologne and toothpaste, she wanted to pull him down to her, to breathe him into her body. But she lay absolutely quiet until he kissed her forehead and was gone.

For the next few days she ate little and slept less. Her mind was torn between shame and anger—anger at David's arrogance, at Nate's loveless temptations, and above all, anger at her own guilt. Her need for self-control had always been paired with a penchant for self-blame. Somehow, the problems in her life were always her fault. She should have been able to manage things better.

Now the Weather Channel was predicting a heavy snow. By week's end, the cabin would be inaccessible, and she would miss her chance to confront David. She wanted to curse and to comfort him, to accuse and to apologize. She wanted to count the hundreds of small ways that he had annoyed her in the course of their marriage. And so, on the fourth morning she dressed in her warmest clothes, walked out to her car, and began her slow procession into the mountains.

The woods looked pale and barren as the road twisted through the foothills. No squirrels hesitated in her path, no birds swooped over her hood. To her right, the river's deep pools lay drowsing beneath blankets of ice, and when she finally reached the cabin's drive and turned off her engine, she heard only the vast miles of stillness. All living things had retreated in the face of the coming storm.

The first flakes began to fall when she tried the door, and they settled on her wrist as she lifted the key from beneath its hiding place. Inside, the air was cold and stale. She turned up the thermostat and walked from room to room, switching on lights and opening doors. David's paint supplies were neatly stacked, his bed made with unusual care. In the bathroom, she found one used razor and a half-empty bottle of aspirin. No shampoo, no shaving cream, no tweezers and Old Spice. She turned on the water, swallowed two aspirin, and stared into the mirror.

David was gone; he had left without her. She was more alone now than when she had lost him in July. A dull misery began to permeate her joints, and she turned off the bathroom light and watched her face in the dark glass reemerge slowly as a featureless shadow. Inside the bedroom that David had left so tidy, Sarah removed her boots and coat and crawled under the covers, thinking, *Now is the winter of our discontent.*

An hour later, thin white stripes had covered the tree limbs. She rose from bed, hoping that David might have returned, but a quick search of the cabin revealed that nothing had changed. Putting on her coat and boots, she stepped outside and found that the world had an eerie glow, all sights and sounds muted except for the hiss of snow falling through pine needles. She descended the stairs and entered the yard, surveying the woods for signs of David returning with his ax, but the forest was darker than she recalled, and the only footprints were her own, crushing the first inch of snow.

Looking down at the river, she noticed something caught at the end of the dock. It appeared to be a gray tree trunk, swaying back and forth like Ahab's arm. One branch, covered with flecks of green, protruded at a right angle from the main trunk, and she walked toward it, snowflakes melting on her cheeks.

When she reached the dock, she paused at the creak of the old boards. Her height above the water blocked the object from view, except for the branch which she followed, counting the twigs that sprouted from its end. Three, four, five—she stopped, her breath catching in her chest. For it wasn't a branch after all, it was an arm—David's arm, with his hand spread wide. Blood roared in her ears, and she staggered forward a few more steps before dropping to her knees at the end of the dock.

The corpse had the phosphorescent beauty of a moonstone, but it had suffered the violations of nature—a cheekbone jutted from its face, patches of the legs were eaten away. This was not a recent death, she realized as she gazed at the bloated skin. This was her husband's seven-month corpse, returned from its odyssey on the river. All this time, he had been waiting in the water.

The current cocked David's head, as if he had a question, and she saw that his flannel shirt was caught on a nail in the dock. It occurred to her that he might want to be set free to continue his journey, but when she leaned over the edge, reaching for the nail, she saw that his eyes were open, staring at her with the same expression of rage and intensity she had seen at her window four nights ago. His mouth opened, spreading into a cavernous yawn, and she leaned closer to the water. The shock of ice pierced her skin as she tumbled into the river, face-to-face with David's raging eyes, his cold fingers tangled in her hair and dragging her down as they sank together into the mud.

Sarah jolted upright in bed, her shirt soaked with sweat. She had been woken by the sound of the back door opening, snowy boots kicking at the deck's entry mat. David was back.

She lay against her pillow and tried to breathe deeply as she listened to his feet approaching down the hall. He did not turn on the lights; his shadow wavered at the room's threshold. Closing her eyes, she pretended to be asleep as he entered and shut the door behind him. For a long time he lingered at the foot of the bed, not moving or speaking; all she could perceive was the shudder of his body with each breath. At the edge of the bed he lifted a pillow from beside her hair, and when she opened her eyes she saw David poised as Othello, the pillow spread in both hands.

"Are you going to kill me?" she asked.

He sighed and propped the pillow against the headboard, then lay down beside her. "No," he said. "Not you."

He was staring at the ceiling, watching the dim light from the window spread into gray polygons. She turned her eyes upon the same dark geometry, and together they formed two stone effigies, listening to the snow blowing across the roof.

"They're predicting two feet," he said after a while.

"Let it come," she replied. "Let it bury us."

• 33 •

The next morning her muscles ached and her jaw was shivering. She recognized the symptoms; for two decades her body had thrived and constricted according to the academic seasons. Adrenaline carried her through each semester's crises, until the completion of exams marked a retreat into illness and exhaustion. These past four days had felt like finals. They were all being tested.

David sat at the edge of her bed and pulled a thermometer from beneath her tongue. His palm felt warm and competent against her forehead as he read her temperature in the window's light.

"One hundred and two. Would you like some Tylenol?"

"No, it's all right." She would let her body burn away its impurities.

"I'll make you some tea."

Five minutes later he brought her a mug of Constant Comment. "Is there anything else you want?" His voice was cold.

Yes, she wanted to talk to him. She wanted to explain that she had never loved Nate, nor did she imagine that he loved her. He had helped her through a difficult winter—that was all. He had forced her to engage with the living world, something David couldn't offer here in this quiet retreat. The cabin was a chrysalis from which David might emerge, transformed, and fly, but for her it was little more than a time warp. David was tied to her past while Nate lived wholly in the present; between the two brothers, she had begun to find her own place in time. But all of this was too hard to explain to an angry man.

"No," she said. "I don't need anything."

For two days David tended her, bringing food and books and blankets and dull jokes about "cabin fever," while she lay in a dim fog, listening to the metronomic precision of his ax. Sometimes the ax's sharp crack was replaced by the crunch of a shovel, scraping away at the driveway bit by bit. He responds to pain with physical labor, Sarah told herself, remembering David poised with a shovel beside his mother's grave. But this pain was of her own making, and she curled her knees to her chest.

On the third afternoon he ran a bath. He helped her rise from bed and escorted her to the tub, leaving her in privacy. When she dipped her foot into the water, her skin turned bright pink. She added some cold and tried again, first one foot, then another. For thirty seconds she stood quiet while her calves grew accustomed to the scalding, then she lowered herself into the tub, inches at a time.

The water burned against her stomach, spreading beads of sweat along her throat and across her temples. She could feel her muscles melting into relaxation; so many corners of her body needed to be thawed. Her forearms bobbed up and down while the steam rose like drowsy spirits, filling the window.

Somewhere in her revery she heard a car starting. David must have finished the driveway—two afternoons of work. But it was strange for him to drive in these conditions, with the mountain road still packed with snow. Strange to drive at all after seven months without a car. We must need groceries, she thought as she heard the tires spinning, stopping, spinning. Her wagon was rocking back and forth, spitting gravel and ice. After a few minutes she sensed that he had turned the car around; the front-wheel drive was now helping him to plow toward the road. The engine paused at the end of the driveway, then the tires spun briefly in a surge of acceleration, followed by a long, distant decrescendo.

An hour later she wrapped herself in a large towel, drained the lukewarm tub, and walked, dripping, back to bed. Sleep came easily, and when she woke the room was dark. Turning on the bedside lamp, she saw by the alarm clock that it was already six, and snow had begun to fall again. Her joints felt stiff as metal as she pulled on some clothes and walked into the main room.

The morning's fire had dwindled into cold ashes and the woodpile was low on kindling. She placed the last four sticks on the ribs of the grate, then reached for David's ax, planning to split more strips from the driest logs, but the ax was not standing sentry at its usual post. Nor was it behind the couch, the easel, the kitchen island. She opened the door onto the deck and stepped outside far enough to see the empty chopping log. Coming back inside, she shook the snowflakes from her hair and began to strip bark from a few pine logs, sprinkling the chips across the four strips of kindling.

Where was David? A trip to the general store should have taken less than an hour. Round-trip to Jackson, with a two-hour shopping spree, should have brought him back by five o'clock. Now it was six-thirty, and as she held a match to her makeshift fire, she imagined her car in a ditch, David trudging home with arms full of groceries. Or perhaps he wasn't able to walk. Perhaps he was lying unconscious in the Jackson emergency room. How long would it take the local nurses to recognize him? He wouldn't be carrying his usual ID; in recent months he had abandoned his wallet, erasing all traces of his old identity. The nurse would wipe the blood from his face and gasp. She would call the doctor and together they would stare at their old colleague, who would slowly open his eyes and find himself discovered.

Or perhaps his eyes would never open. Perhaps the gathering crowd would witness Dr. McConnell's second death. Then once again Carver Petty would come knocking at her door, this time more inquisitive than sympathetic. How did it happen that her dead husband had been driving her car through the mountains on a snowy winter afternoon? Behind Carver she could see the insurance investigators, dressed like morticians, ascending her porch stairs.

Sarah heard footsteps outside the cabin. David entered and placed three brown paper bags on the kitchen counter, and she rose to face him as he hung up his coat.

"I was worried about you. Where did you go?"

"I had to run some errands." He bent down and began to unlace his boots, not looking at her.

"In this weather?"

"The streets are clear, once you get past these gravel roads."

"But you were gone for so long. Did anyone see you?"

"I didn't go into Jackson. I crossed the mountains in the other direction, on Route 29."

Route 29 led to Lynchburg and then Charlottesville, a long way to go for a few bags of groceries. When David lifted his face, she was struck by its pallor.

"You look like you've caught my flu. Come over here by the fire." She spread an afghan around his shoulders as he sank onto the couch, then she walked to the front window and looked out into the driveway.

"I didn't hear the car."

"I parked it at the end of the driveway so we could get out in the morning."

"Are you planning to go somewhere?"

He didn't answer. It occurred to her that David might not want to be near her, after what he had witnessed at their house. He had not asked her to join him here at the cabin, and his tone ever since her arrival had been oddly robotic. His shoveling for the past two days now seemed like the tunneling of an escape route.

"I'll make you some tea."

She filled the kettle and held her fingers above the stove as the burner began to glow. Her legs ached again, her brain still groggy. She wanted nothing more than to wrap herself in a comforter and claim the other half of the couch, where the fire might soothe them both. But she didn't know if David would welcome her there, or if he wanted her in his life at all.

When the tea was ready, she came to the back of the couch and held out his mug. "Here you go."

From underneath the afghan David's right hand emerged, and

as his fingers wrapped around the side of the mug, she felt a sharp pain in the middle of her chest. There, on David's fourth finger, was his father's wedding ring.

A vision of Nate came rushing back, standing in her bedroom in October with that same ring on his finger. "The shape of things to come," he had said, and laughed, his hand spread wide.

When she spoke her voice barely rose to a whisper. "Where is the ax?"

David did not answer. He merely hunched his shoulders and lowered his face to his mug.

"Where is the ax!"

"My God, Sarah, what's wrong?"

He set the mug on the table and stood up, reaching for her with his right hand. As the ring came nearer it winked at her with its golden flash, and she backed away until she hit the wall.

"Oh God."

She ran to the bathroom, locked the door, and turned on the faucet. The cold water, cupped in her hands then splashed across her face, helped ease the surge of saliva in the back of her throat.

David rattled the door handle. "Sarah? Let me in."

What have you done? she thought as she listened to his voice rise.

"*Please,* Sarah."

Her name sounded liked a curse. What have *you* done? she thought as she stared at her dripping reflection. Wasn't this her fault, this clash between brothers? Hadn't she sensed how it would all turn out? She knew the ending of the Frankenstein story, how the monster turned murderous kills the family members. The danger had been obvious and she had not bothered to stop it. Whatever David had done, she shared the blame.

When she opened the door, he stood three feet away, his mouth twisted, just as she remembered it in her basement. He stepped back as she edged sideways, her shoulder blades brushing the wall. She crossed the kitchen floor quickly and pulled her coat off the rack by the door.

"What are you doing?" His voice was muffled, like a man speaking through water.

Sarah knelt to lace her boots. "I've got to go."

"Where?" His voice was louder, but still thick and strange.

She spotted the keys on the kitchen counter, beside the grocery bags. As she reached for them David's right hand came down upon her own. The ring touched her skin like a lighted match, and she yanked the keys away.

"What is it?" he yelled.

"I've got to go!"

"It's completely dark, and you know you can't drive in the snow. You won't make it to the general store."

She opened the front door and was stepping outside when David grabbed her elbow.

"Let go of me!"

She bashed her arm, with his clutching hand, against the doorway, and he jerked it back, holding his knuckles to his mouth. "Jesus Christ!"

And then she was running, with David yelling from the doorway, "You're sick, Sarah! You're feverish. You need to lie down."

The driveway was slick, and the trickle of light from the cabin's entry lamp disappeared after a dozen yards, leaving her in complete darkness. Each time her feet left the gravel, she stepped into leaves and snow and veered back onto the driveway, like a drunk staggering to maintain a straight line. Behind her, she heard the cabin door shut, and when she looked back she saw the beam of a flashlight bobbing up and down. She hurried faster, until her knee smashed into the back bumper of the car. With her hands groping blindly across metal and glass, she felt her way to the handle, climbed inside, and locked the door, just as David reached the window.

"Get out of the car, Sarah!"

She started the ignition and he ran in front of the hood, shining the flashlight into her eyes.

"Get out of the car!"

She jerked the wagon forward and he jumped out of the way, stumbling into the trees at the side of the driveway. Yanking the steering wheel to the left, she skidded sideways into the road, then straightened out the wheels and pressed on the accelerator.

With the snow sweeping into her headlights, she could barely see ten feet ahead. She leaned forward, her chin just above the steering wheel, and wiped at the fog on the inside of the windshield, making a peephole five inches across. For half a mile she tried sticking her head out the window, searching for the tracks left by pickups and SUVs, but the snow lashed her eyes, blinding her even more. Rolling her window up, she concentrated on the few feet of road just beyond the hood of her car, but when the road veered to the right, she turned too late, and her back tires slid sideways off the gravel. She pressed on the gas and the tires spun, digging into the ditch. Two more attempts and she knew it was hopeless.

Sarah pressed her forehead into the steering wheel and fought against tears. With the headlights still on she stepped out of the car, turned up her collar, and looked in the direction of Eileen, guessing that it was a two-mile walk. When she turned in the opposite direction, back toward the cabin, she stopped breathing. A pinprick of bobbing light was coming her way. Quietly, quietly, Sarah backed away from the car, into the woods, and stood behind a large oak.

When David reached the car, he pulled the door open and shined his flashlight inside. She watched him feel the ignition for the keys that she now clutched in her hand, and his flashlight swept away from the car, into the woods.

"Sarah! Where are you?"

The light moved back and forth, and she leaned sideways against the tree, avoiding the touch of the glare. David walked to the other side of the road and repeated the process, shining the flashlight north and south.

"Sarah!" He was yelling at the top of his voice, the sound puncturing the silent woods. "Are you all right?"

Back at the car he began circling, the headlights shining on his torso so that his head was hidden in darkness, a decapitated body. He crossed the ditch and approached the trees where she stood hidden. Twenty feet away, fifteen, ten, nine.

His flashlight leaped up, shining down the road toward the cabin. Then it clicked off. A car was coming. In the darkness she could hear David move behind a tree ten feet to the left of her.

The vehicle slowed as it approached, then came to a full stop. A bearded man in a camouflage jacket stepped out of a pickup and walked toward her car door, peering inside. Sarah bolted out from behind her tree, into the headlights.

"Hello there!" the man yelled. "Are you all right?"

"Yes."

"Looks like you need some help. Do you have any chains, or a rope?"

She shook her head.

"Sorry I haven't got anything to pull you out. I wasn't expecting to meet anyone out here tonight." She guessed he was about fifty-five, gray hair, a raspy voice. "Where are you headed?" he asked.

"Jackson."

"I'm going into town myself. I can take you there and you can call for a tow. The Texaco has a twenty-four-hour service, but they'll probably be busy on a night like this."

"I'd appreciate a ride home."

"Climb on in."

Sarah walked over to her car and turned off the headlights. She climbed into the cab of the man's truck, which was warm and smoky, with country music playing.

"My name's Pete."

"I'm Sarah."

"Nice to meet you, Sarah."

When they arrived at her house, Sarah opened her front door and turned back to wave at Pete, who was waiting to see her safely inside. She watched until his taillights disappeared, then stepped outside again and locked the door. David's Subaru was in the back of the driveway, untouched for seven months. With her coat sleeve she brushed the top layer of flakes off the windshield. Chunks of snow and ice fell at her ankles when she yanked opened the door.

On her first turn of the ignition, the engine shuddered and died.

Five more times it sputtered, coughed, and sighed before holding steady. She turned on the defroster, took the hand scraper from the glove compartment, and began gouging at the layers of snow on the hood and roof. A thin sheet of beaded ice coated the windshield, but the defroster had begun to carve a hole the size of a golf ball, so she left the machine to its work while she went to the basement to get her snow shovel.

As she dug out the tires, Sarah was thankful for David's insistence on four-wheel drive. A doctor could not be snowbound—so he had often explained—and after ten minutes of shoveling, rocking the car back and forth, and shoveling more, she lurched over the last feet of the snowy drive, onto the cleared road, and headed for Charlottesville.

She reached Nate's condominium at eleven-thirty. The windows were dark and no one answered her knock, so she let herself inside with a key hidden in the shrubs.

"Hello? Nate?"

Switching on the living-room lamp, she found nothing disturbed, no chair overturned, no ominous stains on the carpet. She left her boots and coat in the foyer and began searching room to room.

Inside the dark kitchen her sock touched a puddle; warm liquid seeped between her toes. She steeled herself as she brushed her hand up and down the wall, groping for the light switch. But it was only a puddle of water, leaking from the dishwasher. She soaked it up with a sponge, then proceeded down the hall into Nate's bedroom. The covers were neat, the closet empty. Inside the master bathroom, she opened the shower door and revealed a lonely bottle of Prell.

This was no crime scene, this model of tidiness. How crazy was she, to have imagined David as a murderer? Sarah closed the shower door, turned around, and froze. There, in the mirror, scrawled across her reflection: I KNOW WHAT YOU HAVE DONE.

They were written in black Magic Marker, letters leaning to the right in the messy scrawl that David used on every prescription. She approached the glass, noticing how the words scarred her face—black stitches across her forehead, an *A* on her cheek—all meant to disfigure Nate, to let him look into his face and see his brother's condemnation scribbled across his jaw.

But what was David thinking? That Nate would believe a ghost had used a Sharpie? She lifted a washcloth from the towel rack, held it under the sink, then wiped at the letters, streaks of black tears dripping down the glass. When the mirror was clean she wrung the towel into the sink until it was a muted gray, then hung it up and did another circuit of the condominium, checking every mirror, every window, every picture frame, any surface where David might have scratched another message from the grave. By the time she had finished, her brain was throbbing against the front of her skull. Exhausted, she climbed into Nate's bed and shut her eyes.

Early in the morning Sarah woke to a dim apparition—a smiling Nate, standing at the foot of the bed. Garment bag in one hand, laptop in the other.

"This is a surprise." He put down his luggage and stretched out beside her. "I saw David's car outside. That was weird. Is yours having trouble?"

She nodded. "Where have you been?"

"In Washington, on business. When did you get here?"

"Last night."

"Didn't you call first?"

"It was a sudden impulse."

"I like sudden impulses." He ran his fingers through her hair. "Why are you sleeping with your clothes on?"

"I was exhausted."

"You look terrible."

"Thanks."

"Why did you come if you're sick?"

"I wanted to see if you were all right."

He smiled. "Why wouldn't I be?"

Sarah looked at his bare fingers as they pulled away from her hair.

"What did you do with your father's ring?"

"What do you mean?"

"Where is it?"

"How should I know? You're the one who took it."

Nate laughed at her pale stare. "I saw you, when you spent the night back in January, after our New Year's trip. You got up in the middle of the night and were moving around in the dark. I didn't want to disturb you, since you'd told me about your sleepwalking. So I watched you go into my closet and take out David's wool sweater. Then you went to the dresser and took Dad's ring from my top drawer. Don't you remember?"

Sarah shook her head.

"Well, maybe you *were* sleepwalking. Anyway, you walked outside in your nightgown, and you opened the back of your wagon and put them in a box. I could see you from the window. I was a little worried because it was freezing outside and you were walking around in bare feet. When you came back to bed your toes were like icicles. I didn't want to say anything about it in the morning because I thought I understood your reasons."

"What reasons?"

He shrugged. "I have too many things of David's."

It all rang true, but how could she have no memory of walking at night in the January frost? And if she couldn't remember that, what else had she forgotten?

"I do wish you'd give me the ring back," Nate continued. "It would make sense for me to have it now, since it was our dad's."

"Yes," she echoed. "It would make sense."

He walked his fingers down her arm, trying to coax her thoughts his way, but Sarah remained distant. "I'm going to make some breakfast," he said, rising from the bed. "Would you like some?"

"Yes. Some breakfast."

Nate paused in the doorway. "How would you like your eggs?"

She almost replied "over easy," but the question and answer seemed too familiar. "None for me. Just juice and toast."

Ten minutes later, when she walked into the kitchen, Nate was sitting behind *The Wall Street Journal,* her plate of buttered toast lying neatly on a place mat. She took a sip of orange juice and stared at the world news column: budget worries and roadside bombs and motorists trapped in the winter storm.

"I think we should stop seeing each other." She addressed the newsprint.

The headlines sank an inch. "What?"

"I think we shouldn't see each other anymore."

Nate lowered the news and looked into her eyes. "Are you sure that's what you want?"

"Yes."

He sighed and folded the paper. "Well, I knew it wouldn't last forever. I mean, it's not like you and I would ever get *married*." He gave an awkward laugh and scanned her eyes for confirmation. She nodded.

"It's just funny," he said. "I'm used to being the one who calls things off."

Sarah cringed. "Do you want to know what I think?"

"Sure."

"I think you should ask Jenny to marry you. Tell her that you'll have a three-year honeymoon. Time to do all the traveling she wants, and to set up a household. But promise her that by the time you turn forty you two will start a family. That way she'll be a wife by thirty and a mother by thirty-three. What more could she want?"

"I don't think it's that simple."

"It's as simple as you make it."

He placed his hand over hers. "But we'll still see each other?"

"I'm still your sister-in-law."

"And maybe I could see you on a professional level? You might need a financial expert to help manage your assets."

"That's right," and unexpectedly, Sarah laughed. For in the end she was just another potential client, a widow who had inherited a small fortune, in need of an investment adviser. Perhaps that was how Nate had always viewed her. If so, she didn't mind; the thought drained all emotion from their parting. She had no fear of hurting him, no likelihood of guilt.

Still, when he leaned forward to kiss her cheek, she was swamped by a wave of doubt. With the slightest encouragement she would have taken it back, crawled into his bed and stayed forever. Argue with me, she thought. Tell me that I'm wrong. Say that you and I have a future together. But Nate did not even look at her. He finished his orange juice, carried his plate to the sink, and walked away.

• 34 •

Home by midafternoon, Sarah stood at her living-room window, watching a tow truck drag her station wagon up the street. How humiliated the car appeared, its rear end hoisted in the air, the right front fender scratched and muddy.

"You must be Sarah McConnell," the truck driver said when she walked outside, checkbook in hand.

"I must be."

"You'll need to have your tires realigned. Otherwise it seems to be in pretty good shape."

Sarah knelt to pull a chunk of leaves from the grille. "Thanks for bringing it back." Once the man was gone she gathered a bucket, rag, and hose, and rinsed away the rest of the mud, thinking that this whole day had been spent in acts of erasure.

That night she slept restlessly, waking past three to the certainty that someone was watching her. A dim figure sat at the foot of her bed, an echo of her mother, years ago. But there was nothing maternal about this form, and as her eyes adjusted to the bathroom light (she always kept it on these nights) she could discern David's outline.

"I thought you would come." She settled back into her pillows.

"I had to," he replied. "You were sick and crazy when you left the cabin. And you drove off with that stranger."

"I was afraid that you had done something terrible . . . I saw what you wrote on Nate's mirror." David bowed his head, as if his brother's name was a heavy burden. "What would you have done if he had been home?"

David shrugged. "I wasn't going to hurt him, if that's what you mean. I was just planning to give him a good scare. Remind him that Big Brother is always watching. Maybe let him see my face at the window."

"That *is* your modus operandi."

"You're not in a position to be critical." His voice had hardened.

"Neither are you," Sarah replied.

They were silent for a while, David's fingers running over the bedspread. "It's hard to come back here," he said, "after last time."

Sarah was glad for the darkness that hid her blush. "All of that is over. I said good-bye to Nate yesterday. We won't be seeing each other again."

David shook his head. "Who can say what will or won't happen again?"

He scanned the room, as if searching for something. "I'm going to be leaving soon. I've decided I want to go someplace where it's always warm."

Sarah felt the pressure of his hand on her leg. "Come with me, Sarah. We can travel for a month or two, go out west, see the canyons, all the places we've meant to visit. We could find a town with a few art galleries and a college for you to teach at. If you'd sell this house and the cabin we'd have enough money to buy another place without a mortgage. Between our savings and your Social Security, we'd never have to work unless we felt like it. Just paint and write and read."

Amazing, thought Sarah, how all of his sentences were a mirror of her dreams, or at least what her dreams had been three months ago. But much had changed in the intervening weeks.

"I don't know," she said.

"Don't answer right away. Think about it for a while." David rose and walked to the door. "You know where to find me."

Once he was gone, Sarah did not sleep. She turned on the Weather Channel and watched spring arriving with intermittent graphics of snowflakes and sunshine. By six A.M., when the sky had lightened to a purplish blue, she opened her curtains and saw the crocuses tight-fisted against the morning frost.

For the next several days she did little other than read and think. She left the house only at Margaret's bidding, when she insisted that Sarah come for tea. Their Friday ritual had dwindled in recent weeks, with traveling and illness and Sarah's vague excuses. This time Sarah prepared apologies and a loaf of banana bread.

When Sarah arrived at Margaret's door, the boiling kettle sounded like a train whistle ushering her aboard. She sat at the kitchen table and watched the steam form wispy clouds around Margaret's fingers.

"I saw your car," said Margaret. "Last week. Getting towed up the street. Have you been all right?"

Sarah shrugged. "I slid into a ditch during the snowstorm. No harm done." Seeing another question form across Margaret's brow, Sarah hurried to change the subject. "The last time I saw you was at the movies."

"Yes." Margaret smiled. "What an awful film."

Sarah recalled the elementary school teachers watching Nate's hand progress across her shoulders. "I suppose you had a better show to watch than I did?"

Margaret brought the mugs to the table and sat down. "Real life is always more interesting than the movies."

"Well, Nate and I won't be putting on a show anymore. I said good-bye to him a week ago—told him he should patch things up with his old girlfriend."

"So," said Margaret, "should I offer condolences or congratulations?"

"He and I never would have lasted."

"Why's that?"

Sarah smiled. "He's a Republican."

"God forbid." Margaret warmed her fingers around her mug. "So what's next?"

Sarah concentrated on the swirl of cream in her tea. "I'm not sure . . . I might want to travel for a while. Go someplace warm."

"It's getting warmer here."

"Yes." Sarah nodded. "The weather is changing."

"So you want to go to a beach?" Margaret asked.

"Maybe a beach, maybe a desert."

Margaret took a sip of tea. "I have a message to pass along. Adele is hosting the next widows group, and she asked especially if you would come. It's this Sunday evening, and I'm going."

Outside the window Sarah noticed a row of jonquils blooming beside Margaret's driveway. "Adele is a nice old lady."

Margaret nodded.

"But I don't want to become a regular."

Margaret shook her head.

"I suppose I could come for one last time."

On Sunday evening Margaret drove the two of them to Adele's house. Normally they would have walked; she lived less than a mile away. But a late winter freeze had descended, and the sidewalks glittered with ice. Margaret's jonquils bowed their heads to the ground in supplication.

Inside Adele's living room, the wallpaper resembled wedding gift wrap—almond, with white and silver flowers that twined toward the ceiling, where a gold chandelier suspended a dozen electric candles, crystal saucers at their feet to catch the imaginary wax. Their light mingled with the flames from an immense fireplace, five feet tall and framed with Doric columns, its mantel covered in hazy brown photographs—rose-lipped babies in christening dresses, and grim men in uniform, cheeks tinted pink.

Adele presided from a wingback chair, her yellow blouse ruffled at her neck like a daffodil's petals. She patted the divan to her right when Sarah entered.

"I'm glad you've come."

Platters of lemon squares and brownies covered the coffee table, and Sarah took a macaroon from a passing tray. "If I'd known it was a dessert potluck, I would have brought something."

Adele waved as if brushing away a gnat. "The group always insists on bringing food to my house. They seem to think that baking is too strenuous for an old woman. Are you planning to help with the Easter food drive?"

"I hadn't heard about it."

"I think you'd like it. On the Saturday before Easter we pack huge baskets with food for the adults, and chocolate bunnies and toys for the children. We deliver them that afternoon; I was hoping you'd drive with me."

"I will if I'm in town."

"You have travel plans?" Adele asked.

"Possibly."

Around them, the widows were sharing news, the conversation a moving talisman that each woman was required to touch. Ruby's stepson had dropped his lawsuit; in return she had willed the house to him upon her death. She expected the "son of a bitch to knock her off" any day now. Meanwhile, the water-skier's widow had just returned from Florida. She had begun to swim again, and was allowing her children to sail sunfish and catamarans—nothing with speed or deadly propellers.

When the conversation reached Sarah she tried to pass it along lightly—"I don't have much to report"—but the red-haired sociologist wasn't satisfied.

"Have you seen your husband lately?"

"Yes." Sarah hesitated, feeling the women's eyes upon her. "But he's not happy with me. He doesn't like what I've been doing with my life."

"That's classic." The professor took over. "I've been reading ghost narratives from the past seven centuries—real accounts, not Edgar Allan Poe. And from the seventeenth century forward the most common hauntings have been from legacy ghosts who didn't approve of what their widows were doing, either with their money or their children."

"What were the ghosts worried about before the seventeenth century?" Sarah asked.

"Mostly purgatory. They wanted their widows to pray for them or give the church a lot of money to buy their way into heaven." The professor bit into a brownie. "And of course there are the ghosts who don't like their widows' sex lives, sort of like the king in *Hamlet*."

Sarah blushed at the affinity between herself and Shakespeare's Gertrude while Margaret, who had been sitting nearby, rose to place another log on the fire.

"Well," said Ruby, turning to face Sarah. "I don't know about disgruntled husbands, only obnoxious stepsons. But as I see it, it's your life. So *fuck* him."

Adele gave a disapproving cough, and the conversation moved along. Sarah concentrated on her macaroon, until she felt Adele's hoarse whisper at her ear. "You know, dear, I love my visits with

Edward. I wouldn't give him up for anything in the world. But I'm a great-grandmother, and my life is in the past. You've got most of your life ahead of you. If your husband isn't making you happy, maybe it's time to let him go."

Sarah patted Adele's hand. "That's easier said than done."

When Margaret pulled into Sarah's driveway late that evening, she shifted the car into park and lowered her hands into her lap. "There's something that's been bothering me."

"What's that?"

"The things you said tonight about David. How he doesn't approve of what you've been doing with your life."

"I should have said that I don't *think* he *would* have approved."

"It's not your verb tense that's the problem." Margaret raised her hands and gripped the steering wheel. "This has been around for a long time, and I just never thought that I should bring it up."

"Go ahead and tell me." Sarah braced herself while Margaret paused, looking out the windshield.

"Remember three years ago when we went shopping in Charlottesville? We both bought new outfits to wear to the fund-raising dance for the free clinic? And you chose that red dress with the gold thread woven into the fabric?"

"The flapper dress?" Sarah laughed.

"I thought it was lovely," said Margaret.

"I did, too."

"Then why didn't you wear it?" Margaret turned to face Sarah. "You arrived in a black skirt and white satin blouse. I remember it clearly. After all that talk about having some fun with your wardrobe. I never said anything, but I've always had my suspicions."

Sarah remembered it, too—how, on the night of the dance, she had gotten ready before David was home from work. The new dress had inspired her to paint her fingernails red and wear raspberry lipstick. She thought that the colors complemented her dark hair; when she smiled in the mirror she was a woman on fire.

David entered the bedroom just as she was putting on her gold earrings.

"What do you think?" she asked, spinning around so that the dress floated above her knees.

David hesitated for one second too long. "You look great in whatever you wear."

He might as well have said that she looked like the whore of Babylon; diplomacy was wasted on her paper-thin ego. "I guess the dress is a bit much?" She forced a smile.

"Yes," said David, clearly pleased that they were in accord. "That's what I thought too. But what do I know about fashion? You should wear whatever you like."

When Sarah glanced back into the mirror she saw that she resembled a fire truck more than a flame. Her lips were carnivorous, her fingers bloody.

"Maybe on another occasion." She had retreated to the bathroom in search of nail-polish remover.

"It wasn't David's fault," Sarah explained to Margaret. "He told me I should wear whatever I liked."

"But he wasn't wild about the dress?"

"Not even a little."

"So what did you do with it?"

"I gave it to Goodwill two days later."

Margaret sighed. "I figured it was something like that." She flexed her fingers on the steering wheel. "You know I liked David a lot. I admired him; everyone did. But it must have been hard to be married to a man with such a strong personality."

"You think that I deferred to him too much?" Sarah smiled faintly.

"I think you are deferring to him still."

Sarah felt that if she stayed in the car one minute longer she would break down, confess everything, collapse under the weight of the last five months.

"Message received." She opened the car door and stepped out.

"The last stage of mourning is separation." Margaret spoke quietly, as if she were talking to herself.

Sarah nodded. "Same as the last stage of marriage."

• 35 •

In mid-March Sarah drove to the cabin for her final visit. The weather was dry and sunny, which she usually took as a good omen, but as clouds of dust rose from the gravel, she felt a slight foreboding. Here was the ditch where her tires had sunk three weeks ago; there was the tree that had shielded her from David's eyes. Here was the long stretch of road where his flashlight had bobbed like a phantom's lantern. In the face of these dark memories, nature was her only ally. At the foot of the driveway, rhododendrons offered purple nosegays, and when she pulled up at the cabin she saw forsythia in the backyard, shooting fountains of yellow sparks.

Inside, the cabin air was thick with its usual musty scent; the fireplace appeared untouched. But when she stepped out on the deck and trained her eyes upon the river, she made out a man in green flannel at the dock's end.

"Hello!" she called, and David turned.

He approached over mounds of uncut grass bent low from weeks of snow, pausing at the tulipwood tree to push the chicken wire deeper into the earth. At the bottom of the deck stairs he stopped and looked up at her, his posture reminiscent of Halloween.

"We need to talk," she said, and when she opened the door he walked past, into the cabin.

They sat across from each other at the pine table, Sarah squeezing her hands tightly in her lap.

"I've been thinking about what you said, about going away, and you know how much that appeals to me." The slightest hint of a smile crossed David's lips.

"But we can't go together," she went on. "It's impossible. That was never more than a mutual dream." She lifted her hands and hugged her arms around her chest. "It's time for me to get on with my life."

"How do you plan to do that?" asked David.

"I called our department chair yesterday and told him I wanted to get back to work next fall. He's going on sabbatical, so he says that I can teach as many of his courses as I like. British literature mostly—Shakespeare through Dickens. I'll have to do a lot of reading over the next few months.

"I've also decided to sell the house," Sarah continued. "Spring is the season to do it, so I'm planning to put it on the market in another month or so. And this cabin. Too many memories."

David nodded.

"Margaret has invited me to stay at her place for a while. At least until I've found another house. I think it might be a good idea, to avoid being so isolated."

"It sounds like you've mapped everything out."

"There's one more thing." Sarah stared at the table's wood

grain. "I'm going to see about adopting a baby from somewhere overseas. Not right away. It will take a while to work out all the details. But sometime in the next few years."

She looked up and was surprised to see that David's eyes were blurry. "I would have liked to raise a child with you," he said. He pushed his chair back and stood up. "Things never work out the way you plan."

David glanced around until his eyes settled on the easel. "I haven't completed your portrait . . . I don't need you to model, but it would help to have you around, so I can see your profile, and your hands, and your hair. It won't take long."

He's stalling, thought Sarah. Still unwilling to let her go. She rose and walked to the easel, looking down at her unfinished self. Her features were expressionless, her acrylic hands cloudy. Outside the painted window, the world had not yet taken shape.

"I can stay for a few days," she said. "Just until you're done."

And so for three days she stayed at the cabin, sitting on the dock and dangling her feet in the cold water. In the afternoons David painted while she read on the couch, poised so that he could see her face, and the color of her hair. It was strange, how slowly the portrait progressed. Her hands grew fingers, her fingers grew nails. The windowpanes filled with trees and clouds, but her face remained blank, impervious to the view.

Meanwhile, time moved at a geological pace. Across the river the limestone cliffs rose in gray and brown scribbles, each layer another monument to drought or flood. She watched the water carrying streaks of mud into the crags, and felt the real danger of being lulled back into dreams. She was reminded of the cicadas that had surfaced years ago, their brief intermission of activity after years of rest, brown shells left clinging to the pine trees. How well she understood the impulse to burrow, to live in fits and starts and long stretches of retreat. But she had to resist while resistance was possible.

The end came on the fourth morning. Rising at nine-thirty, she padded silently into the living room and discovered David at his canvas, scraping her eyes and mouth with a wet Q-tip. She watched her irises and lips retreat into a foggy cloud, and thought, See no evil. Speak no evil.

"It's not right yet," David explained when he noticed her standing across the room.

"It never will be right," she answered.

She walked up behind his chair, wrapped her arms around his neck, and leaned her lips into his hair. "We've lingered here much too long."

David placed his right hand over hers and pressed it to his chest. She rested her cheek on his head until she felt the tremors in his body settle into long, deep breaths. Slower and slower the breathing came, quieter and quieter, until she couldn't tell that he was breathing at all. Then she felt his body stiffen. A vehicle had pulled into the driveway.

Sarah drew her hands away and walked to the front window.

"Oh God," she murmured. "It's a police car."

She turned back toward the easel, but the room was empty. Outside, she thought she heard the creaking of the deck stairs.

Sarah took a long, shaking breath and opened the front door.

"Hey there, Carver."

"Hey, Sarah. Mind if I come in?"

She swung the door wide.

Carver removed his hat as he entered. "I've been trying to reach you for a couple of days now."

"Did Margaret tell you where to find me?"

"Actually I had my own idea that you might be coming out here."

"Why's that?"

Carver leaned against the kitchen island. "You know your neighbor Rich Haskins? I play poker with him about once a month, and I asked him last November how you seemed to be doing. He told me that you'd asked for the power to be turned back on at this place. That struck him as kind of strange. He didn't think you'd be wanting to come out here in the winter."

Sarah felt the blood rise in her cheeks. "I hadn't thought about Rich."

Carver shrugged. "We live in a very small town." He looked around the room. "I came out here myself last summer. Right after David disappeared. Did you know that?"

Sarah nodded. "I told you where to find the key."

"Actually, the key wasn't in that spot. But the door was unlocked, and the key was on the counter, right where David must have left it."

"I think I'll sit down." Sarah took a chair at the table.

"That's a good idea." Carver paused at David's easel. "I noticed David's painting last time I was here."

"He painted it three years ago," Sarah said quickly. "When we spent a month out here together."

Carver didn't reply. Instead, he sat down beside her and together they stared out at the water. "This is the hardest part of my job," he said.

"It's all right," said Sarah. "I've been expecting you."

Carver reached into his pocket and placed something on the

table—a brown leather object, weather-beaten and torn at one edge.

"What's that?" she asked.

"You don't recognize it?"

Sarah shook her head.

Carver lifted the object into his hand. "Some teenagers found a body four days ago. Washed up from the river, in the woods about eight miles from here. It's pretty badly decomposed, but what's left of the life vest matches the description you gave us last summer. And we found this in the pocket."

He placed the faded wallet on the table in front of Sarah's fingers. Slowly, she opened the leather flap, pulled out the plastic cards, and arranged them like a poker hand. A fading image of David smiled at her from his driver's license.

"I liked David a lot," said Carver. "He was a good man."

His voice cracked, and Sarah saw that his hands were balled into fists on the table's surface. She was amazed at her own sense of calm, a feeling almost of relief; one part of her life was ending so that another might begin. Placing her palm gently over Carver's right hand, she murmured, "Do you believe in ghosts, Carver?"

He wiped his eyes. "What do you mean?"

"It's just a question. Do you believe in ghosts?"

He cocked his head, as if expecting a trick.

"As a matter of fact I do."

"What would you say if I told you that I've been seeing David's ghost out here, in this cabin? That I come here to talk to him, and spend time with him, and he sits in that very same chair where you're sitting now . . . Would you say that I'm crazy?"

She ended with a laugh, but Carver's face was intent, studying her in silence. "I'd say you weren't the first person to report such things . . . But if I were you I wouldn't tell anyone else."

Sarah nodded.

"I'll tell you something more, that I've only told two other people." He leaned toward her slightly. "I was with my father at the hospital when he passed away four years ago. He was eighty-two and full of pneumonia, so I knew it was coming. But when he died I sensed something, like his spirit was moving around that room, and I'd swear to this day that I felt a hand on me." He reached up and grasped his left shoulder. "He always rested his hand on my shoulder like that, ever since I was a boy, and I sensed the weight of it in that hospital room. After a while it faded, like my shoulder was just heavy. But I know what I felt, and nobody can tell me that it wasn't real."

Sarah smiled. "It's real for me, too—but afterward it feels like I've only been sleepwalking."

She looked out at the river. "He's here now, outside. I should go and talk to him."

Carver shifted uncomfortably. "I don't like the idea of leaving you alone out here."

"This won't take long." She rose and opened the deck door. "If you'll wait I'll follow you back to town when I'm done."

David was seated at the end of the dock, peeling a long sliver from the railing at his side. He tossed it into the water as Sarah sat down beside him.

"Carver brought your wallet," she said. "They've found your body. I suppose there will be a funeral, now that there's something to bury."

David threw another strip of wood across the water's surface. "I prefer cremation. Scatter my ashes in the river."

Sarah watched the small bits of pine float downstream. "Remember what you told me you saw from the bottom of the river, at the moment when you were drowning? You said you saw me calling you back, telling you to come home? . . . I think that's right. I think I wanted you back so that I could apologize for the last few years of our marriage."

David shook his head. "You have nothing to be sorry for."

Sarah shrugged. "There's always something to regret." On the back of her left hand she traced the letters *S-O-R-R-Y*. "I was angry for a long time," she began. "Angry at the world for not giving me everything I expected. Angry at you for getting on with your career while mine was going nowhere . . . You never did anything wrong—never drank or had affairs, or flirted with your students. I think I wanted you to do something wrong, just to bring you down to my level."

"I've done plenty wrong—" David objected, but Sarah stopped him.

"Do you know the last act of *The Crucible*? When Elizabeth Proctor is talking to John? He's deciding whether to confess—it's a question of life or death—and she's thinking about their marriage. She says, 'It were a cold house I kept.' That's the line that came back to me, when you disappeared: 'It were a cold house I kept.' "

"You blame yourself too much," David replied. "I never helped you. After your second miscarriage, I put all my energy into my work, and I left you on your own. Too many evenings you were alone in the house. That's a lot of time and reason to be angry."

There was truth in it, thought Sarah. Truth and contrition, and maybe that was all she had ever wanted from him. "I'm not angry anymore," she said.

"Neither am I." David stared into his hands, and for a few minutes they remained silent, watching the river.

"You know," he said eventually, "there's somebody else who's been calling to me."

"Who?"

"Another woman." David watched Sarah's eyebrows raise, then he grinned. "It's my mother."

Of course, thought Sarah. How silly of her, all these months, to have imagined David as immeasurably lonely. The dead always had company, generations upon generations.

David took her hand, and for once his palm was warm as the sun spreading across them. He leaned over and kissed her cheek, so softly that she felt she could dissolve into his body, as if he had always been permeable; she had only imagined the boundaries of skin and bone.

"Good-bye, my beautiful wife."

Sarah remained seated, watching the current, while David walked off the dock and across the grass. Only when he had reached the edge of the woods did she stand and look back. "David!" she called. "Wait!" He turned, waved, and was gone.

Another ten minutes passed before she left the dock, the sun tipping into the trees as she waded up the yard. Inside the cabin, Carver was on the couch, reading a *National Geographic*. He rose when Sarah entered.

"Are you ready?" he asked.

"Yes," she said quietly. "I am ready."

Afterword

The history of English literature is haunted with dead husbands. Sometimes they appear as ghosts, like the King in *Hamlet,* as troubled by his widow's sexuality as by his own murder. Other times they appear as living men who have faked their deaths in order to spy on their wives. Chapman, Molière, Behn, and Steele—to name only a few—create husbands who leap from the wings when their widows take new lovers. Finally, there are the husbands who exist as figments in widows' minds, because women have been encouraged, in conduct books and educational treatises from medieval days forward, to imagine their husbands' spirits as ever-present beings, whose eyes, joined by the eyes of God, see everything.

Acknowledgments

The idea for this novel grew from a favorite chapter in my dissertation on widows in English literature, and so first thanks go to the director of that project, Patricia Meyer Spacks. From there, many readers helped to shape the story. The inaugural members of the Southern Inn writing group, Chris Gavaler, Molly Petty, and Paul Hanstedt, read the first draft as it emerged chapter by chapter. Stephanie Wilkinson, Anne Davies, Beth Colocci, Kerry Humes, Marian Bouchard, Leigh Shemitz-Winters, Tinni Sen, Marsha Heatwole, Carolyn Capps, Michael Matin, Carol Howard, John Leland, and Laure Stevens Lubin all gave advice and encouragement; and Rod Smith, editor of *Shenandoah*, has been very supportive. Special thanks go to Rosemary James and Joseph deSalvo for their unflagging promotion of new writers through their work as co-founders of the Pirate's Alley/Faulkner Society, and to Michael Malone, who chose *The Widow's Season* for the Faulkner-Wisdom

2005 prize for Best Novel-in-Progress. The novel would never have been published without the combined efforts of Gail Hochman, my agent, who saw the promise in the story and encouraged me to keep writing, and my editor, Jackie Cantor, who has been unfailingly enthusiastic.

Closer to home, my neighbors, Jeanette Coleman and Catherine Tomlin, provided free childcare that gave me the time to write, and I am always indebted to my husband and daughters, to whom the novel is dedicated.

The Widow's Season

by Laura Brodie

READERS GUIDE

1. What are some of the meanings behind the novel's title? Why do you think the author chose it, and how does the plot follow the holiday seasons?

2. Why do you believe the author tells the story both from Sarah's and David's point of view?

3. This novel stemmed from the author's graduate dissertation on widows in English literature—in particular, a chapter about "dead" husbands (either ghosts or men who fake their deaths) watching their wives. Take a look at the novel's epigraph, which comes from that study. Do you think that today's widows still feel that their husbands are watching them? Does society encourage them to keep their husbands present in their lives?

4. What are some of the underlying reasons that Sarah and Nate have the affair? What do they gain from the relationship? Why do you think Margaret encourages it?

5. At one point Sarah wonders, "What could be extraordinary in the life of a small-town upper-middle-class white woman" like her? Why does she think her life is so mundane, and what is ironic about her question?

6. Sarah is mourning more than just the loss of David when he disappears. Explore why she is in such a dark place in her life. Can she pinpoint when it happened and why?

7. After learning that David survives the storm on the river, and hearing his explanations for his actions, do you think his "hiding out" was a selfish act or a reasonable option?

8. Sarah thinks, "Age . . . does not appear first in wrinkles or gray hair, but in the dulling of one's smile." How does this sum up the life she was living with David before his disappearance?

9. Why do you think David is so real to Sarah? Why does she need him to be?

10. At the end of the novel, we discover what really happened to David. Did Sarah create an alternate reality, or is David a real ghost?

11. What did Sarah expect to gain from her life with David? Was it for her peace of mind and healing, or to give him the chance to live the life he had always dreamed?

12. What was needed both from David and Sarah in order for his ghost to finally leave?

13. Sarah feels angry and frustrated about many of the things in her life—the downfall of her marriage, her inability to carry a child to term, David's disappearance. How does she finally find peace with herself?